Lily's Secret

Kirsty Ferry

Book 2 – Cornish Secrets

Where heroes are like chocolate – irresistible!

Published 2022 by Choc Lit Limited
Penrose House, Crawley Drive, Camberley, Surrey GU15 2AB, UK
www.choc-lit.com

A CIP catalogue record for this book is available
from the British Library

ISBN 978-1-78189-514-6

Printed and bound in Great Britain by Clays Ltd, Elcograf S.p.A.

To my family, as always.

Acknowledgements

As always, the inspiration for this book came from several sources. The idea of the 1895 'Pageant' that the children hold in the book started to germinate when we visited Mount Grace Priory in North Yorkshire and saw some black and white photographs of the children who used to live there, dressed up for their very own pageant. The idea cemented itself when we visited Suffolk in the autumn, and went to The Museum of East Anglian Life in Stowmarket. One of the buildings there is called Abbot's Hall, and again there were some photographs of the children of the family, all dressed up for some amateur dramatics, looking very important. A few years ago, Lyme Park in Cheshire – better known as Pemberley in the Colin Firth *Pride and Prejudice* series – also had some splendid cine film of the children putting on a play, and the way my character Elsie started to develop just cried out for her to do something similar!

Elsie's heroine, Lily Valentine, is an amalgamation of Evelyn Nesbit, Lillie Langtree and Ellen Terry. All three of these women were quite scandalous stars in the late nineteenth and early twentieth centuries, and it really is worth a look into the Google rabbit hole if you want to learn more about them. Evelyn, for instance, was part of a love triangle that resulted in murder, and the court case was deemed the 'Trial of the Century'; Lillie was a Royal Mistress, and had an illegitimate child, but basically just went all out for whatever she wanted to do, in whatever career or social strata she fancied; and Ellen also had affairs and produced illegitimate children, but was one of the most renowned actors in the world. Her entry in the *Oxford Dictionary of National Biography* states, rather marvellously, that she "became a cult figure for poets and painters of the later Pre-Raphaelite and Aesthetic movements, including Oscar Wilde." I must also thank my good friend Elspeth, who allowed me to pilfer her daughter's gorgeous name – hence my "Lily" fitted in beautifully with the floral theme of the Pencradoc stories so far.

The idea of someone coming over from Ireland and changing their identity was also something that occurred to me after some digging into our own family history. My husband's grandma came over from Ireland and married his granddad – but nobody knew until after she died that she had been using a different name the whole time she'd been in England. There were family stories about how and why she might have come over, including the fact she may have run away from home and travelled with her sister, but it's something I doubt we will ever know the truth of. We think we've found records of her when she was a child, and we have one piece of beautifully copied out piece of Sunday School work we think her mother did in the late 1880s, but nothing else. Her story is going to have to remain a mystery, and to be fair that's probably what she wanted. But to honour her memory, I decided that Lily Valentine should come from the same area of Ireland – County Meath.

As always, I have lots and lots of people to thank, who all helped bring this book to life. The wider team at Choc Lit, who are forever supportive and always on our side, my editor, my cover designer and all the extended Choc Lit family. Thanks so much for being part of this. I'd also like to thank the panel who passed this book and said it combined some of my very own favourite elements: humour, mystery and a touch of horror. If that's all managed to come through in the writing, I'm so pleased! Special thanks to those who passed the manuscript and made publication possible: Luise Piri, Anne Eckersley, Barbara Wickham, Carol Fletcher, Dimi

Evangelou, Donna Morgan, Emily Seldon, Gill Leivers, Hilary Brown, Isabelle D, Jenny Mitchell, Jo Osborne, Joy Bleach, Margaret Marshall and Sharon Walsh. Also huge thanks to the Choc Lit Stars who selected the very, very beautiful cover – and of course to the readers of *A Secret Rose* who asked for more. And here it is! I hope you're not disappointed.

The biggest thanks as always must go to my long-suffering family, who must have thought they were living with a particularly snappy dog during some of the time I spent writing this. I'm back to normal now – I promise … well, as normal as I'll ever be, I suppose! Thanks again, and I love you all.

There, in a never-ceasing round,
In the slow stream, by noon, by night, by dawn,
An ancient, hidden water-wheel turns on
With a sad, reiterant sound.

Most eerily it comes and dies,
And comes again, when on the horizon's breast
The ruby of Antares seems to rest,
Fallen from star-fraught skies.

Extract from 'The Old Water-Wheel'
by Clark Ashton Smith

Lily's Secret

Chapter One

Cordelia Beaumont was fed up. She was fed up with the summer heat in London. She was fed up with her deathly dull and boring temping job on reception in a PR firm – which should have been exciting, but really wasn't – and today she was fed up to her back teeth about the fact that Roland, her upstairs neighbour, had caught her at the bottom of the stairs and told her that her much-loved flat in the nice new block in Kentish Town, had flooded. Apparently he'd had a burst pipe in his bathroom, the floor had collapsed and the water had found its way down to hers.

She looked up at the block of flats and sighed inwardly, even as Roland assured her his insurance would be paying up. The flat she was renting belonged to her best friend Merryn, who had now gone to live with her partner, Kit Penhaligon, in a tiny cottage in Marazion, Cornwall. Kit was an artist and owned a business in Marazion, and he also taught art courses. The Arts Centre Kit taught at was attached to Pencradoc, which was his and his brother Coren's ancestral home. Once Kit and Merryn had become serious, it was a no-brainer for Merryn to move down there and let out her flat to Cordy, who was fed up – again – of renting a shoebox-sized room in a shared house.

Cordy's heart lay in acting, and acting was what she had come down to London for from her home in Oxfordshire, but the jobs were few and far between. Temping, although boring at times, did bring in a bit of money to help her out.

Today, however, Cordy was considering the fact that she was spending an awful lot of time feeling fed up. She was also considering the beaches and the moors in Cornwall; the coastal breeze blowing through her hair and tickling the back of her neck; the idea of launching herself into the sea at a moment's notice and getting thoroughly soaked and salty in the ocean.

It was the one thing she absolutely yearned to do right now. She'd attempted to bathe in the ponds at Hampstead Heath once, but it was a bit of a chore getting there, and the tube full of hot, sweaty people on the way home had promptly destroyed any serenity she'd achieved through the experience.

But a beach.

In Cornwall.

Oh God.

Perfection.

'How long do you think it'll take to sort it all out then? The flood? My flat?'

'The assessor is coming out immediately. Hopefully it won't be long.' Roland smiled at her, his eyes wide and hopeful. He hated upsetting anyone.

'Good. Okay.' She nodded. What else could she do really? It wasn't Roland's fault. 'Thank you for sorting it. I guess I should find somewhere to stay for a few days while they do their thing. I'll need to pack some things and I'll let you know where and when I go.' She knew, deep down, she had already made that decision of where to go. She'd call the agency first thing, work the day out so she didn't leave the PR company in the lurch and see if she could stay with her friends Ash and Paul for the evening. 'I think I'll be staying with some friends for tonight, but maybe I'll take a little holiday if I have to.'

'I'm so sorry,' said Roland again. 'If there's anything I can do …'

'No, it's fine.' She smiled at her neighbour and lifted her phone up. 'Look. I'm already on the case. Oh – hi Ash!'

'Hello Cordy! How's things?' Ash asked, sounding delighted to hear from her. Ash and Paul lived in Pimlico, and were always happy to have her bunk down the odd night if she was near the West End.

'Darling Ash. They could be better – so I have a small favour to ask you.'

'Anything you want. Are you back with Toby though,

because if you can get us tickets to his latest show, I shan't at all use the words "bribery" or "corruption".'

Cordy pulled a face. 'No. Toby and I are over, as you well know.' Ash and Paul had been delighted and a little star-struck when she'd been with Toby Fowler, her most recent ex, who was something of a West End star. The boys hadn't liked it at all when they'd broken up – Toby Fowler was very good at buying friendship, and Ash and Paul, gorgeous as they were, were suckers for free West End tickets. 'You need to be nice to me without that carrot dangling in front of your nose.'

'Damn. Oh well – it was worth a try.' Ash sounded just a little disappointed, but she knew he would be fine.

'I need somewhere to stay – just for a night or two as my flat is flooded. Just until I call Merryn and try to arrange something else …'

It really was worth a shot. She could almost taste the fresh air and the clotted cream, even as she chatted to Ash and sorted out the next couple days in the stifling heat of London.

Matt Harker put the last thing into his car: his easel. It lay on top of the suitcase and buried the selection of paints and teaching materials he had stashed in there beforehand. Kit and Coren always found it amusing that he had a favourite easel.

'We have enough here you can borrow!' Kit had told him the first time he ran the workshop at Pencradoc Arts Centre. 'You really don't need to bring your own.'

Matt had grinned and shaken his head. 'Come on – you know yourself that you need the correct tools to work efficiently.'

'Well yes, but still!'

'Let's agree to disagree. I'm doing you a favour after all.'

'Yeah – and I do appreciate it.'

Matt and Kit had been to art college together, and since Kit and his brother Coren had inherited Pencradoc and converted it into an Arts Centre, Matt had been coming up to the old house from his home in Newlyn to teach workshops and short courses to help the brothers out.

He was happy to do so – Pencradoc was a beautiful place and he always felt a strong sense of belonging there, almost as if he was part of the family.

Matt smiled to himself as he shut the boot of the car and prepared to drive up to Pencradoc. It was perhaps a busman's holiday for him, as his 'real job', according to some of his un-creative friends, was an art teacher in a secondary school – and helping out with the drama classes, when he couldn't get out of it. It wasn't quite the future he'd envisaged when he'd stayed up all night drinking and chatting with his fellow students, making grandiose plans for their successful galleries and businesses in the future, but it was steady work, he enjoyed it and, most importantly, it paid the bills.

And, this time, he was booked at Pencradoc for a couple of weeks in the summer holidays to teach regular short courses and workshops, which meant he'd be staying over in one of the little guest apartments that had been created in the old attic spaces of the house.

He couldn't think of a better way to spend his time before he returned to real life, and he wanted to forget all about Layla anyway. It had been a few months since they'd split up, but he hadn't managed to get away and let go of the memories properly until now. He was looking forward to just being himself and doing what he loved, and not watching his back any more.

No, he wasn't looking for anything beyond a nice, relaxing holiday and some time spent at one of his favourite places.

'But pleeeeeease!' Cordy was clutching the office phone as if her life depended on it. 'I'm homeless!'

'No, you're not.' Merryn's voice was mildly amused at Cordy's plight. Typical Merryn. 'You've had a minor flood which will mean a soggy residence for a while, but it'll sort out. You've just told me you're bunking with Ash and Paul

4

who love having you. You've got that PR job with all the celebs. Why on earth do you want to come here so desperately anyway? So desperately, that you want our sofa?' Merryn and Kit were redecorating and renovating, and the tiny fisherman's cottage in Marazion was, apparently, in chaos. 'We have one usable room at any one time, and we might need the sofa ourselves at some point!'

'But I'm fed up. I'm bored out of my tiny mind, and—' Cordy lowered her voice and covered her mouth with her hand, just in case she was lip-read on CCTV '—my boss is a cowbag.' She cast her eyes nervously around in case her boss had, indeed, bugged the Reception area for any reason. 'And I really don't want to bump into Toby in this place. He is a client after all!'

Frankly, she was pleased to be out of such a misguided relationship. Toby's ego was rising with his stardom and she'd caught him erring towards the metaphoric casting couch one too many times.

And she was positive that there were hidden cameras in this place. The PR office had some high-level clientele, higher than Toby Fowler at any rate, and nothing was left to chance. One time, before she had worked there, a group of teenage girls had stormed the place as the lead singer of the newest indie rock band had come to sign up. Apparently security had been on the girls almost immediately.

Now *that*, Cordy thought, would have been a fun day.

This, however, was not a fun day. Her boss had grumbled and groaned at the announcement that she was leaving, but at least Cordy had given them the courtesy of finishing the week – she might have just decided to not turn up.

She tried one last angle with Merryn. 'I have no job to go to on Monday.' She tried to inject the correct amount of sadness into her voice.

'You work for an agency. It's called flexibility. Sorry about Toby.'

'I'm not sorry. But are there any jobs at Pencradoc I can do? Please?' Look – I just have to get away. I mean it.'

'You love London. You love your life. Fair enough, you maybe don't love Toby …'

'I do, I do, I *don't*. But I'll be honest. It's summer and it's stifling and we are in a heatwave. I need some sea air and some water I can paddle in.'

Merryn finally laughed, caving in good-naturedly. 'Fine, whatever. To be perfectly honest with you, we *could* use some help in the Tower Tea-Room. There's a big exhibition coming up about the actress Lily Valentine. She did a little pageant here for the Pencradoc children on the 10th August 1895 and we've got some trips and tours booked in to celebrate that, but Sorcha is off poorly at the minute. Remember Sorcha? She runs the place? Well, she's had an operation and she's laid up for a couple more weeks. We've got her niece Steph and Steph's boyfriend Josh helping, but then we're sort of taking turns to jump in when we have to – and we've had to close it the odd time during the week, which isn't great. Anyway, as I say, we're building on the Lily Valentine visit. Pushing the arts connection a bit to encompass drama and the stage – Wheal Mount have a big Ruan Teague thing going on this summer, so we don't want to compete with them painting-wise, and my sources tell me there's something of a Lily Valentine revival going on in your world. Am I right? So, we're capitalising on it. Blame Coren. He's the mastermind.'

'Yes – they're redoing *The Black Rose* as a musical – Lily's most famous role was Rosalee the gypsy girl, and I've been reading up on her loads. She's so interesting. See, it's fate that I need to be at Pencradoc when you're doing something about her. But ohhh, let's talk about Ruan Teague.' Cordy smiled. Ruan Teague had been a famous artist who had fallen in love, rather scandalously, with Zennor, Duchess of Trecarrow in the 1880s. The Pencradoc family had owned Pencradoc itself and their other property, Wheal Mount, a little further south, and the two former homes were now arts centres and worked very well together. Merryn always spoke very highly of Sybill Helyer, the manager of Wheal Mount, and everyone seemed to get on well. Cordy had met her on a couple of occasions and she had liked her too.

'Yes, Ruan Teague. He wasn't around when Lily came, though. I believe he and the fabulous Zennor were on honeymoon. Accompanied by four of their children. Then they had a few more later, when they settled back here.' Merryn sounded amused. 'Apparently it was a quiet wedding – but at least they eventually got around to doing it. Lady Elsie, the Duchess's daughter to her first husband, was bridesmaid.'

Cordy smothered a laugh. 'Fair enough. Okay – I think I'm equipped to work in a tea-room to help you out. I don't mind; it'll be fun. When can I start? Poor Sorcha, though!'

'It was appendicitis – she's fine now but, like I say, she's going to be off for a couple more weeks. Can you be here for Monday? And can you get down here over the weekend? And, more importantly, can Ash and Paul bear to see you go?'

'I bet they can't really bear to see me go, but I shall sweet talk them. I'll take some gin home tonight and they'll be happy.'

'Great. We're almost finished renovating the old Mill House which we're going to turn into a guest cottage on the estate, so next time you come you can stay there if you want water nearby. Remember how horrid it was inside? You'll not recognise the place soon. It's almost done, but there's a problem with part of the flooring. We're just waiting for some repairs, then it'll be all sorted. For now, are you happy to stay in Pencradoc itself? You can have one of the attic rooms for a couple of weeks until your flat gets sorted.'

'You're not putting me in Rose's room, then? Dammit.'

'You don't mean that. You're terrified of that room!'

'That's true.' Cordy grinned into the phone. Rose had been a Duchess, a young woman from the nineteenth century who had created a beautiful Gothic garden, and then died on the estate under mysterious circumstances. Cordy hated Rose's old rooms; she was convinced the girl would come out and haunt her, although Merryn had often told her Rose would do no such thing.

'You can go in the attics and be grateful,' Merryn continued, the amusement still in her voice. 'You could have had a retreat room, but we're saving them for proper guests. Don't interrupt – I'm teasing! Seriously, when we have people running courses or working with us for an extended period, we let them use the attics. I often nip up and stay during the week anyway, so we'll still see each other loads.'

'I can *definitely* tolerate a garret, I am a starving *artiste* after all. And it will definitely be okay. I'm so looking forward to it!'

'Great.' Merryn's voice was warm. 'Let me know your plans and we'll hopefully see you on Sunday.'

'Hopefully.'

Cordy couldn't bloody wait.

1895

'I absolutely do not think it will be a problem,' Lady Elsie Pencradoc announced imperiously. Elsie Pencradoc was, Alys knew, very much Mistress of Pencradoc while her mama and step-papa – Alys' cousin Zennor and her husband Ruan – were away on their honeymoon. The honeymoon entourage included Elsie's younger siblings; which was utterly baffling to some of the more decorous ladies of Society, but completely normal to eight-year old Lady Elsie – despite the fact that her next-youngest brother was seven and Zennor and Ruan had only been married three months. 'It's not a problem at all. Everyone can stay here.'

Elsie flapped her hands haughtily up the stairs as Alys, the new Duchess of Trecarrow, looked at her, a smile threatening to break through her almost-stern expression. 'And where do you propose we put "everyone"?'

Elsie stared at her as if she was quite mad. 'Well it is quite obvious, Aunt Alys. Myself and my cousins will stay in the nurseries, of course, and you and Uncle Jago may use Mama and Step-papa's suite.'

'I don't think so, Elsie.' Alys reached down and ruffled the child's dark, curly hair. 'I am sure Uncle Jago and myself can use one of the other suites. It's bad enough that we're having to stay here whilst your mama and step-papa are away, without taking over their bedroom as well. Why, what if the work on Wheal Mount takes longer than expected? There was quite a lot of water damage to the ground floor, you know. But Uncle Jago is certain it isn't a problem for us to stay here. He has, out of courtesy, of course, written a letter to your mama explaining the situation—'

'— but because Pencradoc is really Uncle Jago's house, we have to let you stay. I know very well.' Elsie frowned. 'We live here because you prefer Wheal Mount, which is *also* Uncle Jago's house.'

'It is the Duke of Trecarrow's house,' chided Alys. 'Currently, the Duke is your Uncle Jago. Should one of our daughters have a son, he will become the Duke. If they don't, and you have a son, why then *he* will be the Duke. We really can't predict the future. Apart from the fact that we will all be living here for a little while.' She pulled a face and looked at the large portrait of Jago's half-brother, Ellory, who had been the previous Duke. And who, Alys knew, would have hated the way the inheritance of the title and the property had happened: the brothers had never been close.

'Anyway,' Alys continued, turning away from the previous Duke and looking affectionately at the little girl. 'Had it not been for some certain little girls playing "The Three Billy Goats Gruff" by the ha-ha at Wheal Mount and accidentally opening the floodgate from the river, we would not be in this situation, would we now?'

Elsie had the grace to look ashamed. The ill-fated game had, everyone knew, been her idea. 'I did not quite know how fast the water would flow, and how much of it there would be. I *am* sorry.'

'I know. And there wasn't anything too important harmed, so we shan't become cross about it again, shall we?'

Elsie shook her head. She had, Alys knew, disliked intensely the fact she had been scolded so very soundly by Uncle Jago – Jago rarely lost his temper, but when he did, it was a very unwelcome experience for the person on the receiving end.

'Cross? Who's becoming cross?'

Alys turned to the door and saw Jago coming in with their smallest daughter, Nancy, sitting on his shoulders.

Alys smiled. 'Nobody is cross with anyone. Elsie and I are simply working out who should sleep where.'

'Well, do you think you could add an extra two people to that equation, perhaps?' Jago dipped down and Nancy slid off his shoulders, running off somewhere after planting a big, soggy kiss on her papa's forehead. 'Can you remember the letter I received from my old friend Edwin Griffiths? He's sent another one – a response to mine.' He looked at the letter and half-smiled. 'When he was fighting in the Semantan War, correspondence to me wasn't his priority, but it seems since he was invalided out of the army and spent some time recovering in France, he is making up for lost time.'

'Oh what a shame – he wanted to come to visit us at Wheal Mount, didn't he?'

Jago cast an amused glance at Elsie. 'He did – but he's happy to come here – if, of course, Madam here allows it? And even better, he wants to bring along his new bride and would very much like us all to meet her.'

Elsie flushed but stood up a little straighter anyway. 'Of *course* I shall allow it,' she said. 'Why, we were just discussing accommodation, weren't we, Aunt Alys?'

'We were.' Alys nodded seriously. 'And what, may I ask, is the new bride's name? I don't believe he mentioned that fact to us.'

'His new bride,' said Jago, his eyes twinkling as he deliberately didn't catch Elsie's eye, 'is called Lily Valentine.'

Alys watched in amusement as the child's jaw literally dropped and her eyes became as round as saucers.

'Lily Valentine?' The name was whispered, almost reverently. 'Lily Valentine from the Paris Opera? I'm sorry – I mean of course, the *Théâtre National de l'Opéra*. Oh my goodness! I must write to Mama. I must tell my dear friends ...' Lily Valentine was Elsie's heroine. She was a star of the stage and played all sorts of characters; some, Alys thought wryly, that weren't acceptable idols for an eight-year old girl. However, Lily had recently been in Paris, as Elsie had said, and the little girl had collected pictures and newspaper clippings of that lady for several years and pasted them all carefully into her scrapbook.

'Not so fast, Madam Elsie.' Alys could tell Jago was trying to sound serious. 'Edwin says they are here for a holiday, and they will want to be peaceful and quiet. Lily is in an ... interesting condition.' He shot a glance at Alys and she dropped her head, trying to hide a smile. She knew full well what that meant. And Elsie would as well, as she had so many small siblings and four small cousins. And if she was just a 'new bride', Alys wondered if perhaps the marriage may have been organised rather hastily. 'They don't want any bother,' Jago was saying. 'And that bother includes you, Lady Elsie Pencradoc. I know how much you admire Miss Valentine, but you must be considerate.'

'Will she want to see my collection of pictures? My scrapbook, perhaps?' Elsie was not listening at all.

'I think she might like to see them – but not immediately, eh?'

Elsie nodded. 'But I have a very good collection of them and perhaps she may sit for a portrait for me?' Elsie was quite an accomplished little artist for one so young. Strangers may suggest that her step-papa, Ruan Teague – who was himself quite a famous artist by now – had taught her well. Others, like Alys and Jago, thought it was more of an inherited talent, but who were they to suggest that outside the safe walls of Pencradoc?

'Perhaps she might. But you must respect her and Mr Griffith's right to privacy – actually, I have a suggestion.' Jago lifted a finger and pointed it in the direction of the front door. 'I think it may be best all-round if Edwin and Lily stay in the Mill House. Do you think that is sensible, Alys?'

Alys nodded. 'Yes.' She deliberately didn't look at the small child next to her. She had a feeling that there might be steam coming out of the top of her head if her prize was snatched away quite so brutally. But she knew Edwin had suffered in the conflict and now sported a rather dashing eye-patch, as well as some other injuries to the left side of his body. The idea of giving the poor man no respite from an enthusiastic Elsie, as he came here for some peace and quiet and to look after a newly-pregnant wife, did not seem like a good one.

'I say, that is *rather* unfair!'

Elsie's voice was shrill, and Jago quelled her with a look. 'Why is it unfair?'

The quelling did not work. 'Because I shall *never* see them. *Never*. Not if they are all the way at the Mill House!' She very nearly stamped her foot, but must have remembered that it was very unladylike and thus restrained herself.

'I'm fairly sure you *will* see them. But this way, they have some privacy.' Jago relented and tweaked her nose. 'They don't want to be looking after a little girl for the whole holiday, do they? Now, why don't you go and find your pictures and your scrapbook and make sure it's all presentable for when they arrive?' He looked at Alys. 'Shall I write back and tell them they should report to us as soon as possible?'

'Yes. Yes, I think that would be a good idea.' She cast a glance at her niece. 'As soon as possible really. Or I do think Elsie might just simply explode. And I don't really know how I could explain *that* to her mother.'

Chapter Two

'Matt! Good to see you.' Kit waved at him from the driveway. He had, of all things, a wheelbarrow with him.

Matt grinned as he climbed out of the car. 'Diversifying, are we?' The two men shook hands and Kit clapped Matt on the back.

'Just helping out. Have you seen the newest sculptures on the trail? We needed to clear some undergrowth away to put the theatre in at the end of it.'

'How could I have seen the sculptures? I haven't been for weeks,' Matt teased.

'You read the news don't you? Surely you haven't missed the media storm about the Lily Valentine exhibition?'

'Now that I *have* seen.' Matt smiled. 'So it's an installation to complement that, is it?'

'Yes. The theatre – well, it's more of a vintage stage, really – is in Rose's Garden. The idea is that kids can dress up and play there if they want to. There are some noticeboards up about the girls who were here at the time Lily visited, and you've probably seen that great photo of them in the advertising materials, all dressed up to do a summer pageant. They seem to have been in the Rose Garden, looking at the background, so it's fitting. They created a stage, and it's all done up for something intriguing in that photo as well. We've had the picture blown up and copied onto one of the boards.'

'Ah yes, that's a great photo! I thought it looked familiar. I recognised the stage. With the flowers around it? The lilies? And the ivy draped over it all?'

'Familiar?' Kit looked at him curiously. 'You can see the floor, and there are curtains behind the kids, with a couple of props outside the curtains – a tree stump and a chair. It looks as if they're standing on wooden floorboards, but you can just see the path leading to the fake ruins through a gap in the curtain. There aren't loads of flowers draped everywhere – of course, we don't know what's behind the curtains, so you never know.'

'Really?' Matt frowned. He was sure he'd seen the flowers. 'It must have been a different picture.'

'That's the only one we have.' Kit was still looking at him a little curiously.

'Oh. Well. Maybe I've seen similar things from other old houses when I've been researching for school. No matter.' He shrugged. It really didn't matter. One year his school had put on an Edwardian Variety Show. He'd had to read up on it all. It must have been from that. 'Regardless, it's a great picture.' He grinned at Kit. 'I'm looking forward to seeing the girls more clearly on the enlarged picture anyway!'

The girls he referred to were the children of Kit's nineteenth-century relative Jago, the Duke of Trecarrow and his wife Alys, whose 'official' residence was Wheal Mount. Clara Bronnen, Mabel Gwenna, Lucy Ebrel and Nancy Verran had been regular visitors to Pencradoc and had more or less grown up with their cousin Elsie. It was clear that the girls had enjoyed dressing up – as Coren's friend Sybill had discovered from her access to the old family collection in the attics of Wheal Mount.

By all accounts, Elsie had been a very creative little girl and, if the black and white photograph reproduced in the newspaper article was anything like reality, she had seemingly loved being in charge of the little ones. She stood in the middle, eldest by only a few months, surrounded by the others in stiff little poses, staring straight ahead at the camera. A sharp-eyed person might have noticed that Elsie had stood herself on a box and casually draped her long dress over it to make herself quite a bit taller than the others. It was a picture Matt had laughed at, and he was looking forward to seeing it properly.

'Come with me,' Kit was saying. 'You can help me unload

this lot in the compost heap and we'll swing back by Rose's Garden so you can see it all. Sorry about Layla, by the way. How are you doing?'

'I'm actually doing great, thanks. It's a relief not to go home to an atmosphere every night to be honest. And a trip to the compost heap via Rose's Garden sounds fine.'

Matt fell into step with Kit as he pointed out things that might have changed since Matt's last visit and talked about the plans he, Merryn and Coren had for the Arts Centre. Pencradoc was both a labour of love and a work in progress, and small things altered each time Matt came.

There was, he noticed, the beginnings of a gravel path snaking through the woodlands towards the Tower Tea-Room; he assumed to prevent too many muddy feet trekking into the building. The tower was an old folly, and the top level held temporary art exhibitions while the tea-room was situated on the ground floor. Some nineteenth-century graffiti by Duchess Rose, written when she was a child, had been lovingly preserved behind some Perspex and was always a talking point for anyone who visited the folly for the first time.

'We're renovating the Mill House as well,' Kit told him, 'but we've got some issues with the floor in one of the rooms. It's almost finished though.'

As well as the burgeoning paths, there were some new plants growing in the flowerbeds laid out in the formal gardens, copying the original plans as far as possible, and once more a fountain was tinkling happily in the middle of it. It was in the original place they knew a fountain to have been, but it had been designed with a far more contemporary feel to suit the Sculpture Trail around the estate.

Here and there, boards told stories about Pencradoc and, according to Kit, they'd also printed up some glossy maps to guide visitors through the grounds, rather than relying on A4 photocopies.

'We've also pencilled in space for a second-hand bookshop

and a gift shop in the gatehouse,' Kit said. 'Nothing too commercial, as we don't want to spoil the feel of the place, but Merryn has done some visitor feedback questionnaires and a lot of them have come back and said that.'

'You're certainly getting the place on the map.' Matt grinned, looking at a sculpture in the style of Henry Moore beneath a tree. 'It's great. And thanks again for inviting me up.'

'No problem. Your classes have some of the best feedback questionnaires we get.' Kit looked at him askance and winked, teasing. 'Better than mine, some of them.'

'I wonder why that is.' Matt laughed at the irony of it.

'Because you're single and I'm not. They still think they have a chance with you.'

'And Merryn would kill anyone who tried to flirt with you?' It was Matt's turn to tease.

'Not quite. But she'd make it quite clear where they stood.' Kit smiled, apparently thinking of such a situation.

'They'd stand at the back of a very long queue, I guess. How's Lowenna?' Lowenna was Kit's assistant in his gallery and shop in Marazion. She'd had quite a thing for Coren, and then Kit, then realised she was out of luck. Kit and Coren weren't naïve. They knew it was Pencradoc more than the Penhaligon brothers she had a fancy for.

'Lowenna is Lowenna. She's a good friend. Harmless. Now she *does* know where she stands with Merryn. They're fine with one another now.' Kit laughed, shaking his head. 'Better than it was in the beginning. Look. Here we are. One compost heap, then around that corner is the stage. Come on. Get your hands dirty and give me some help, then we can move onto the fun stuff.'

'No problem, sir.' Matt grinned and tugged at an imaginary forelock, then they began to empty the wheelbarrow.

Cordy almost fell out of the taxi, so eager was she to run up the steps of Pencradoc and see her friend. 'Merryn!' she yelled and waved frantically, as Merryn hurried down the steps to meet her and the taxi driver struggled with her luggage. Cordy never packed light.

'Cordy! Honestly, I'm cross with you!' Merryn hugged her friend. 'Talk about springing it on a person. Did you have to wait until you were in the actual taxi before letting me know you were here? We could have collected you at the station. And what if I *hadn't* been here?'

'I hazarded a guess. And I know I'm a day early and it's only Saturday – but once I got it into my head, I wanted to get here quite quickly. What can I say? I'm impetuous. And Coren would have been around anyway.' She shrugged, nonchalantly. What was the problem? She knew Coren. She'd met him before, and he lived in an apartment on-site.

'But still,' Merryn chided. 'What if nobody was around?'

'There would have been somebody around. And I would have sat and waited on the steps until one of you guys found me anyway. You're open to the public, aren't you? You have *staff*, darling, *staff*.' Cordy put her best *Downton Abbey* voice on. She'd been an extra in a ball scene. She'd had no dialogue, but she'd had to smile at a footman and take a glass from the silver tray he proffered. She'd loved that flouncy frock she'd had to wear, *loved* it. She'd made Merryn watch the footage over and over and pointed and exclaimed delightedly each time she appeared in the background.

'Hmmm.' Merryn grinned. 'Look, pay your poor taxi driver and we'll get you settled in.'

'Oh! Yes. Yes, of course. Sorry.' Cordy directed a bright smile to the taxi driver and tipped him generously. Then she looked about her and threw her arms out in delight. 'God, you are *so* lucky.'

'I don't live here! I work here!' Merryn laughed and grabbed a vanity case. 'But yes. It is beautiful. Kit and Coren have really worked hard on it. And I'm so excited about this Lily Valentine exhibition.'

'She was the quintessential Gibson Girl, wasn't she?' Cordy waved her hand around her head, indicating the elaborate hairstyles of the 'It Girls' of the late nineteenth century.

'Yes. A Tiller Girl, a member of the Folies Bergère, a singer in the Paris Opera. Actress, model, singer, dancer. Most little girls at dance class dream of that life, don't they?'

'I did. I still do. Closest I'm getting at the minute is the reception desk at the bloody PR agencies.'

'And how's that working out?' There was amusement in Merryn's voice. 'Have you ensnared any other clients, or just the one?'

'Just the one. Not enough room for two egos in that relationship. Needed to move on.' She shrugged.

'I wouldn't say you had *that* big an ego,' said Merryn in surprise.

'No. But who says they were both mine? There was Toby's ego and Toby's Fame's ego. Ugh. Plus the ego of the props girl he serviced. Oh. And the set girl. And the one who fed him his lines because he could never remember what the hell he was supposed to say.' She paused, halfway into the grand hallway. 'And the ego of the third violinist as well. Or maybe second. Hmmm. Maybe both. Oh well. And – oh *look*! Look at little Elsie. Just *look* at her!' Butterfly-minded as always, Cordy dashed over the tiled floor and drew to a halt in front of the marble bust depicting Lady Elsie Pencradoc when she was a little girl in the late nineteenth century. She had curls that made you want to tuck them behind her ears, and a smile so mischievous that you couldn't help smiling back. 'Hello, Beautiful,' said Cordy, running her fingers over the sculpted curls. 'You really are adorable.'

'Isn't she? You should head up to Rose's Garden later. You can see the little theatre set up and Elsie's photo for the exhibition. She seemed to have a starring role amongst all her cousins. We have such a sweet photo of them all. Of course you might go wild on the stage. We'll have to restrain you if so.'

Cordy laughed. 'I haven't been wild on a stage for months. I miss it. Hey – I meant to ask, have you got any acting going on to celebrate Lily? Any plays you're producing that she might have done? That would be rather cool.'

Merryn shook her head. 'No, although it would have been nice to do one. We know she did a scene from *A Midsummer Night's Dream*, and sang some songs from the music halls, but we haven't pulled anything together properly.'

Cordy paused for a moment, her fingers lingering on Elsie's cheek. 'Would you like *me* to try and pull something together for you? I've been studying scriptwriting, and it'll be fun to do something like that. I was thinking on the train here about what I could do to enhance it all. I don't mind getting up on the stage and delivering it either – we could give it a real family focus, considering the little girls were involved.'

'That would be brilliant. But won't it literally just be a scene from that play and some music hall songs? Having said that, you're more than welcome to do it.'

'Thanks. I can add a monologue or something – make it into a bit of me telling everyone her story ... I think it's definitely got mileage. But I need to research her a little bit more to get it right.'

'Good luck on that one.' Merryn smiled. 'As far as we know, she just burst onto the scene at the age of twenty and worked her way up the ranks. Nobody knows much about her before that.'

'So we go with what we know and start from there. Excellent.' Cordy clapped her hands. 'I have a project. As well as a new summer job.' She grinned at Merryn. 'I can stay longer if you want – you know, hang around and help?'

'Thanks. We might take you up on that, depending on whether Lily Valentine brings us hitherto unimagined footfall.'

'Great. I shall not let you forget.' Cordy nodded, satisfied. She pointed upstairs. 'Where am I? Point me in the right direction.'

'Attics. On the left. Turn along and keep going.'

'Fab-u-lous. Oh, just leave the vanity case. I'll come back for that and the rest of my stuff. It's in nobody's way. You go off and do whatever you need to do. I'll be fine. I know my way around this place. Yay for floods!' And she bounded upstairs, two at a time, bouncing one of her suitcases behind her.

1895

The carriage pulled up in front of Pencradoc, passing the gatehouse and trundling up the long driveway to draw up before the imposing grey building. Lily Valentine peered out of the window and saw a small figure dotting around on the top of the steps. They were a little early, and it wasn't surprising that there wasn't a bigger welcome party. To be honest, she didn't really want a big welcome party anyway.

The excited little figure was, she saw, a girl of about eight years old, her dark hair brushed neatly and teased into ringlets, blue ribbons tucked into it at each side just above her ears. She was clutching a book of some description and seemingly finding it difficult to stay in one place. A dog bounced around at her heels, wagging its tail furiously and looking up adoringly at the girl. The dog appeared to be some kind of cross-breed, and Lily raised her eyebrows at it in amusement. It had the short body and long ears of a Spaniel but the snout and face of a Labrador.

'*Someone* is excited,' she said. 'I'm not sure who is the most excited though – the child or the dog.'

'One of them wants your attention more than the other,' the man next to her responded. 'The child, I think.' Edwin Griffiths nodded to the window as the child stopped stock-still at the top of the steps and drew herself up to her full height, as if she had remembered a particularly important deportment lesson.

'Possibly.' Lily was aware that the girl was staring at the

20

carriage, her eyes round, completely star-struck by the visitors. 'Edwin – thank you. Thank you for doing this. For bringing me here.' Lily turned to the man beside her. She twisted the ring on the third finger of her left hand. It still felt odd and was very, very shiny.

'Nobody will ask questions here.' He half-smiled, his one good eye navy-blue and, for a brief moment, sparking with amusement. 'I've known the family for a while. They don't hold too much with tradition. And it's the best place we can be at the moment.'

Lily nodded. 'Well then.' She took a deep breath. 'Shall we alight?' It was time, she knew, to call on all of her dramatic skills. She was, to all intents and purposes, a new bride. It had been a whirlwind romance, acted out in the most romantic city in the world, culminating in a wedding granted by special licence …

Even if that wasn't entirely the truth. They both knew that special licence was still crisp and unused but, despite all that, she had to look and behave just like a new bride.

A new bride with – oh God – a child on the way. The thought still made her feel sick, even though she wasn't feeling physically sick quite as much as she had been about a month ago. She mentally calculated that she had about five months – less than half a year – left of being her own person.

But there wasn't much time to prepare herself, as the little girl with dark hair ran down the steps towards the carriage and now stood right next to the door.

'Shall I fend her off?' Edwin's voice was amused.

'No. I can manage.'

Lily went to open the door, but Edwin put his hand on hers gently. 'The coachman will do that for you.'

Lily felt her cheeks heat up. She was so used to doing things for herself that it was difficult to factor in any help. But she had to do that now. She needed Edwin and whatever help he could offer to her.

'Yes. Quite.' She swallowed and folded her hands neatly on her lap, even as her heart pounded madly in her chest.

In another moment, the door opened and the coachman stepped to the side, bowing.

'Miss Valentine! Welcome! Welcome to Pencradoc!' The child curtsied elaborately, not even giving Lily time to climb down. 'Biscuit says hello as well.' She indicated the dog who sat nicely and wagged his tail happily.

'Oh! Oh, well thank you so very much.' Lily's professional side switched on and she smiled at the girl. 'And who do I have the pleasure of speaking to?'

'Lady Elsie Pencradoc.' The child curtsied again. 'Or perhaps I should call you Mrs Griffiths?' She frowned. 'I wasn't informed what I should refer to you as.'

'How about you just call me Lily? I'm quite happy for you to do that.'

'*May* I?' Lady Elsie Pencradoc stared at her for a moment, barely suppressing her joy. 'Thank you. *Lily*.'

By now, Edwin had appeared behind Elsie. Leaning heavily on his cane – Lily knew the long journey hadn't been kind to him – he smiled across Elsie's head and cleared his throat gently so she turned to him, instead of simply gawping at Lily. 'Lady Elsie. It's a joy to meet you. I have heard so much about you from your uncle. Aren't you the eldest of the Pencradoc children?'

'I am. I am *indeed*.' Elsie smiled up at Edwin, and Lily took the opportunity to take his outstretched hand and clamber out of the carriage whilst Elsie was otherwise occupied. 'I have four younger cousins who are here as well.' She waved her hand in the direction of the house. 'And I have three younger siblings.' She frowned. 'Half siblings, that is. I am so sorry that Mama and my step-papa aren't here to greet you. They are on their honeymoon. We had a splendid time at the wedding.' She smiled up at Edwin and Lily. 'I fully expect to have *four* siblings when they come back. People do tend

22

to have more babies just after they are married, don't they?'

Lily almost choked and Edwin squeezed her hand. *You see*, he seemed to be saying, *we won't be judged here*.

'It is often the case, I believe.' Lily's voice was, even to her ears, faint. She was aware that the Irish lilt she had tried to gloss over for her stage-work was more noticeable in that phrase. The child had thrown her, completely thrown her.

'Are you expecting a baby?' Elsie's face was guileless. 'I suspected that you were, but I would just like to be sure before I congratulate you.'

'Ummm – yes. Yes I am.' Lily felt a little ill. It was stupid. She couldn't hide it, and there was no need to, was there? She was a respectable married woman now, for God's sake!

'Congratulations,' Elsie said warmly. 'My Aunt Alys will be able to talk to you about it, should you need reassurance. She has, as I say, four children.' She nodded sagely. 'But! Have you a moment, I wonder, to look at my scrapbook? It's very special and I hoped we could spend some time looking at it together—'

Edwin's voice interrupted her, amused. 'Thank you, Lady Elsie. I'm sure once we are settled my wife will be very pleased to look at your scrapbook with you. But first, I think, we need to find an adult and let them know we are here. Do you think you would be able to help us do that?'

'Oh! Oh, most certainly. Yes. I shall find someone immediately. Come – come with me to the house, and we shall find my uncle or my aunt – the Duke,' she said importantly, 'or the Duchess.'

'The Duke or the Duchess. Quite.' Lily nodded and was pleased to feel Edwin press her arm reassuringly again. This was all new to her; very new.

Who, back at home in County Meath, would have thought that she would ever be spending time in the company of a Duke and a Duchess?

*

Edwin indicated that Lady Elsie Pencradoc should precede them into the house. It was one way, he reckoned, to stop her chattering to Lily. The child meant well, but he could tell Lily was rather overwhelmed with it all, and it wasn't surprising, really. Just a few weeks ago she had been on the stage in Paris, finishing her last performance of Rosalee the Gypsy Girl in *The Black Rose*.

Nobody knew it was her last performance, though – she had simply packed her things after the show and clambered into Edwin's waiting carriage. He had purchased a special marriage licence and then contacted his good friend Jago Pencradoc; the man he had met in India several years ago, when Jago had found himself in a very dark place indeed.

Now, however, the roles were somewhat reversed – the Semantan War had been one of the worst things Edwin thought a man could ever endure. He was away now, out of the army, but he bore scars both physically and mentally. Recovering in Paris, he had found solace in the theatre. He didn't need two functioning eyes to sit quietly in the audience. He didn't need a full range of movement to enjoy the performances. He didn't need daylight and shop windows and mirrors around every corner to remind him that his face and body were scarred by his experience; although, he did thank God that the worst of the scarring was hidden beneath his clothing and his face had healed better than anyone had expected it to.

What he could do instead was close his eyes and listen to the music, until he decided that Lily Valentine was far more intoxicating than the music she sang or the roles she played. He'd been in the audience for many of her performances, ensuring he had the same seat every night. He fancied that, on occasion, she would look down and see him; and one unforgettable evening, he knew that was the case. She looked down into the stalls and his heart exploded as she smiled directly at him.

The next night, she did the same. And the night after that.

Then he took a bunch of lilies into the theatre and sat with them on his knee. After the show, he took them to the stage door and left them there in the care of a theatre attendant.

The next night, she smiled down at him as usual. She mouthed the words '*thank you*' and he tumbled deeper into the void ...

He still couldn't believe that she was here with him as his wife. His *wife*. After the war, he despaired that anyone would ever want to be with him again, but here she was. Lily Valentine. It was incredible.

Chapter Three

Matt seemed to be wearing much of the leaf mould and soil that he'd helped Kit get rid of.

Kit took pity on him and, laughing, pointed him back towards the house. 'Go on, get yourself cleaned up and I'll finish up here.'

'It's not a visit to Pencradoc without getting your hands dirty, is it?' asked Matt, ironically.

'Not really. That's what makes you part of the team.' Kit grinned. 'You're in your usual room.'

'Just like coming home.' Matt laughed and wiped his hands down his jeans, smearing dirt down to his knees. 'Okay, I'll go and unpack and sort myself out. I didn't even get that far before you waylaid me.'

'Part of the team, you see.' Kit winked and nodded again towards Pencradoc. 'Off you go. See you later.' And, still smiling, he turned his attention to the compost heap.

Matt strolled back to the car and brought out his luggage. One case of clothing, one case of art equipment and of course his easel. Balancing them all carefully, he headed up the steps, feeling his way with his toes, unwilling to trip as he went inside the Hall.

He made it as far as the bottom of the grand staircase, but then his toe connected with another shambolic pile of luggage and he stumbled over it all.

He dropped his case of clothing, but saved the easel and his art equipment – despite a few choice curses echoing around the hallway as the case crashed onto the floor and burst open, scattering his T-shirts and socks all over the floor.

'Hmm. Sorry about that …'

Matt snapped his head up, anger bubbling up inside him as he opened his mouth to respond to the speaker and direct a few of those choice curses towards them.

'... but you really should have been looking where you were going.'

He stopped, the words dying on his lips as he tried to formulate an answer. On the bottom of the steps was a tall, graceful redhead. Her hair was held back from her face by a green polka dot hairband, and she had a definite 1960s vibe going on with her black-and-white checked capri pants and green halter-neck top. She was a woman who didn't appear to lack confidence as she stared at him out of bright blue, curious eyes. He blinked. He knew her from somewhere; he was pretty certain he'd seen her before.

The words finally came out, but they quite possibly weren't the ones he had originally intended to use; there was no swearing, for a start. 'Is that stuff yours? Just dumped at the bottom of the stairs? Where anyone can fall over it?'

'Perhaps you should have been watching your step.'

'A person doesn't expect a month's worth of luggage at the bottom of a staircase.' He edged around her cases and dumped his own things down. He bent down and began to scoop his possessions untidily into the case.'

'Do you ... ummm ... want a hand?'

'No. Thank you.'

'Then if you'll excuse me, I'll just get my things.'

'I do hope *your* cases don't burst.' He knew he sounded sarcastic, but her cases were absolutely bulging. She was obviously here for the duration. Or she'd moved in permanently and was someone Coren was keeping quiet. She looked like one of those arty, dramatic types that had thrown themselves at Coren when they were all a bit younger in the hope of making him take notice – the sort of girl who Kit had been more than happy to date and console when they realised they'd get nowhere with Coren, unless they appeared naked,

27

apart from a spreadsheet and some financial statistics draped strategically over their bodies.

And she wasn't here for Kit, who was happily settled with Merryn, so she could well be with Coren. Stranger things had happened.

The redhead edged around him and Matt was aware of a dragging sound as she pulled her stuff away from him and then a bouncing sound as she headed up the stairs: *thud, thud, thud*.

He paused for a moment and stood up, watching her retreating back as she negotiated the stairs in six-inch stiletto heels.

He sighed. 'Do *you* want a hand?'

'No. Thank you.'

She didn't even bother to toss the comment back over her shoulder or flip her hair around, which was the sort of thing he might have expected her to do, given first impressions. Rather, she just headed up the stairs, ramrod straight, thudding her cases behind her.

'Please yourself,' he muttered, and went back to the task in hand.

Cordy poised on the landing at the top of the stairs, looking down at the man in the hallway as he shovelled things back in the bag. She would have, actually, quite liked a hand with her cases; they were so damn *heavy*! But she wasn't going to give him the satisfaction.

She grimaced a little as she wondered whose fault it exactly *was* that her cases were ridiculous, but nothing good ever came of blaming oneself, so she quashed the thought down. The man would have been nice looking if he wasn't scowling. He had tousled, light brown hair, and she'd seen that his eyes were soft, dark and chocolate-brown before he had drawn his eyebrows together and glared at her. Well, if she was honest, he *was* good-looking. Very much so, in fact.

She supposed she wouldn't be very happy either if she'd fallen over someone's abandoned luggage – but he had his arms full of ... *stuff*. So it wasn't surprising. He really should have been looking where he was going. He looked a bit scruffy and his jeans had been covered in dirt – so chances were he was one of the gardeners or a member of staff or something, helping someone carry their luggage indoors; in which case he should have been expecting piles of luggage in the hallway.

Not to worry. He wasn't her concern, and hopefully she'd have nothing more to do with him. No, her priority now was to get her things up to her room – which meant thudding up even more stairs – and then she'd have a poke around the old house and grounds and see what they'd done to it since her last visit, familiarise herself with the tea-room, perhaps. She smiled to herself. It wouldn't be so bad if she treated herself to a cake and a cuppa there today, would it? For research purposes, of course.

She paused in the hallway, which was simply an excuse not to drag her cases any further right at that moment, and read some of the signs on the noticeboard. There was a big sign about the Lily Valentine exhibition, and some about workshops they were running over the summer: watercolours, painting flowers, sketching and the like. She smiled. She'd enjoyed art when she was younger, but had abandoned it for drama, so perhaps it would be nice to sit in on some sessions here and reconnect with her inner Berthe Morisot – if she was going to be down here for a little while.

But first, she thought, as she began to drag her luggage along again, she would get this little lot to her bedroom and then go and check out the tea-room.

1895

The Duke and Duchess had been delightful, absolutely delightful. Lily wondered why she had been so worried about seeing them, although she supposed they were almost royalty. The Duke, Jago, had become Duke due to a tragic set of circumstances. He had never been born to the job as he told Edwin wryly.

'However, it is because of my position here that I can offer you the Mill House to stay in.' Jago smiled in the direction of Elsie who was sitting in the corner of the room, sketching. Her younger cousins had greeted Lily and Edwin with awe and shyness, stared in curiosity at his eye-patch and his cane, asked if he was the pirate Long John Silver (Mabel), been scolded and told to *shush* (Clara), then been corralled outside by their nursemaid. Jago had laughingly suggested that perhaps the little girls needed to run around outside and burn some energy off. 'Elsie would have had you sleep in the nurseries with her and her cousins, but we intervened.'

'Our niece means well,' added Alys, the Duchess, pouring another cup of tea for Lily and pushing the cup over to her, 'but she is only eight and you are quite the most exciting visitor we've ever had. Her scrapbook is full of clippings about the theatre and musicals and the arts.'

Lily was a little stunned. 'Some parents would deem musical theatre rather inappropriate.' She flushed as she recalled some of the parts she had played in the very early days; scantily clad dancing girls, enticing prostitutes and siren-like mermaids to name but a few. She shuddered. She was glad those days were over. That and the modelling. And oh my, *that* photograph of her with her breast almost exposed. Oh God! 'Has anyone seen the contents of that there scrapbook?' she asked in a rush. 'Does anyone know what the pictures are she keeps in it?'

Alys smiled. 'What a beautiful accent. Do I detect a little Irish in there?'

Lily felt her cheeks heat up even more. She really had to stop slipping into the brogue …

She took a deep breath and tried again. 'Yes. Yes I am, but as you can imagine it's not looked upon too kindly in certain quarters, what with the Home Rule argument. People usually think I'm from somewhere in England, and I don't correct them unless they guess.'

'We don't judge here at Pencradoc. People are entitled to their political opinions. We take people as we find them.' Alys took a sip of her tea. 'And yes, we have looked at Elsie's scrapbook. Many, *many* times.' She looked at Lily, amusement in her eyes. 'There's nothing inappropriate in there, don't worry about it. I suspect my cousin Zennor and her husband would be the last to judge anyone on the content of art anyway.'

'Good.' Lily dipped her head as her cheeks burned up even further.

She raised her head to make a further comment, when Elsie slipped off the stool and walked over to her. 'My step-papa is the artist Ruan Teague,' she announced proudly. 'As you can see, he has taught me well.' Elsie thrust her sketchbook under Lily's nose and a faint scent of leaded pencil and wet ink drifted up to her. 'I have more of my pictures upstairs. And some at Wheal Mount, where my uncle and aunt live most of the time. Would you like to see some of my work?'

'I'd ... love to.' Lily, not having much of an option to decline, looked at the proffered picture and she could hardly believe what she saw. It was an image of herself and Alys, sipping tea and talking. Loose lines suggested the men on the edge of the room, where they were, indeed, looking at something on a desk by the window, but the focal point was Alys and Lily. There was a smile on Alys' lips and her unruly hair was sketched in, along with the welcoming, warm expression in her eyes. Lily herself was drawn with more care, it seemed; every curl of her own red hair and every twist of the ribbon tied around her bodice, tumbling to the ground until it skimmed the floor was there. There was a look in her eyes that she didn't like, though. Startled, afraid and wary were the words she would have used had she been pressed.

'That's ... incredible.' Her voice was more controlled than

31

she thought it would have been. 'And you say your step-papa taught you this skill?'

'He did.' Elsie nodded comfortably. 'Mama says I have a natural talent.'

'And does your Mama draw so well?'

'Oh no. Not at all. Nobody in my family draws at all. My step-papa says I have a unique talent.' Her words were blithe and unconcerned.

'Elsie, would you like to ring the bell and get more tea for us please?' Alys interjected. 'Oh! In fact, I'm sure Lily would love some little cakes as well, perhaps? Would you be a very good girl and run down to the kitchens to ask Cook?'

'Of course!' Elsie performed a small curtsey and hurried out of the room.

'That's one way of getting her to leave,' Alys said. 'She is utterly taken with you. But we need to discuss practicalities and we shall get nowhere with her monopolising you. How long, for instance, do you think you will need to stay here? The Mill House has three good-sized bedrooms, plus of course the attic rooms if you prefer the servants to live in.'

'Servants?' Lily was thrown again. 'I never thought ...'

'The opportunity is there for you to have a housekeeper and a nursemaid for the baby – should you wish to extend your stay. It's entirely up to you, of course. My husband didn't say what your plans were beyond coming to see us.'

'That's because my ... husband ... isn't sure himself.' Lily felt her lips twist into a wry smile. *Her husband*. The word was still very new to her.

'In that case,' said Alys gently, 'let us not plan too far ahead.' She reached over and patted Lily's hand. 'Just enjoy your stay at Pencradoc for now, have your meals with us should you choose to, and I'll make sure one of the maids comes daily and cleans the Mill House and sets your fires and everything else, but she won't stay. So you and Edwin can simply enjoy some time together.'

'Thank you.' There was nothing else to say, really. 'I will take some time to look at Elsie's scrapbook as well.'

'Yes, I think she'd like that. Her pictures are really very good. I'm sure you'll find yourself drawn and painted and sketched at every conceivable moment. She's bored of using me as a model, Jago humours her so much then they both begin arguing, the rest of her family are away and my girls won't sit still long enough, but she tries anyway.'

'She's wonderful.' Lily's voice was, genuinely, warm. She felt her guard slip a little. 'She reminds me of myself when I was small. Never still, dramatic and full of confidence.'

'I suspect you would need all of those talents and more to become a success in the theatre.'

'Yes. And to be able to sing and dance helps.' She smiled, briefly. 'And to sit still for studio photographs.'

'That is where Elsie would fail spectacularly.' Alys was mock-serious. She smiled at the door as it opened and Elsie strode back in importantly, having delivered her message to Cook.

'What? What would our delightful niece fail at? She has never failed, in all her born days.' The men had finished their conversation and had walked over to the women. Jago came up behind Alys, and put his hands on her shoulders. He dipped down briefly and kissed the top of her head. Edwin stood beside Lily, then took a seat opposite her.

'Sitting still. Lily is saying how similar Elsie is to her younger self. I doubt Elsie would pose quietly for anyone. Would you, darling?'

'I am similar to Lily?' The child's voice was strident. 'I am *similar* to Lily?' Her face lit up. 'Of course I could sit still. Or stand still. Or pose for any number of photographs.'

'Practically every photograph we have of you is blurred,' Jago said with a smile. 'Apart from one or two where we have captured you sitting drawing. I recall my most favourite – the one with your boots up on the table and your head bent over your artwork.'

'I did not know that one was being taken.' Elsie was serious. 'Had I known I would have posed properly. I do think photography is the most magical form of art. How one can press the mechanism and have a plate with an image on and then have an actual picture of what you looked at – without even having to *draw* it? I do think it is almost *magical*.'

'I have a camera,' said Edwin. His voice was quiet, yet it commanded attention. 'It is indeed magical. I have no talent to draw anything beautiful – I could not even capture my wife in pencil the way you have done, Lady Elsie, so I am afraid I bought a camera to help me. I got it on the Continent some time ago. I was hoping I could find some suitable subjects here, in Cornwall, to try it out on.' He smiled at the little girl. 'If you wish, I can show you how it works.'

'Would you? That would be most kind.' Elsie returned his smile. 'Perhaps I could take some photographs of *you*, Miss Valentine? As well as produce some portraiture, of course ...' Elsie stared off into the distance, tapping her finger on her chin, seemingly preoccupied with the work ahead of her.

'*How* old is she?' Edwin whispered to Lily, amused.

'Eight, I believe.' She fought back a smile. 'Perhaps they grow up quicker in Cornwall.'

'Perhaps they do.'

For one moment their eyes met, and she felt a wider smile break through. Edwin matched it, and she thought, for the first time since Paris, that this might be bearable.

Present Day

Matt eventually managed to get his things together and head upstairs. He was in his usual place – up in the attics on the right-hand side, then all the way along, and in a room that had a pretty splendid view of the moors cresting the horizon, and a glint in the far distance which may have been the sea. It was a view he'd sketched many a time, sitting on a chair facing the window, his bare feet resting on the sill as he balanced his sketchbook on his knees.

Today was no different. He threw the window open and leaned out, breathing the soft moorland air, noting the colours of the trees as the foliage blended together, the negative shapes formed by the sky in the dips of the trees where they touched, almost like the tips of fingers reaching out to one another. The scent of cut grass was blowing in, along with a waft of roses from the Duchess Rose's Gothic garden and he smiled at nothing in particular. It was a day that made him glad to be alive.

He scanned the gardens and saw a figure pushing along an empty wheelbarrow: Kit, no doubt. A woman appeared out of the gardens with a mug in each hand and gave one to Kit. Matt's old friend dropped a kiss on her forehead, and they sat down on a bench. That was Merryn, then.

Further along, he saw a figure running through the gardens, towards the Tower Tea-Room. The running figure had red hair, flying out behind her. Matt blinked. He could have sworn it was that woman from the hallway, but she'd changed into some sort of floaty frock; green, long-sleeved with a ribbon tied under her bust, the ends fluttering free. She disappeared behind some bushes and, despite himself, and the fact he thought she was pretty much the most abrupt and arrogant person he'd ever encountered, something made him watch a little longer to see if she appeared again.

She did. But he blinked and squinted, confused. It was definitely her, but she was wearing the cropped trousers and green halter-neck. Not a floaty frock. He shook his head. Must have been a trick of the light. Being an artist, he was pretty observant but also, being an artist, he knew how a ray of sunshine or a shaft of light could change the look of something in an instant.

Not to worry.

Whoever she was and wherever she was going was none of his concern.

He'd unpack, he decided, then go for a walk himself. He quite fancied the idea of seeing the Mill House Kit had told him about. It might be nice to capture a drawing of it before it got renovated. A little bit of genteel ruin always made for a good charcoal sketch, or even a pen and ink one …

Yes. That was a damn good plan.

Cordy bought a takeaway coffee. It was too beautiful a day to be stuck inside, she reasoned. If she was going to work in the Tower Tea-Room as of Monday, then she would have plenty of time to be inside the lovely old folly. So today, as she was on her own time, she'd be a customer.

She smiled at the girl behind the counter, Sorcha's niece, apparently, and the niece's boyfriend, who was enthusiastically steaming milk from the coffee machine whether the coffee required steamed milk or not. Everything was a latte.

Cordy smiled widely at the pair of them and headed upstairs with her cup to have a look at the exhibition. Lots of local artists exhibited here, and Kit had already organised plenty of exhibitions. Today there was an exhibition complementing the Lily Valentine story. Grainy images of the area as it would have been during her visit jostled for space with picture postcards of the sort late Victorian ladies would have sent to friends and relations. Someone had been a keen photographer as there were lots of photos of Pencradoc itself, with the Wilderness Garden and Rose's Gothic fantasy captured beautifully. In one photograph a woman in a floppy, wide-brimmed hat sat on a rock overlooking the waterfall while a little girl played with a small dog beside her.

Cordy frowned. The woman sat with her back to the photographer so she couldn't see her face. How annoying. The little girl's face was also not visible, so she couldn't even say if it had been one of the little Pencradoc girls from Wheal Mount.

She would like to think the woman was Lily Valentine, but her dress wasn't tightly corseted as Cordy would have expected from those days. It was much more of the flowing Arts and Crafts style favoured by the freer thinking woman. Cordy pulled her phone out of her pocket and did a quick Google search for Lily. There were, as expected, some studio shots of her. It was impossible to see if the gypsy or the harem girl or the can-can dancer depicted in those posed shots and portrait studio images was the lady on the rock.

Ah well. It was nice to see the photos, regardless.

Cordy switched the screen off, took a swig of coffee and headed downstairs. Time to explore the estate. Hadn't Merryn said something about the Mill House being renovated? That might mean that it would be roped off to the paying visitor. But Cordy was a member of staff – or at least she would be in a day or so – so it was fine for her to be there, she reasoned with herself. Staff had to keep an eye on things, didn't they? She would be doing Merryn a favour, really.

On an impulse, she bought a notebook and a pencil from the small stash by the till and confused the young lad who looked longingly at her takeaway cup as if he really, *really* wanted to froth some more milk up for her coffee. Taking pity on him, she asked for a refill while she looked at the other items for sale. There were postcards depicting some of the photos upstairs. She grabbed the one she had admired of the woman by the waterfall and added that to her purchases. Inexplicably, she felt really drawn to it. Since her appearance in *Downton Abbey* she'd had a fondness for all things dress-up. If she was to perform the Lily Valentine monologue, she'd use this lady as inspiration for her costume. It might be easier to get a dress like that, rather than perform as a belly dancer or can-can dancer. It would reflect the real Lily – not the character she was portrayed as in the media—

'—bloody hell,' she muttered to herself. 'Where the hell did that thought come from?' The place was already stirring her imagination. Which was good. *Very* good. She could hardly wait to start on it all properly and put some of her ideas into practice. Thanking the young lad for her drink, she bounded out of the shop, her mood lifting by the second. Soon she'd be in orbit. She *loved* it here. She really did.

Cordy walked through the grounds, barely looking at the signs they had put up to discreetly guide people through the Sculpture Trail, tossing the empty takeaway cup into a waste bin halfway there. She'd been to Pencradoc a few times and was fairly confident as to where she was heading. She paused at an overgrown area and looked along it, knowing the stream was beyond it. She could hear it rushing past, and she knew that the stream led to the Mill House. However, wasn't there a pathway along here? Through this undergrowth? Off the main pathway? It was a shortcut of kinds.

She was certain she'd walked along it before, because there was a giant white buddleia halfway, and you had to fight with the butterflies to get past it. She stared at the undergrowth, then shrugged. It must be a bit that they hadn't got around to cutting back for this year. But as she was *staff*, she would be able to go through there without risking an angry shout from Coren. She smiled to herself. He was a lovely guy, but was pretty focused on what he did. Pencradoc Arts Centre was largely his baby and he had very precise views on where it was going and, she imagined, shedloads of planning spreadsheets and charts in his office, ticking off each bit as he completed it. Kit was much more easy-going and Merryn was the voice of reason between them. That was why it all worked so well. Cordy was looking forward to joining the team, even if it was just briefly.

As she pushed her way through the undergrowth, she grew hotter and hotter and more and more grumpy. It really hadn't been looked after at all for ages. There were brambles and branches lurking in the most annoying places, and she had to perform some strange contortions to get under them, then jump over more of the same a metre later. Eventually she reached the bit where she could have sworn that the buddleia ran rampant and stood, confused, looking around for it.

'Don't say they dug it out!' she cried to nobody in particular. 'I *loved* that bloody thing!' Swearing to herself, she continued through the foliage until she broke out onto the other side. Surprisingly, though, she had to draw herself up quickly and grab onto a low-hanging tree branch nearby. Her toes were literally balanced on the edge of a stone where the edge of the path had sheared into the stream below her. Much further along, to her right, she could see the waterfall tumbling down into the depths. To her left, she knew the Mill House awaited her. But what the hell had happened to the pathway?

'Buggeration!' She jumped back a couple of feet, using the branch as leverage, and edged her way around some more bushes until she stood on a firmer piece of ground. Walking more carefully, still clutching her notebook, the postcard tucked inside it and the pencil in her pocket, Cordy picked her way along. This must be why the path wasn't in public use.

Walking more sedately, and staying well clear of the edge, Cordy made her way down the winding, overgrown pathway to the Mill House. She just had to round a little corner, she knew, and she'd see it there. An image of the building came into her mind and she smiled at the recollection. The wheel on the side was big and creaky and old, and served no purpose nowadays, but, if she stood here, and listened very carefully, she could hear the welcome *splash, splash, splash* of the old mechanism turning around, spraying up water from the mill race, a steady stream of droplets spattering the river again as the wooden wheel spun slowly around. She heard, above the splashing noise, a shout of children's laughter and the pounding of feet on the soft earth as they ran towards her, smacking at overgrown branches with sticks.

The laughter came closer and she jumped back as a whirlwind dashed past her, rustling branches and leaves, shaking petals from the wild roses that drooped sleepily from the branches above her ...

Yet that was all it was – a whirlwind. No people. No children. Nobody.

Not one person had run past her, yet she could hear the footsteps and the laughter echoing and fading into the distance as she stood, squashed against a rhododendron bush, looking in the direction she knew, she just *knew*, they had gone.

Cordy's heart was pounding in her ears and for a few seconds she just stood, frozen to the spot, staring back towards the waterfall before sense and reason began to return.

The acoustics around here were mad. Absolutely bonkers.

Those kids must have been playing over the other side of the gardens, the sounds carried across on a summer breeze ...

Water did that, didn't it? It reflected noise in all sorts of ways. It was the same in a covered swimming pool, with the voices and shouts of the swimmers echoing all around the area.

'Stupid,' she scolded herself. 'Don't be so *stupid*.' It was kids playing elsewhere, of course it was.

She stepped out from her makeshift shelter and continued towards the Mill House. The wheel had fallen silent now, and she guessed it was on some sort of timer, or the workmen in there had stopped it while they did something because, sure enough, when she rounded that corner and came face to face with the building on the other side of the stream, the wheel wasn't moving at all.

That was a bit of a shame, as she'd been looking forward to seeing it in motion. Ah well, plenty of time. She hurried up the few stone steps onto a narrow bridge that spanned the stream and ran across it, ready to say a big hello to the workmen and introduce herself as, hopefully, a future tenant of the property.

However, she couldn't see anybody to actually introduce

herself to. They must have stopped work and buggered off for lunch or something extraordinarily quickly.

'Hello?' Cordy tried anyway, pushing the old wooden door open and peering into the building. Last time she'd been here, it had smelled damp and old and a little bit rotten. It was a lot better now, although some tools were lying abandoned in the hallway, and a stepladder was laid up against the wall; evidence of the last bit of renovation. But at least the inside seemed largely sorted, and out of the three rooms on the ground floor, two looked finished, but one was still quite empty. She stared around. There was the hallway, obviously, and then the kitchen. Another room, with the water-wheel just visible in the window, was all furnished out as a dining room, although she was certain it had, at one time, been a sunroom – and this room here, the one to her left, overlooked the water out of a big picture window. It looked like this was the lounge. It was also obviously the one which had the problem with the floor, as there was a big 'Keep Clear' sign in the doorway.

She wondered where the problem was. It all looked pretty solid to her, but what did she know? Well, she'd never been great at being a 'Good Girl', and a forbidden room was a lot more exciting than an accessible one. So she edged around the sign and walked across the room.

Ahhhh – *now* she could see it – the workmen had been replacing some floorboards, which meant that—

But she never got a chance to finish that thought, as the particular floorboard she had stepped on gave way beneath her, her foot disappeared into a void and she ended up half-in and half-out of the floor, hanging on for dear life as one leg dangled into a cellar and one was bent, very uncomfortably, beneath her chin. If she let go, she'd slide right down into that cellar – and it would *hurt*.

Chapter Four

1895

As they made polite conversation with Alys and Jago over tea and cakes, Edwin could still barely believe he was here with her: with Lily. There were some things in his life he was working hard to forget but he remembered, very clearly, the night he had proposed to Lily. It was just after she had realised she was with child. She had never mentioned her suspicions until then.

'Who will want to see a pregnant Rosalee on the stage?' she had wailed. 'I can't play her any more like *this*, can I? I simply can't. I'm so stupid, so, so stupid – why did I let it happen? *Why*? Oh *God*. Oh, why did I let it happen? How long can I hide it, do you think? Just how *long* can I hide it?' She had tugged at the gypsy costume in despair, pulling it away from her still slim figure, ripping a lace trim and bursting into a fresh wave of tears.

'I know it's not what you want to hear, but you don't have to play Rosalee. You don't have to play anything else. You can marry me instead. In fact, you *should* marry me—'

'—I can't. I can't marry you. How can I do that? Look – just look. This is the *Théâtre National de l'Opéra*. I'll never get another chance like this. I've spoiled everything—'

'—Lily – Lily. Please.' He had taken her in his arms and stroked her hair away from her face. 'Think about it, at least. Please?' It hadn't been the most romantic proposal in the world; they both knew that. 'I can get a licence quite quickly. At least come away with me. My old friend inherited some estates in Cornwall, and we've been corresponding. I know that he would let us stay at Wheal Mount, or at Pencradoc. Wherever he can accommodate us. I can take you away from all of this and nobody will ever find you, unless you want to be found.'

'But Edwin. It might not even be yours! How can I put that on you? How?'

That, he admitted, had been a shock – but then she had spilled the whole story out, and the shock had gradually abated and turned into horror. At the very least, he had to protect her. At the very most, he had fathered a child.

He was a man of honour, but his war experiences had made him wary and scared to love in that all-consuming way he hoped, deep down, he was capable of. He adored Lily – he couldn't imagine his life without her. But something stopped him from allowing himself to love her as much as he wanted to; to express those feelings, and to let her know his life, strangely, meant nothing if she wasn't in it.

And beyond that, he wasn't about to walk away from his mistakes.

After the war, his emotions had been dark and erratic. He'd felt removed from the world around him, and he had refused to let anyone in. His horrors were his own to bear and what was left of his life was his own to forge out, the best way he could. Lily had been a beautiful and very necessary distraction, and he felt that if he could only learn to trust himself and give himself to her fully that they could somehow move forwards, and to hell with his crazy mind.

Now his hand had been forced – there was no way he could walk away and leave her to her fate, even if there was a chance the child wasn't his. So, that night he kept asking her to marry him.

And eventually she had agreed. And here they were. At Pencradoc. As newly-weds.

Edwin cast a glance at Lily. Beneath the dignified façade, she looked terrified.

He suspected it would prove to be an interesting visit and a shiver ran up his spine. Which was entirely ridiculous.

He cast another glance at Lily and hoped his fears were unfounded.

The idiot was draíocht, *moonstruck, bewitched. The night that sap proposed to her, Francis was watching, hiding in the shadows outside her dressing room. Her dressing room! Who the feck did she think she was?*

He wasn't a fool himself – he'd seen the clippings, the news stories – who could fail to see so much about Lily bloody Valentine? He knew it was her, saw it in the way she looked at that damn camera. She was taunting him from every cursed picture he saw, looking right at him, defying him to go and take what was rightfully his. He hadn't been sure at first, but one picture, one in particular where she was dressed in nothing but a bed-sheet told him for sure it was her. Her hair was different, her face looking less round and more defined where the light cleverly fell across her cheekbones – but they were her eyes, the look in them the look that she had given only him, the one she showed him as they made love in the early days.

And it was more than just sheer begrudgery. She was his. Always had been. Always would be.

He had travelled to Paris, toiled and fought his way across the water to find her, and here he was.

He had, of course, already seen her. He had told her she was his, and made sure she would never forget it. That was the way to do it – leave just enough time between visits so she thought she was safe, so she thought he had forgotten – and then strike again.

And tonight, he had come to make her his once more.

But now – now it seemed as if she was defying him and going back across the water to England, with this weak half-man. To some mad place in Cornwall, of all places.

No matter.

He could travel too. He could bide his time and find her there. He would let her go this time.

Because, thanks be to his God, it appeared that he had even more leverage than he had hoped and he intended to use it.

Present Day

Matt was enjoying exploring the grounds. Already, he'd found an apparently little-used pathway, away from the Sculpture Trail and paused as he looked along it. Someone had been through there quite recently. Branches were broken and foliage was crushed; he could smell the fresh scent of greenery and sniffed appreciatively.

There was another scent along there, something a little stronger; almost like a perfume. He sniffed again. Lilies. He could definitely smell lilies.

Curious, he walked into the undergrowth. He didn't know much about plants, but would be surprised if there was a crop of lilies under this lot. But perhaps there was, perhaps the fact that the branches above were broken had suddenly let some sunlight in there, and the petals were releasing their fragrance. He had an image in his head of a group of flowers nestled in some sort of secret grotto and felt his heart quicken. It would make an amazing picture if that was the case – pencil? Or watercolour? Or pastels? He'd sketch it out first and see what it looked like.

Then, all of a sudden, the scent was gone. Nothing except that sharp, natural – *green* – smell of broken branches and sap and slightly damp soil.

Something caught his eye at the far end of the disused pathway as he looked along it; a group of kids running along the pathway by the stream – he could hear the water and the kids' laughter. Shrugging, he headed further along the pathway and, breaking out onto the other side, was stunned to see the edge shear away into the water below him.

His heart lurching, he looked over the edge, hoping desperately that he wasn't going to see a gaggle of kids spinning around in the current. Thank God he didn't, but that scent was back. The lilies. It was coming from his left, and so was the thrum of a water-wheel. At least, then, he was heading in the right direction.

Well of *course* he was.

The thought was as surprising as it was definite. But, just to make sure there were no flailing kids anywhere, he had a proper look along the path to his right and another look into the water. Nothing. They must have been on the other side of the stream, then. Oh well. So long as nobody was in trouble, he'd continue his saunter towards the Mill House.

As he rounded the corner and the old building came into sight, he registered that the wheel wasn't in motion. Odd. Never mind. There was, though, a figure moving around behind the upstairs window; a woman leaning out of the window. A redhead with a green dress on, if he wasn't mistaken. The window was flung open wider and it seemed that she made to climb out, but then another figure appeared behind her. A pair of hands appeared on her shoulders, almost as if they were about to push her. Then he blinked and the image disappeared.

Matt's heart began to pound. Was there someone in there? And if there was, what the hell was happening?

With no thought for himself, he shouted and ran across the stone bridge. 'Hey! Hey! Who's in there?' He pounded across and burst through an old wooden door which was standing open, then drew to a halt as two realisations struck him almost simultaneously.

Firstly, there was definitely no sound of a struggle from up the stairs, no sign that anyone had trekked up that pristine carpet.

Secondly, in a room just off the hallway, a girl was hanging onto the floorboards, half stuck in a hole, her knee bent up under her chin and looking as shocked as he felt. It was the redhead from the hallway, the one with the month's worth of luggage.

'Thank *God*. Please – get me out!' she cried. 'I'm falling!' She twisted her head around and her eyes widened. '*You!*'

Matt stared at her for a split second, then reached her in a couple of strides. 'Yes. Me. But I have to know – is anyone upstairs? Anyone except us in here?'

'No, no. It's just me. Or someone would hopefully have hauled me out by now. I've been shouting long enough!'

A sob caught in her throat, which seemed to embarrass her, and Matt bent down. 'Okay – it's okay, I'm here now and we can get you out. I might have been earlier, but I had to step over some suitcases in the damn hallway before I could even leave the house. Here. I've got you. Grab my arms. I'll pull you up. Can you move your leg okay?'

The girl nodded, her face white. 'I think so. It's just dangling in the hole though. And this one is *hurting*. I don't know if I've pulled a muscle or I've got cramp.'

'Okay. You're fine, you're fine. Nothing's broken. Come on. On the count of three: one, two, *three* …' He hauled the redhead out, pulling her onto the firmer floorboards, dragging her, almost, out of the hole.

'Ouch! *Ouch*!' she moaned as she lay on the ground. 'God I feel so *stupid*! Then she started shaking, and Matt bit back what might very well have been a sarcastic retort. He sat with her until her breathing steadied and she had calmed down.

'Oh dear. I suppose I should thank you for getting me out. I'm sorry. Thank you for getting me out. Thank you … but I do feel really, *really* stupid!'

'No problem.' Then, he couldn't resist it. 'A person should really look where they're going, shouldn't they?' Well, he justified to himself, she looked pretty much okay, despite her enthusiastic protests otherwise he'd have said nothing of the sort.

'Yes. I guess I deserved that.' She took a deep, shaky breath and half-smiled at him. 'Seriously, though. Thanks. I don't know what I would have done if you hadn't come. I suppose

I would have had to drop down there and wait until the workmen came back. I think they're on their lunch-break.' She looked around as if they'd appear out of one of the other rooms. Obviously, they didn't. 'I wouldn't have been down there forever.' She peered over the edge of the hole. 'I don't think it's that deep, now I've seen it. And I'm quite tall.'

'And there's definitely nobody up there? I thought I saw …'

His voice tailed off as she looked at him curiously. 'There's nobody here. If there was, I think they might have come down and made themselves known. I really was shouting quite a lot.' She pulled a face and blushed, a rosy pink that made her cheeks glow.

'Ah. I thought … never mind. I clearly thought wrong. Too much imagination. I was looking for the kids that were playing around here. Followed a path. Heard the water-wheel going.' He shrugged. 'And then I came running over here.'

'No. There's just me. Being a stupid damsel in distress. Oh – bugger!' The girl suddenly patted her pockets. 'My phone. It's fallen out of my pocket. I bet it's down there.' She got onto her hands and knees and peered into the hole in the floor. 'Yes. There it is. I can see it. Oh *bugger.*'

Matt crawled over and peered down next her. She was radiating heat and a soft scent of suntan lotion, lilies and another fresh floral fragrance. Ah. *That* was the smell he'd followed along the pathway, and it was an oddly familiar one at that.

'Can you see it? Just down there?' The girl pointed to a bright pink rectangle on the floor, perched on what looked to be some old hessian corn sacks that must have been put in the cellar for some reason.

'Yes – yes, you're right.' Matt sat back on his heels. 'Well, there's two ways we can do this.'

'Two? Okay. What do you suggest?' The girl sat back on her own heels.

'One, I go down and get it. Two, *you* go down and get it.'

There was a pause then the redhead surprised him by laughing out loud. 'Oh, I like it. I like it. Yeah. I can't see any way else we can do it.' She held a hand out. 'If we're going to be going on an expedition together, we'd better introduce ourselves. I'm Cordelia Beaumont. I'm Merryn's friend. Do you know Merryn? She works with Kit and Coren? Lives with Kit? My flat in London flooded so I came down to help out in the tea-room and do some work with the guys on a summer show. People usually call me Cordy.' She smiled at him properly then, dazzling him with it, and that was when he realised when he'd seen her before – seen that smile before.

It was in the gossip columns – wasn't it? Her name definitely rang a bell but, when he thought about it properly, he couldn't recall actually seeing a photo of her. Rather, he'd seen some headline on a gossip mag in the teacher's lounge at work: *Toby Fowler and Cordelia Beaumont. Why it Works with this West End Girl*. Or some such nonsense.

'Aren't you the girl who's with Toby Fowler? The guy from the musicals?' He couldn't help himself, even as he took her hand. He started as a little zip of electricity shivered up his arm – plus, it felt very much as if he'd held that hand before.

Cordelia Beaumont's eyes widened slightly, and he wondered whether she had felt the same as him. If she had, she'd hidden it pretty well, but seemed in no hurry to let go of his hand. Instead, she spoke again. 'Was. He's an idiot. Half of the West End was with him. He deserves to get a nasty disease, he really does.' Then she did let go and his hand felt strangely empty.

But, despite the odd sensations and the feeling that certain images seemed to be knocking on the side of his mind's eye for access, Matt couldn't help but respond. 'He always seems like he's going places. He's been in a couple of shows I've seen.'

'Hmm. I could say he's been in a couple of showgirls as well, but that would make me sound jealous and annoyed and I'm not. Well. I'm maybe annoyed. But he can get stuffed, he really can. I don't want no disease, Mister.' Her accent had changed from cut-glass British to Southern American as easily as that. 'He's one of the reasons I'm here. I worked at his PR agency. It got a bit awkward when I was fielding calls from weeping girls who he'd *wham, bam, thank you ma'am*-ed.' She sniffed in disdain. 'Plus with my flat flooding, I'm technically homeless at the minute until Roland sorts it out.'

'Roland?' Matt was thrown again.

'Mmm.' She nodded. 'My upstairs neighbour. Long story. Anyway. Yes. I'm here. Sorry. I talk too much. And anyway – you are …?' She flushed again and looked at him politely.

'Oh! Sorry. Yes. I'm Matt.' He had been far too busy studying her face and listening to that surprisingly musical voice to concentrate on anything as mundane as his name. 'Matt Harker. I'm Kit's friend. We went to art college together. I teach art at a secondary school.' He gave her a thumbs-up. 'Yep – my friend is your friend's partner. I know Merryn. I'm staying at Pencradoc for a couple of weeks as well. Doing some workshops to help out.'

'Oh! How wonderful. I thought you were maybe a gardener when I saw you in the hallway. All muddy. But no. You're not. Again, look, I really am so sorry about my luggage.'

'Forget it. At least it was only my clothes. I wouldn't have been so forgiving if it was my art stuff or my easel.' He was, actually, deadly serious about that one. 'Let's think instead about how we can get your phone out of that hole. There must be a stepladder somewhere. We could maybe lower it down and one of us could climb into the cellar.'

'Yes. Good idea.' Cordy looked around and her gaze settled on the discarded tools in the hallway. 'I see one over there.'

She made to stand up, but Matt put his hand on her shoulder. 'You stay there. I'll go and get it. Hopefully we won't find any more dodgy floorboards.'

It was odd, though, because the layout seemed a little off to him. The dining table shouldn't really be where they'd put it – it was supposed to be a sunroom, wasn't it? So they needed a table right *there*, and maybe a comfy chair right *there* ... and part of him was still wondering what he had seen upstairs. He shivered, involuntarily, and got to his feet. 'Okay. I'll be right back.'

'Okay.' Cordy nodded. She sat down and crossed her legs with an expectant look on her face.

Cordy watched the man, Matt, head towards the tools. He was a lot nicer than she'd expected, now they'd cleared the air a bit. He didn't look half so angry for a start. When he smiled, he looked quite friendly, in fact – despite having a strangely conflicting demeanour of teacher-type authority and easygoing creativity. Cordy suspected his art was his outlet and it wasn't just restricted to teaching children.

Interesting.

She was still pondering when he came back with the stepladder, as promised.

He smiled at Cordy. 'This should work. Shall I do the honours?' He shifted the weight of the ladder and eased it into the hole in the floorboards. 'Ha. I'm not sure I'll fit down there, having said that.'

There wasn't a lot of room in the narrow space, once the ladder was in place, and Cordy shuffled over. 'I think I might.' She looked at Matt and assessed his build – he was quite slim, yet broad-shouldered and she thought he might indeed get wedged in there – his top half, anyway. Cordy, on the other hand, had what she deemed the skinniest shoulders in the world. And no real hips to speak of.

'I'll manage,' she said. 'I think I can wriggle down there.

'If you're sure. We can always pull a couple more floorboards up.'

'Ha! I've been here less than two hours. I've already wrecked their renovations – I don't really want Coren to get super cross with me if he finds out I've *deliberately* ripped up some floorboards. I'll manage.' She took hold of the ladder and looked up at Matt. 'Just hold onto the top for me, would you please?'

'Of course. Be careful. I don't want to have to explain why you got stuck down there properly. Then Coren would be cross with me.'

'True. Okay. Here we go.'

Cordy shimmied down the ladder and pulled a face as her feet touched the bottom. The floor was stone, but the hessian sacks had, thankfully, broken the fall of her phone, and it was seemingly fine. As she dusted it down and looked around her, she wrinkled her nose; it felt quite damp and smelly down there, and there was a definite rushing sound to her right. She listened carefully and realised it was the sound of the river flowing past them – the bit where the wheel mechanism would be, she guessed.

As her eyes adjusted to the gloom, she started to make out some old joists and machinery and, curious, she walked carefully over to them.

'Is everything all right down there?' Matt's voice was strangely far away, the acoustics odd as she went further into the cellar.

'It's fine, thanks. I've got my phone back, but I'm just going to have a look at the machinery. It's fascinating.' She found the torch on her phone and switched it on, lighting her way through the cellar.

Then: 'Oh.'

Cordy stopped and trained the light on the mechanism. She was no engineer, but even she could see that the wheel, if that indeed was what was attached to the side of the building here, couldn't have worked for a very, very long time. The wooden beam spiking through the wheel, and through the cellar wall – the wooden beam which would have been attached to the cogs inside and helped the wheel to turn – was rotten and a big chunk had come off. Someone, probably many moons ago, had hammered a big cross-beam across the mechanism to stop the thing spinning out of control with the power of the water. So, basically, there was no way that wheel would turn.

'Oh,' she said again and pointed the torch a little longer at it, confusion making her frown. 'Matt?' she called, turning to face the gap. Her voice echoed weirdly through the gloom, and she was more relieved than she could say to hear him answer.

'Yeah? Are you okay? Do I need to come down?'

'No. No, I'm okay. Just ... did you hear the water-wheel turning when you came along here?'

'Yeah. Loud and clear.' There was a smile in his voice.

'But it wasn't working when you actually reached the cottage?'

'No – not that I can recall.' There was a pause, seemingly where he was thinking. 'Definitely not. It must have been switched off. On a timer or something maybe?'

'I – I don't think so.' She turned back to the pieces of old wood and walked closer still. No, there was no way that thing had moved in forever. The cross-beam was full of rusty nails, hammered in eons ago, and liberally coated with spiders' webs that had clearly been there for a very long time, judging by the crispy husks of flies entrapped in them.

She flashed the torch up and down and saw something stuck in one of the cogs at the top, trapped between the teeth and the wall. There was a chink of light just above it, almost illuminating it as if to say, 'hey there, come and see what this is!' Cordy blinked and, her heart speeding up and then slowing down, realised it was a crack between two of the floorboards above it. The light must be coming in from a window – perhaps that big picture window in 'her' lounge – and dust motes danced around the crack like a swarm of fireflies.

'Ummmm – Matt?' Her voice was even more echoey.

'Yeah?'

'I don't suppose I could bring that ladder over here, could I?' She turned to the mechanism again and swung her light upwards to the cogs.

Matt laughed. 'Not sure how that'll work – unless we manoeuvre it a bit ...' There was a thoughtful sort of silence, then a loud *crack* and some creaking as someone came down the ladder, and then footsteps behind her.

'That's better.'

Cordy yelped and jumped, turning and flashing her torch right in Matt's face. 'God! What a shock!'

'That light is *bright*.' He turned his face away and held his hands up in front of his face, blinking as Cordy quickly swung the torchlight away from him.

'How did you ...?'

'Slight accident with another floorboard.' He shrugged. 'They all need replacing in that bit anyway. It's dangerous. I'll go back to the hole and get the ladder for you, if you show me what you want it for.'

'For that.' She swung her makeshift torch around and illuminated the cog and the object stuck in it. 'I don't know if I'm mistaken, but it seems as if this mechanism hasn't been working in ages. But I definitely heard the wheel turning when I came this way.'

'So did I.' Matt moved closer to her and faced the beam. 'You're right. That's certainly been out of commission for a long time. What's that, I wonder?' He pointed up at the item which had caught Cordy's attention.

'That's what I'm wondering. Hence I wanted the ladder. Might it be that it's stopping the wheel from going around? It's dropped in there and stuck it. Like in the last twenty minutes or something?' She looked up at Matt, almost hopefully.

'Not in the last twenty minutes, no. Maybe in the last twenty years ...'

'I want to get up there and check.'

'Okay ...' He didn't seem convinced. 'Maybe I should go up, though. It's looking a bit creaky.'

'Creaky!' Cordy scoffed. 'Creaky is the flying harness thing I had to use when I was the Fairy Godmother in *Cinderella*.'

She didn't expand on the fact that the show was at one of the little community theatres in the suburbs. She'd had to stay at a hotel for the three nights of the production because it would have cost more to commute there and back every day. But that, at least, was the joy of temping. She could be flexible like that if an opportunity came up – and, as she always told herself, it looked good on her acting CV.

'Fairy godmother? So you're into drama are you?'

'Into drama?' She laughed. 'My dream is to be an actress; well, an actress that people have heard of, not just a bit-player that's known for sleeping with Toby Fowler. But sadly, I haven't really commandeered the stage in a proper production yet. I've done chorus things. Crowd scenes. Extras. I was even in *Downton Abbey*, you know. Blink and you'd miss me, but I was there.' She smiled. 'That's part of the reason I'm here. I'm resting, as they say. Hence the temping. And I couldn't resist Lily Valentine.'

'Few people could, or so I hear.' Matt smiled back. 'Well, one of us should go up there and—'

'—And I'm definitely the lightest, no offence, so if I fall and crush you, it shouldn't be too terminal.'

'I guess. All right. But I'll hold the ladder again, and you come straight down if it's looking dangerous.'

'I will. And thanks.' She turned to him, and felt her cheeks colour. 'Thanks for indulging me on this one.'

'I'm as intrigued as you are. Especially considering it looks as if this thing hasn't moved for years.'

Cordy looked back at the mouldering cogs and beams. Deep down, she really hoped they weren't *too* rotten – or this may very well be her final curtain call.

Chapter Five

1895

Jago had suggested they might like to walk to the Mill House, given that Edwin and Lily had been in the carriage for quite a while, and he would send someone over with the luggage later. Lily had thought that a wonderful idea. It was all astonishing, and although she had thoroughly enjoyed meeting Alys and Jago, she was longing to have some time to herself. Which was an odd thing for an actress to long for, when she was so accustomed to being in the public eye.

But Lily was tired and emotional, which equally surprised her, and she leapt at the chance to get away to the sanctuary they had been promised. She and Edwin had walked arm in arm across the estate, through the winding paths and old follies in an ancient rose garden and by the clear, refreshing river that tumbled over some rocks in a dancing waterfall. She felt her spirits lift immensely, even on such a small walk. It was comforting in a way to be able to walk with Edwin as well and have no expectation on either side.

They eventually reached the Mill House, and Lily stood as Edwin opened the door, then he bowed and indicated that she should enter. 'After you, please,' he said.

'Thank you.' She made to walk inside, then she heard a little voice: 'Ohhhhh. Oh no.'

Lily looked behind her, astonished at the disappointed little noise that came out from the bushes.

Then she realised. 'Elsie? Is that you?'

'Miss Valentine. Yes. I'm sorry. It's me.' The bushes rustled and moved and Elsie appeared, clutching a book. The scrapbook again, it seemed. 'I did so want you to look at this, and I am so very sorry to bother you, but if you have it now, we might be able to talk about it tomorrow?'

'Oh. I see. Well, I can certainly take it from you to look at.'

'Thank you.' She handed it over, but then there was yet another lusty sigh. 'I did so hope that ...' Then she shook her head, her dark curls bouncing on her shoulders. 'Forgive me. All the adults in my life would tell me I am disagreeable and to be quiet.'

Despite herself, Lily found it difficult not to smile. 'What is so disagreeable about you giving me that scrapbook right there?'

She held out her hand and Elsie gave the book to her willingly, then pressed her palms together. 'It's not the scrapbook. I just – I just hoped—' Here she raised her hands, still clasped, imploringly, and Lily heard Edwin turn what might have been a laugh into a cough, '—that as you have just been married, that Mr Griffiths would carry you across the threshold. I have never seen that happen in real life, although I have heard it does, when someone gives someone one's heart.'

'Elsie!' Lily was speechless.

'Why Lady Elsie.' That was Edwin, seemingly recovered from his coughing fit. 'That is a splendid idea. It is, as I understand, a tradition that is kept for the newly-weds as they enter their own home for the first time. This is not to be our home, so I cannot say that the thought had crossed my mind. However, as it is, indeed, the first homely place we have visited together, then if Miss Valentine agrees, I shall attempt to do so.'

Lily looked up at him in surprise. 'But your leg. Your injuries. Don't be such an eejit.'

'If I can't take two or three steps without this damn cane to carry my wife over the threshold, what does that make me?'

'Edwin ...'

'Elsie, sweetheart, would you be so kind as to hold this for me?' He handed over his cane to the delighted, astonished little girl whose eyes widened as she clasped her hands together even more tightly, clutching the cane between them.

'Miss Valentine? Or should I say Mrs Griffiths? Lily …' There was a glint of a challenge in his eye, and Lily understood the importance of this.

It was twofold. They needed to make it seem as if they were indeed deliriously happy newly-weds, but Edwin also wanted to do such a silly thing as carry her over the threshold to prove that he was not going to be beaten by his injuries.

'Very well.' She nodded and stood in front of him. 'Go ahead, Mr Griffiths.'

And to her surprise, and apparently Elsie's delight, Edwin picked her up. Squaring himself to face the challenge, he took three hesitant steps over the threshold and into the hall of the Mill House.

She slipped out of his arms to set her feet back on the floor, but rested her hands on his shoulders for a little moment afterwards, his gaze locking on hers.

'Thank you,' she said.

'No. I should thank you,' he replied quietly. Then he half-smiled. 'Small victories.'

'Small victories.' Then, to both their surprise, she stood on her tiptoes and kissed him briefly.

'Oh that was so romantic!' Elsie thrust the cane back at him and clapped her hands. He didn't even look at the child; just took the cane and thanked her. He was too busy just staring into Lily's eyes. That kiss had been gratitude and perhaps a hint of congratulation, nothing more. He had walked into this relationship without any illusions; it had been necessary on many levels for them both.

Lily was trapped and desperate, and he knew he could offer her a way out. He was trapped and desperate in his own way – and Lily was his way out. If he had a wife and child to think about he would focus more on them than his inner demons. He just knew it had to be that way or he would sink somewhere dark that nobody would ever reach him.

So here they were, at Pencradoc. The newly-wed couple, so happy and positive about the future. Carrying her over the threshold was a small thing, but again necessary.

'It *is* quite romantic.' Lily moved her attention away from him and focused on the little girl. 'And thank you for the scrapbook, but I think you perhaps need to go back to your family now. I'll look after this for you.' She held up the scrapbook. 'And we shall talk about it tomorrow.' Her smile was brilliant, and he saw the little girl melt with the force of it. 'My husband and I need to rest and settle into our little holiday house.'

'Of course.' Elsie curtsied quickly and smiled. 'I will see you tomorrow, Miss Valentine – I mean, Mrs Griffiths.'

'Please – call me Lily, as I asked.'

'Lily.' Elsie smiled even more widely. 'Until tomorrow. *Adieu*. One day, I'm going to write and illustrate things about the arts. You'll see.' She nodded and turned on her heel, bouncing off through the undergrowth.

'A singular child,' murmured Edwin.

'Singular. But well-meaning and full of romantic notions, I suspect.' Lily sighed and flicked through the scrapbook. She raised her eyebrows as she turned the pages. Edwin glanced small, visiting-card-sized black and white pictures of actresses and stage stars. He barely recognised any of them, except of course for Lily. There were also clippings from newspapers and periodicals, theatre programmes and ticket stubs he assumed people had sent the little girl from their travels – or she had been taken to a *lot* of shows, and he somehow thought that might be unlikely, given her age and where she lived.

'I think I'll take this up to my room and I can study it in peace up there.' Lily looked up and smiled.

'Of course.' Edwin nodded and bowed. 'Let's go upstairs and you can choose which room you want. I'll take another one.'

'Oh.' She stared at him. 'Of course. Thank you. It's not …

not that I don't *want* to share a room or a bed with you, it's just ...'

'It's just the same reason I'm *not* going to share a room or a bed with you, Lily.' He leaned down and dared to kiss her, gently. 'It's just that I don't think either of us are quite ready to be married ... yet.'

'I hope we might be, though. At some point.'

'We will be, I'm certain about it. But for now, you're safe. And that's all that matters really.'

'And you're safe too.'

'I am.'

'Good.' Her hand slipped into his. 'Shall we go upstairs and choose our rooms then?'

'Yes. I'm following you.'

'What about the luggage? What shall we tell them?'

'We don't need to tell them anything. It's not unusual for people of this social rank to have separate rooms.' He grinned at her, suddenly.

'Well that's not the way it works where I'm from!'

'Nor me!' He laughed. 'Who'd be a Duke, eh?'

'And who'd be a Duchess? Do you think a disgraced old actress and a dashing wounded soldier will ever fit in here?'

'Everyone fits in at Pencradoc,' he told her. And you're anything but a disgraced old actress. Have no fear.'

'I don't think I will. Not so long as we fit in here together, somehow.'

He nodded. It seemed the best prospect he could hope for himself as well. And that seemed like a small victory in itself.

Present Day

Matt held the ladder tightly and watched Cordy climb up it. They now had his phone lying on the floor, the torch beam on that illuminating the rungs, and she had her phone with her to get a better look at whatever was stuck in the cogs.

It was a mystery as to why they had both heard the water-wheel churning. There had been definite splashes and creaks going on, and Matt was puzzled. Half of his mind was trying to work out what it might have been, and half of it was silently urging Cordelia Beaumont to grab whatever it was that was stuck and come back down. As he looked around, he fully realised how old and decrepit this cellar was; there was a sense of damp and dirt all around him, and if that item she was now easing out of its trap was indeed paper or card, as he suspected having looked at it in a bit more detail as he stood here, then it was fortunate that it hadn't landed on the floor itself. It would have been ruined, for sure.

But then again, it might just be an old flyer or advertising leaflet; perhaps a label that had fallen off something and slipped between the gaps in the floorboards. It was unlikely to be anything special, but he kind of understood Cordy's desire to retrieve it. The workmen might have dropped it earlier, or those kids he had heard might have thought it fun to post it through a gap ... his stomach lurched as he remembered the people upstairs. Perhaps they had been real after all. Perhaps they had clambered out of a window and back down – of course! Of course. There might be an outside staircase – sometimes these old buildings had them, didn't they? – and those people could have come up that way. And disappeared the same way. He was still a little uncomfortable thinking of the fact that one of them had seemed about to push the other out of the window, though.

Bizarre. Very bizarre.

'I think I've got it. It's pretty much stuck tight. I don't want to tear it,' came Cordy's voice, breaking into his thoughts. It sounded strangely echoey, with all the weird acoustics down there.

'If it's just a bit of litter that's jamming the cogs, then I don't think it matters too much if you tear it,' he called.

'But that's the thing. I don't know if it is just litter. It's a bit thick to be one sheet of paper, and I'm doing my best to ease it out. Oh God! I've just had a terrible thought.' She looked down at him. 'What if it was put here deliberately. What if it's here to serve a purpose? Like to stop the wheel from turning?'

Matt laughed. 'I don't think a bit of paper would be a very effective wedge. It's not like you're going to remove it and the thing is going to start moving again—' He stopped that train of thought as he remembered the noise of the water-wheel turning. It couldn't have been this piece of equipment, it just couldn't have been, judging by the state of the nails hammered into the beams and the thick planks stopping anything from moving.

Matt shivered and suddenly wished that Cordy would hurry up and retrieve that thing, then they could get back above ground. The whole atmosphere had seemed to change down suddenly and, if he wasn't mistaken, there was a shadow breaking away from that wall along there …

'Cordy. Hurry up. I think we need to get out of here.'

'Yeah. Got it. I think – yesssss!' She waved the piece of paper or whatever it was in the air. 'It looks like an envelope, but … oh!' She looked down and seemed to stare at the exact point where Matt had thought he had seen that shadow.

'Shit.' Cordy scrambled down the ladder like the devil's dog himself was snapping at her from the top of the wheel. 'Come on. I don't like it down here any more.' She jumped the last few rungs, and Matt didn't need telling twice. He ducked down and retrieved his phone, then lugged the ladder up and ran after her, quite awkwardly, it had to be said, until they reached the hole where they'd come down earlier. He managed to get the ladder propped up and stood back briefly. 'You go. I'll follow.'

Cordy didn't need telling twice. She scrambled up, and Matt followed her. As he leaned down and pulled the ladder up, he was fairly certain he saw a face staring up at him … and a hand reaching out.

*

Cordy ran straight out of the Mill House, Matt close behind her. They didn't stop until they were on the other side of the bridge and she was horrified and embarrassed to see that her hands were shaking, even as she held her phone – with the torch still on – in one hand, and the envelope she'd retrieved in the other.

Feeling rather foolish now she was away from the old building, certain her imagination had been playing tricks on her, she looked up at Matt. 'Well. Sorry about that. I think I set you off as well, didn't I?' She attempted a laugh. 'I felt pretty sure that … yes … okay. Maybe not.' She choked out another, rather strangled, laugh.

'There was something down there with us?'

Cordy stopped laughing abruptly. 'Yes. Um. Yes. Actually.' She pulled a face. 'Not too sure what it was.'

'Hmmm. No. Me neither.' Matt attempted a smile and shoved his hands in his pockets. 'I feel pretty stupid myself, to be honest. It was probably a rat. Or an owl.' He pulled a face which, Cordy was sure, would match hers.

'Ugh! Not rats. Anything but rats.' She shuddered, but part of her thought that big, black shadow she'd seen was not really a rat at all, unless it was a six-foot tall one, and she was also quite sure that said rat was walking on its hind legs. Perhaps, upon reflection, she would rather it had been a rat? 'Do you think we need to 'fess up about the holes in the floor?'

'No. Not right now.'

'Good. Shall we see what we've got here instead?'

'That sounds like a better plan.' Matt flicked a look back at the Mill House and Cordy shuddered again.

Deliberately turning her back on the place, she pointed towards the clearing where they'd both broken through into this little secret part of the garden. 'Over there?'

'Over there,' Matt agreed, and, falling into step with one another, they walked, quite quickly, to the pathway and the overgrown bower.

The scent of lilies drifted past on a breeze, and, without knowing why, Cordy shivered.

It was good to be back. It was good to see daylight again. To breathe sweetly scented fresh air. Her perfume was still in the atmosphere and he closed his eyes to breathe her in. Lilies. Like her name.

Opening his eyes again, he fixed his gaze on the distance and began to walk.

They reached the part of the garden where the overgrown pathway ended and, by unspoken agreement, they kept walking towards the waterfall. As the distance increased between them and the Mill House, Cordy felt her heart rate return to something like normal.

'I think we should be okay to stop just over here.' She pointed towards a better maintained pathway which headed up towards a flat rock overlooking the waterfall. 'Every time I've been here, I've found this spot really peaceful – and actually, this is the spot that's on this postcard I just bought. Look.' She stopped and fished the postcard of the lady and the little girl and the dog out of her pocket. 'I'm glad that didn't drop in the cellar too. Although I suppose a notebook and a postcard and a pencil would have been easier to replace than a phone. I probably wouldn't have decided to climb down there for just those.'

She handed the card to Matt and their fingertips connected slightly as he took it from her. There was a little tingle, something like a tiny electric shock, that jolted up her arm and for a split-second she caught his eye. It was just like before, in the cellar. It had taken her by surprise then just as much as it did now…

But she thought it best not to mention it, and smiled instead, drawing on all her acting training. 'I'm not sure if it's Lily, but it would be nice to think so.'

'That's a beautiful postcard. I wonder who the little girl was. Maybe it was this lady's daughter?'

'Maybe. Like I say, I'm not convinced it's Lily. Her dress looks a little Arts and Crafts. I would have expected her to be more ... flamboyant, somehow.'

'Yes, but if she was trussed up like a turkey for her day-job, don't you think she'd be happy to chill out a bit and be a bit less ... corseted ... on her holiday?' He smiled. 'They didn't have to worry too much about the paparazzi catching them unawares in those days.'

'True.' Cordy laughed and took the picture back, being very careful to ensure her skin didn't connect with Matt's again. 'There. Shall I see what this is then?' She lifted the envelope up. 'It's probably something and nothing, but I get very curious about things like this. Just in case they're super exciting.'

'Possibly old receipts or invoices for the work carried out when they boarded up that wheel.' Matt raised his eyebrows. 'Because I really don't think it's worked for years.'

'Hmmm.' Cordy didn't really want to pursue that line of thought. 'Okay. I'm going to open it.' She dipped her head and carefully eased the flap away from the envelope.

Inside, there were a few pieces of paper, and Cordy saw that some of them were thicker and shinier than the others. 'Photographs! I think someone put some photos in here. They're sort of tucked inside this leaflet ... oh! Oh look!'

In her hand was an exquisitely painted, hand-written theatre programme, made up of one messily folded sheet of paper. On the front was a watercolour of a stunning redheaded woman standing on a flower-strewn stage, gazing pensively into the distance. She was surrounded by a bower of trailing lilies and ivy, and despite the fact that there was a definite childish, untrained look to the picture, it had been beautifully done. Written carefully in best copperplate handwriting was the legend: 'Miss Lily Valentine Appears at Pencradoc in a Pageant'.

'It's Lily Valentine!' Cordy laughed. 'Oh my goodness. It must be from when she was here.' She peered at some writing on the bottom. '"*A Midsummer Night's Dream*, a play by Mr Wm. Shakespeare, produced, directed and programme drawn by Lady Elsie Pencradoc." Wow. That little girl was *busy*.'

'And talented ... may I?' Matt reached out for the delicate paper.

'Sure. Just let me rescue the photos ...' Cordy slipped the pictures out of the programme. A little squiggle of a thrill was starting to creep through her body. Photographs! They might be of Lily as well.

But, even better than that – 'Yes!' She held one out. It was, more or less, a companion picture to the one she had bought as a postcard. This time, it showed the woman in the hat – most *definitely* Lily, she could see now – facing the photographer. She was smiling, a true professional, posing for the camera. She was on her own though, with no dog and no child – but her dress and her hat were the same. So even if it had been taken on a different day, it was quite obvious that the model was the same. The angle of the photo, however, was tilted upwards. Then realisation dawned, and Cordy smiled.

Because there were a couple of other photos as well – all taken, Cordy noticed, looking up at Lily, as if from a child's vantage point. There was also one of a dog, the same dog the child had been playing with, and he sat very nicely, his tail a blurry mess as he apparently wagged it at the photographer. One picture was of a collection of small girls, the smallest one looking cross and folding her arms, while the other three posed just like Lily; chins out, noses in the air, clasped hands and even, in one case, a dramatic pose as one child knelt on the floor and raised her hands, wringing them like a tiny Lady Macbeth.

Cordy shuffled the photos around and was delighted to see that one was of Lady Elsie Pencradoc herself; it was obvious to anyone who knew the marble bust in the hallway and, she was even more delighted to see, that she was also dressed the same as the child in the postcard. 'It's not her daughter – it's Elsie! How wonderful. And how lucky we found them.' But the best one, in Cordy's opinion, was the picture of Lily. 'They're in good condition for being stuck down there!' commented Cordy.

'If they'd been on the ground they'd be mush,' Matt observed wryly. 'Just as well that machinery *was* stuck in place.'

'It mustn't have been that water-wheel we heard, then. There must be one further along the river.'

'Perhaps a newer one. Or perhaps it was a recording of one they've got set to go off to create ambience.'

'Ah – yes. That's a good suggestion.' Certainly, it was better than agreeing they'd both heard a water-wheel that had been stilled for years turning.

'Lady Elsie was quite the little artist, wasn't she?' commented Matt.

'Her step-papa must have taught her well.' She knew there was a note of amusement in her voice.

'Very well. And I think, looking at the ages of the girls, these pictures were taken the same time as the one they've displayed by the stage.'

'The stage! Of course. Merryn mentioned it. I'll have to get myself up there ...' But Cordy didn't quite understand why she suddenly felt a strange sense of anticipation or why there was that drifting scent of lilies again, blowing past her on the breeze, and instead looked down at the precious photographs and smiled. Then she frowned as she peered more closely.

'Oh – hold on. There's one more thing.' She unfolded a scrap of paper that was tucked behind everything else. It was a note that was dreadfully faded – something that looked like marriage lines or an extract from a parish register. 'Looks like it's a record of Evelyn Sullivan and Francis O'Hara, who got married in November 1887. From County Meath. That's Ireland, isn't it? Intriguing.'

It was oddly familiar, standing by the river with the sound of the water-wheel going behind them ... no ... there wasn't a water-wheel turning, was there? Matt listened again, just to make sure, and of course it was silent, apart from the usual summer noises of bees and soft leaves rustling and the river flowing lazily by, the tumbling waterfall upriver from them.

He looked down at the girl next to him. She was a little more dishevelled now after her adventure in the cellar and what with falling through the floorboards, of course, but her eyes were dancing and there was a pink tinge to her cheeks – whether it was from the sunshine or the fizzing excitement he could sense from her find down there, he didn't know. She looked a lot better, in an odd way, with her hair coming loose and the smudge of dirt on her nose. Not so polished – so much more natural.

He just stopped himself from rubbing the smudge off her nose and was pleased he had done so, as she looked directly up at him and grinned. It would have been very peculiar if his forefinger had been centimetres away from her nose at the time, he thought.

'Well. This has been fun, hasn't it? I'm glad you didn't damage yourself when you fell over my luggage.'

'Me too. I'm glad I managed to pull you out of that cellar.' They started walking back on the path they'd created through the overgrown foliage. Matt looked over his shoulder and shivered; there was no trace of the way they'd come. The branches had seemed to close behind them silently and secretively, shutting the world of the Mill House and the mysterious water-wheel sounds off from real life.

'Oh, I don't suppose I would have damaged myself too much. It wasn't that deep in the end, and the workmen would have got me out, I guess,' Cordy was saying as they broke into the main area of the gardens.

'I guess.'

There was an awkward moment where they both stood and got their bearings. Matt felt odd, as if he was readjusting to the real world after returning from the place they'd just been to.

It was more than awkward, in fact. The atmosphere shifted and, unaccountably, the conversation seemingly dried up between them, to the extent that Cordy was suddenly shuffling the photos and the home-made theatre programme nervously, not looking at him. It was beyond weird and even he didn't quite know what to say to drive the conversation forward. He was not usually stuck for words, but nothing seemed quite right ...

'Okay. I'm going to find Merryn and show her these, I think. Once again. Thank you. I'm sure we will see each other around.'

'I'm sure we will.'

They stood facing each other for a moment longer, but then Cordy dropped her head and stuffed the photos back in the envelope, then tucked them all inside her notebook. 'I'm heading ... that way.' She pointed vaguely in the direction of Rose's Garden. 'I'm going to have a look at the stage, I think. Make the most of my day off, before I start doing proper work.'

'Sure. I was heading this way anyway.' Matt nodded in the other direction. Cordy was still studying the pathway intently, deliberately, it seemed, not catching his eye. 'See you ... around.'

There were a few murmured words of assent and they took leave of one another.

As Matt strode away from Cordy, he scowled. What on earth had just happened there? He looked back, intending to perhaps go after Cordy and say he'd changed his mind and he'd have a look at the stage with her, but she'd disappeared.

His eyes drifted to the overgrown pathway they'd come through – but unless he had completely lost his bearings, there was no access there at all. In fact, a neat row of lavender hedges lined the gravelled pathway and there was no part of that which was broken. He frowned again.

He *must* have lost his bearings. It was the only logical explanation.

But then something nagged at the back of his mind: a voice, a woman's voice with a slight Irish lilt to it seemed to whisper a comment: *There's nothing logical about Pencradoc!*

Irish? How the heck had he conjured up that sort of accent – even if he did agree with the sentiment? It must have been that slip of paper Cordy found with the names on it.

But how that had got there, in the cellar of a house in Cornwall, was anyone's guess.

And how it got there, along with the photographs of Lily Valentine and a programme from her visit here, was another story entirely.

Chapter Six

1895

Once Lily and Edwin had established themselves in the Mill House, they fell into a routine of sorts. They continued to sleep in different rooms, of course – hers was at the back, overlooking the water-wheel and the river; his was at the front of the house, a smaller, less fussy room altogether. His clothes and possessions were laid out with military precision, a fact noted by Lily on the rare occasion she glimpsed inside the room.

In contrast, her space was much more chaotic, with clothes and bright blankets covering practically every piece of furniture, the top of her dressing table littered with bottles of perfume, hairbrushes, combs and jewellery. The maids came in every morning to tidy and clean, as Alys had promised, but Lily and Edwin had soon made it clear that they neither wanted nor needed someone in the house all the time. Edwin was the one who laid the fires and Lily was the one who usually made lunch: soup or sandwiches or something quite simple. Breakfast was the same. They ate together, quite companionably, in the sunroom while Edwin read the paper and Lily read a book. Daytimes were taken up with walks or trips into the towns and villages thereabouts, and quiet times were to be had where she lazed on the rocks by the waterfall, or tracked little pathways through buddleias and the lilies, in places where nobody ever seemed to go.

At times, Lily would be enjoying the peace and the scents in the rose garden, and Elsie would materialise out of nowhere clutching an art box and draw endless studies of her, whilst Edwin wandered off with his camera or went out with Jago, keen to understand more about the estate. Lily understood he needed his own space, just as she did, and they were happy to grant that privilege to one another.

Each day, when they could, they met up for afternoon tea, which might be a picnic, or involve a stroll to Pencradoc, and evening meals were taken, without fail, with Jago and Alys and the girls up at the house. Alys' suggestion of only dining there when they wanted to had soon been negated. Lily did, actually, enjoy the chit-chat and friendly atmosphere to be found in the Pencradoc dining room. It took her mind off herself and her own problems, and it was nice to feel safe, surrounded by people who actually seemed to care about her.

Lily was quite sure most families of the Duke and Duchess's social standing didn't have children around the dinner table, but she was soon learning that no such rules existed at Pencradoc. The girls were given enough freedom to enjoy themselves, but enough boundaries to make them understand how to behave in polite society. It was, she acknowledged, a good way to bring them up and she determined that she would be the same with her child.

It was getting a little more obvious that she was with child now, to her at least, and she was grateful for the loose and flattering style which had been christened Arts and Crafts. It was exactly what she needed at the moment – she was just a little too large for her usual clothes, but not big enough to have special clothes made or her old ones let out. She shuddered, thinking of it all, and tried to tell herself the result at the end would be worth it, despite the way the child had been conceived.

She also told herself repeatedly it was Edwin's baby, but whether her heart and soul believed that, she didn't know. Everyone else did, though, thank God, and Edwin was happy to accept the situation, and he did genuinely care for her. She knew, however, that they both needed to let go a little more, but at least they seemed to be moving in the right direction which was a positive thing.

On one particular evening as they were seated around the dinner table, Elsie leaned over and asked, very politely, if Lily would consider something which had been on her mind for a little while.

'I do hope you don't mind me asking,' the little girl continued, 'but I was wondering if it would be at all possible for us to stage a pageant?' She looked at Lily hopefully. 'You see, it has always been my dream to be involved with something like a pageant, but my cousins are still rather small to direct in such important roles.'

'A pageant?' Lily was surprised. 'Wouldn't that be rather a big thing to do?'

'Usually it would. Some pageants are very big and have very many people in them, but I was thinking that this one could be much ... smaller.'

'It would have to be smaller,' said Alys. 'You don't have a lot of people who could go in your pageant!'

'I have, actually. I have you and Uncle Jago. My cousins. Mr Griffiths. And—' she ticked the names off importantly on her fingers '—Lily Valentine. And myself. Of course. Oh! And Biscuit. How many is that? Ten? I have ten people.'

'Biscuit isn't a person,' muttered Clara. 'He's a dog.'

'He's a person to me.' Elsie dismissed her cousin with a look. 'So I think that is quite a good number for a small pageant.'

'I'm not sure Mr and Mrs Griffiths would want to join in,' chided Jago gently. 'Mrs Griffiths is not here to amuse you. She's here to have a little rest and a little holiday, and not to be bothered by little girls. I think you bother her quite enough by drawing her all the time and demanding she discusses your scrapbook at any given moment.'

'Oh, it's really not a bother,' said Lily quickly. 'I think it might be quite fun, actually. I have sort of missed the theatre. I think I'd like to do it very much. Edwin? Would you like to be part of it?'

She smiled at him, and his eye sparked with amusement as he smiled back. 'Who could resist that offer? A beautiful young lady asking me to be part of a pageant – and the renowned actress Lily Valentine asking me the same thing. I would very much like to be part of the Pencradoc Pageant. Thank you.'

'Oh no, thank *you*!' For a moment, the slightly serious expression of Lady Elsie Pencradoc disappeared and a light came on behind her eyes, a wide smile breaking across her face showing off the bright eight-year-old to her best. 'I have a few ideas. May I perhaps talk to you about them after pudding?'

Lily swallowed down a giggle. 'Yes. After pudding would be perfect.'

Later that evening, after pudding, and after Elsie's ideas had been brought forth in an excited babble, supported by a notebook full of carefully drawn images and concise notes, Edwin and Lily meandered back to the Mill House. They were arm in arm; Edwin had offered his arm, as he always did, but tonight not only had she taken it, but she had moved closer to him as she did so. He could feel the warmth of her body next to his and he took a chance and drew her closer still. She didn't object.

'Thank you for agreeing to be in Elsie's pageant,' Lily said. 'I wasn't sure you'd want to.'

'There's no reason for me *not* to want to.' He smiled down at her. 'I'm enjoying spending time with the girls. It makes me think that children aren't quite as terrifying as I believe them to be.'

'Those ones are adorable. Do you come from a big family, Edwin? I never thought to ask you.'

He laughed. 'I never thought to ask you either. How strange. One imagines that when one marries, one should know everything about that person.'

'We clearly married in haste.' Her voice was wry, but not accusatory. They both knew it had been very much in haste; a marriage of convenience in more than one way.

'We did. But I for one am glad. I'm not sure I ever thanked you properly for accepting me.'

'You don't need to thank me. I should be the one thanking you. I hate to think ...' She dropped her head and refused to continue.

So he continued for her. 'You hate to think what situation you would have been in had I not offered myself. Yet I think I was the one who put you in that situation in the first place.'

'You were not. You surely were *not*.' Her voice was firm. 'I was at fault. You know what happened – what happened before you came ...'

'And again. You did not put yourself in that position, Lily.' His voice was firmer now. 'And in answer to your question, I have no siblings. There's just me, so I was never used to a large number of children. I was brought up by my grandmother. My mother died when I was young, and my father couldn't cope. When she died, I joined the army. I haven't seen any of my relatives for years. I don't miss them. I'm not even sure if my father is still alive.'

'Oh Edwin. I'm sorry.' She squeezed his arm. 'I've been so wrapped up in myself I never gave anything beyond your ... recovery ... a thought. I too had only a father. No brothers or sisters. And the rest you know.'

'We can become our own family, Lily.' He wasn't even sure he should have mentioned that, if they were still thinking along the lines of a marriage of convenience. 'Or at least that's what we can show to the outside world.' He frowned, hoping that she would see the sense in the arrangement and wouldn't come to regret her choices.

'We can.' She surprised him by tucking herself into him even closer. 'I think that's the most sensible solution for us all at the moment. I still worry, though. I still think that—' She stopped herself and shook her head. 'No. No, I can't think like that.'

'You can't.' He stopped, making her stop with him. 'Look. Just look around you. We're at Pencradoc. You're safe. Nobody will bother us here.'

'I long to believe you, Edwin. I really do. I just can't help thinking that it's all going to come crashing down around my ears.' She looked up at him, and it was one of those very rare moments that she looked scared and helpless; this wasn't the woman he had seen on stage every night. This, he knew, was the real Lily. 'It won't come crashing down, Lily. Not if I can help it.'

'I know, Edwin. That, I actually know.'

And, to his surprise and delight, she stood on tiptoe and kissed him, properly, on the lips. He hesitated a moment, then pulled her towards him and she nestled into his shoulder. They stood like that for quite a while, watching the summer sunset turn the world of Pencradoc rose-gold, listening to the waterfall tumble far beneath them, aware of the distant thrum of the water-wheel on the banks of the river, next to their temporary sanctuary of Mill House.

Present Day

Cordy walked, quite sedately, until she felt she was a reasonable distance away from Matt Harker. Then she ran and scurried behind a huge piece of topiary, peering out from between the branches, until she saw him finally disappear. He'd stopped, then looked around him as if he was searching for her, and she felt her skin grow warm and embarrassment curl her toes. It just felt different, now they were away from the Mill House. She felt completely embarrassed for a start. *God!* What a way to be found.

What if she'd needed a pee whilst she was suspended between the floors? That would have been a zillion times worse. She shuddered at the thought and followed his gaze. He was looking at the borders, and she wondered why. It wasn't as if that little pathway was visible. There was that lavender hedge, for a start. Odd, though. She didn't think she'd veered that far away from the entrance to the pathway.

Never mind.

76

When she was sure he'd gone, she snuck out from the topiary and continued towards the area where the stage was. She noticed a little flight of steps winding down to the river down a gentle stretch of riverbank, and she looked back along the direction she'd come. The Mill House did look beautiful, to be honest. The sun was in just the perfect position to make sure the building and the greenery around it were reflected perfectly in the smooth, glassy mill pond, and the water-wheel appeared to be balanced ever-so-carefully on the surface.

There was no way she could have envisaged that moving – it was quite clear from here, even, that there were massive struts attached between the back of the wheel and the building, just to make extra sure that the thing wouldn't turn. Even so, it was a thing of beauty and she decided to walk down the steps and take a photo along the river. It would be a good opportunity, she thought wryly, to make sure her mobile was still working after its tumble into the cellar.

She picked her way down the steps and raised her camera-phone, framing the shot. So far, so good. She took several photos, one after the other. The phone seemed to be suffering no ill-effects.

'Well that's one good thing,' she muttered, switching it off and tucking it back in her pocket. It was as she turned to head back up the stairs that she saw it, half-buried in the mud at the side of the river; something glinting silver in the sunlight that bounced off the water.

Her head filled with possibly romantic, possibly silly images of discovering someone's long-lost ring – did they toss it in, in a fit of pique, or did it slip off their finger as they lay back in a little boat, trailing their hand through the water – or was it, more likely, a ring-pull or a piece of scrap?

Smiling wryly to herself, and hoping it was the former, she bent down and eased it out of the mud – but it was neither jewellery nor ring-pull. Cordy felt a little sick as she looked at it; a ring-pull would have been better than this. A bullet. A bullet which looked misshapen enough to have hit something. And if that something was not a sentient being, because even a rabbit-type something was a sentient being, then that would not be too bad …

But as she held the bullet in her palm, she felt even more sick, because she knew, she just *knew*, that it had hit something living and definitely very sentient, and the images burst into her mind …

She saw them there, facing off against one another as she ran towards the riverbank.

'No!' She drew up close to them and raised the gun. 'Leave. Just leave now and never come back.'

There was some more conversation, some denials; then she fired the gun—

'Cordy? What are you doing down there?' Merryn's voice startled her out of the scenario her imagination was painting – for it had to be her imagination, didn't it? 'Oh, I *see* what you're doing. Taking photographs.'

Cordy looked up, forcing a smile onto her lips as Merryn came down the steps. 'The Mill House looks lovely in that light,' continued Merryn. 'It'll be so nice when the work's finished on it. I think Coren's hoping that they can get the water-wheel going again when it's all finished.'

'So it's really been out of action for a while then?'

'A good long while.' Merryn jumped down the last step and came to stand next to her. 'I think when they looked into it, it was stopped about 1895 or thereabouts.' Merryn pulled a face. 'The rumour was that a labourer was killed, but then again that sort of thing happened all the time, didn't it?'

'There was no health and safety, that's for sure.' Cordy still had the bullet in her hand. She was just about to show it to Merryn, when something stopped her. Instead, she slipped it into her pocket, and then thought about the photographs she had discovered in the cellar and felt her cheeks grow warm as she knew they were tucked inside her notebook. But again, did she really want to show Merryn them just yet? Chances are they'd be taken straight to Kit or Coren and – selfish as it seemed – she wanted to hold onto them a little longer; perhaps even sit on the stage and have a better look at them.

She decided against handing them over.

Then Merryn was talking again. 'Can I see the photo then?' She nodded to the phone. 'If it's a good one I might ask you to send me it. I don't think I've got anything from this angle. I was always more interested in the tower. Before it became a tea-room, of course.'

'I'd be equally interested in the tower as a tea-room. And not just to work in. To be a customer in as well,' said Cordy with an attempt at humour she didn't really feel.

Merryn laughed. 'That *is* a point.' She waved her hand towards the overgrown shrubs and foliage lining the path. 'We're planning on doing some work around here quite soon, anyway.'

'Oh, sorting out that overgrown pathway would be a good start.' The words were out before she could stop them. 'The bit where the side of the path's all crumbled away.'

'Crumbs, isn't it *dangerous* around there?' It wasn't really a question; Merryn was simply stating a fact. 'That's one reason why we've never done it. Lots of work to be done to make it safe before we can allow the general public on it.'

'Really? Because I heard children playing there before, so they must have found a way in.'

'Oh *no*. Honestly, some people will totally go where they're not supposed to.'

Yes, it was definitely not a good time to show Merryn the programme and tell her where she'd found it ...

Quickly, as some sort of distraction – although to be fair, Merryn was blithely chattering away and had no idea what Cordy felt the need to distract her from – Cordy swiped open the Gallery app on her phone: 'Here – which picture do you want sending through, then?' She'd taken three pictures, and she thrust the screen under Merryn's nose so she could see them.

'Oh! Oh ... ummm ... let me see.' Merryn leaned a little backwards, away from the extremely close phone.

'Sorry.' Cordy moved it away slightly. 'You just have a look and let me know if there are any good ones.'

Merryn smiled. 'Thanks. Okay ... may I?' Cordy nodded as Merryn swiped the pictures along. 'Hey – who's that?'

'Who?' Cordy looked at the area on the picture Merryn had pointed to. There was a dark figure, walking along the river bank: the shape of a man, but too far away to be recognisable. He was only in the one shot – the other two photos were just simply the delightful bucolic scene of a mill and a mill pond and the Cornish landscape of Pencradoc surrounding it.

'Gosh ... I don't know.' She had a feeling though – maybe it was Matt – perhaps he'd gone back to have another look at something? 'Just someone out for a walk on that side of the river? Maybe he'd gone behind the house for the other two?' She wasn't going to drop Matt in it as being equally explorative as her.

'Like I say,' Merryn grumbled, 'some people will totally go where they're not supposed to.'

'Definitely. I wouldn't though. I wouldn't do that.'

'Ha!' Merryn laughed. 'Well, these steps did have a sign at the top saying no access – but you know.'

She grinned and Cordy felt dreadful. 'Really? God, I'm sorry—'

'Relax!' Merryn patted her arm, and too late Cordy saw the glint of mischief in her friend's eyes. 'Of course they don't. Okay – I'll have that third picture then, if that's all right with you. The first one is a little wonky, the second one has that chap on it – but the third one is perfect.'

'You naughty thing, Merryn!' On safer ground, Cordy

grinned back at Merryn, then pressed a few keys. 'Super. The picture is on its way to you.'

'Splendid. Thanks a lot.' Merryn pointed back the way she'd come. 'I'm guessing you're heading to the stage area – you're on the right track, it's all the way along there, and you need to get off this but just a little further along. It's all set up. You'll love it.'

'Thanks. I'm sure I will,' she replied warmly. Determinedly, she put the thought of that mysterious bullet out of her head. There was no place for it in Rose's Garden, she was quite sure.

But she was certain she *would* love the stage there – but exactly *why* she'd love it, she wasn't quite sure. Perhaps, she thought wryly, there might be a bit more of Lily Valentine over there, doing what Lily Valentine did best.

Or perhaps it was just simply because it was a stage.

And that was quite exciting in itself, really.

Matt let himself back into the house and took the stairs two at a time up to his room in the attic. The only way he knew how to deal with so many odd things was to do something he was totally confident in, and totally understood. And that had to have something to do with art.

For once, he yearned to have a pile of schoolkids' portfolios with him, clogging up his lounge until he got around to marking them over the weekend, but that was not the case, of course. And anyway, the courses he ran for Kit didn't involve anyone getting marks out of ten. They were supposed to be fun and relaxing and, to be fair, he did enjoy doing them.

So, based on that principle, he decided to set one of the classrooms up in preparation for the first course he was going to run. That would take his mind off phantom water-wheels and imaginary people hanging out of windows and black shapes creeping around dingy cellars … it might not necessarily take his mind off redheads who looked like the actress Ann-Margret did in the sixties. But it was a distraction of sorts.

The stage area was just as wonderful as Cordy had imagined.

'Wow.' She walked up the couple of steps at the side and found herself on the stage itself. She stood, quite deliberately, in the middle of the boards and looked out. If she closed her eyes, she could imagine herself standing there and performing.

So she did.

Yes, if she scrunched up her face and concentrated really hard, she could truly imagine someone was playing the piano; a jolly tune that was the introduction to 'Daisy Bell' – one of Cordy's childhood favourites. If she listened closely, she could almost hear someone singing it: *Daisy, Daisy, give me your answer do ... I'm half-crazy, all for the love of you—*

The voice was soft and tuneful, and Cordy kept her eyes closed, smiling. She imagined herself wearing an oyster-coloured satin dress with creamy lace sleeves. Her shoulders were exposed, which might have been a little *risqué* anywhere else, but not here, not at Pencradoc. She smoothed the fabric down and curtsied prettily, waiting for the applause to die down. It wasn't quite the *Théâtre National de l'Opéra*. but then again, she'd had enough of that place to last a lifetime.

And she knew he was standing in the wings, just out of sight. He would walk onto the stage with her very soon. She just had to smile and accept the applause. Then she looked to the side of the stage and held her hand out, inviting him to join her.

And Matt walked on, smiling at her, but it was the oddest thing, because there was something just a little strange about his appearance, and he looked rather dashing in a way ... then someone tugged at her skirt and she looked down and a small, fair-haired child was staring up at her.

'*I was told I was to be a fairy, and that must mean I can*

come and stand next to you now. Even though I do not think Mustardseed is a proper fairy name.'

'Of course it is, and of course you can.' She leaned down to the child, hiding a smile and whispering to her as giggles rippled through the audience. 'But why don't you take my hand, and we shall wait here until the others come on as well ...'

Cordy jumped as she came out of the reverie she'd imagined herself into. It felt awfully like someone was still clasping her hand and she quickly looked down – just long enough to see the wavery image of a little girl fade away, but not so fast that she didn't see the tumble of golden curls, the curious brown eyes and the strange little costume she was wearing; a green robe, more like a Grecian tunic tied with a bright yellow sash which had no doubt once been a curtain ...

She stared at the spot where the image had been, her heart thumping as the modern world flooded back.

'Hang on. Just *hang* on a minute,' she said to nobody. She sat down heavily on the stage before her legs gave way and rummaged through her notebook with shaking hands. She pulled the envelope out of its hiding place and, her fingers barely functioning, started to take the photographs out of the package.

Sure enough, there was the picture of the little Pencradoc girls, clasping their hands dramatically. One of the smaller ones was wearing an identical costume – although, clearly, Cordy wasn't to know what colour it had been.

But that was it. Her imagination had kicked in – it had been a long day. She'd been trespassing like there was no tomorrow. She'd found a collection of old, hugely exciting pictures. And she'd been trapped in a hole in the floor.

And all that on two cups of coffee and no lunch.

Her head began to swim. It wasn't surprising her mind had played that trick on her. She'd seen the picture, got too carried away with her role-playing and had magicked up a little girl.

She squeezed her eyes shut and dropped her head onto her knees.

She opened them after a moment and was just trying to calm down and rationalise it some more, staring at the floorboards in the gap between her knees, when the overpowering scent of lilies swept past her on a gust of wind, accompanied by the swishing of a long skirt.

And then she saw the skirt – she saw the damn, pale green skirt and a glimpse of the white shoes beneath as it came closer, and then, seemingly, the whole thing went right through her.

And then she truly was frozen to the spot.

Chapter Seven

1895

'I thought that this would work quite nicely.' Edwin straightened up and weighed the hammer in his hands. Lily was standing in front of him, her perfume alerting him to her presence before he'd even seen her. 'Jago was brave enough to let me loose with some tools to try and get this scenery sorted.' He raised his eyebrows. 'I'm not entirely certain why he thinks I can be trusted with such deadly weapons.'

'Deadly weapons?' Lily smiled and it was like the sun came out. 'I'm not sure what damage one can do with a toolkit.'

'Enough, I should think.' He shrugged and laid the hammer down. 'My own thumb, for instance, sadly connected with the hammer as I held a nail in place. A great tragedy, I think, for that thumb – and played out on the very stage I'm trying to create.'

'I am very grateful for your sacrifice,' Lily said gravely, and he felt a smile curl the edges of his lips.

It was a warm day, a very pleasant day in fact, and he had already discarded his jacket. His shirt sleeves were rolled up, held in place by silver armbands, and he saw her eyes go to the scarring on his left forearm. Self-consciously, he began to roll his sleeve back down.

'No – don't.' Lily reached out and placed her hand on his forearm. 'It's too hot. You'll melt, I swear it. Sit down instead. I've brought us some lemonade. Elsie said you were here.' She flushed and nodded towards a basket she'd placed on the grass, just beside the makeshift stage.

'Ah, Elsie. Yes. I had to chase her away. She was determined to be helpful and pass me some nails after the thumb incident, but then all her cousins drifted across and I had to fend off five small girls instead of one, so I sent them to the house and told them to design their costumes and ask Alys what could be used as fabric, because that would take an equally long time as knocking a stage together. And it was something they could, hopefully, find more pleasure in.'

'And more to occupy their time. Don't lie, Edwin.' This time the smile was wider. 'Thank you for doing this. I know it's more of an amusement for the girls than anything you anticipated doing over your summer.'

'This summer has turned out quite differently to how I ever imagined.' He looked at her wryly. 'Differently for us both, I think. But it's good to be doing something physical again. One can spend too much time in a sort of recovery that isn't really a recovery, if you understand.'

'Oh, I think one needs to work through a sort of recovery for one's mind as well as one's body. I can't imagine what you experienced abroad is a pretty thing.'

'Not pretty at all. Shall we?' He indicated the steps up to the platform and offered her his arm. His right arm.

Lily, however, smiled and went around to his left side, and she linked him there instead. 'The lemonade is freshly squeezed – by myself, I hasten to add. As you have just pointed out, it was nice to do something practical. I don't think I was made for genteel invalidity, and when one is with child it's inevitable that people treat you as such. I'm desperately bored, if I'm honest. I was never meant to spend sunny days draped fetchingly on a chaise longue.'

'People are just looking after you.'

'I'm not the only one that needs looking after. Here we are. There may be cake in there. Don't know how that got there.' The Irish lilt was back as she peered into the basket.

'Then we'd best not confess we found it.'

'No. No we won't. But it's rather nice. I may have just sampled some in the kitchens when I was preparing the lemonade.'

'Then it would be rude not to try some.' Edwin unfolded the rug Lily had placed on top of the basket and placed it on the grass. He helped her sit down, then joined her. It was indeed a pleasant half-hour or so – pleasant, that was, until a shot rang out on the other side of the waterfall and a flock of birds flurried out of the treetops.

'Oh! Oh my – do they have to do that today and ruin the peace?' Lily scowled as she watched the birds take flight.

'I suppose if there is need to do so, the gamekeepers have to react when it's appropriate.' He knew his voice was strained, and he had clutched the glass of lemonade so tightly when he heard the shot, he was astonished that the container wasn't shattered. He made a great effort to release his grip and place the glass on the rug. His hand shook a little as he withdrew it but Lily, thank God, didn't seem to notice.

'It's still uncalled for. I mean, people have to eat ...' She trailed off and looked intently at her own glass.

'Actually, I agree. And I somehow think that Jago's family feel the same, so your guess is, as they say, is as good as mine.'

'Perhaps it's an itinerant labourer – someone passing through who fancied a little sport.'

'Perhaps. Whatever it was, I don't think it's any concern of ours. Now – drink and eat, and I must get on or we'll never have the thing completed. Not that I'm in any way wishing for you to leave,' he added hurriedly. 'You can stay and help, if you wish. There are probably a few more nails required, and I somehow think you might be a greater help than the girls.'

He smiled at her gently and she flushed, then smiled back. 'It is for my benefit.' Then she raised her glass solemnly. '"May there always be work for your hands to do".'

'And yours.' He nudged her playfully, surprising himself.

'Aye. And the work won't do itself, so come on.'

They helped one another to their feet, holding hands maybe a little longer than necessary as they did so – but Edwin wasn't going to complain. Far from it.

Rather, he pushed his sleeves further up his arms and guided Lily Valentine onto the stage.

At one point, he cast a glance across the river and was surprised to see the gamekeeper, or whoever he was, apparently staring back at them from the other side. But the figure was in shadow, his features unclear, and Edwin didn't really give it a second thought.

Dismissing it as a slightly curious gentleman wondering what was happening with the construction work in the rose garden, he turned his attention back to Lily and concentrated instead on the companionable work they found themselves happily involved in.

Lily, however, was not quite as assured as she appeared to be on the surface. She was, after all, an actress, and that skill had come in quite handy recently.

She passed nails to Edwin, chattering and laughing at his comments, helping him where she could and even holding a ladder steady for him as he made his way slowly up the steps. She looked up at him as he worked and found herself daydreaming about how things might have been different had she just met Edwin a month or two earlier than she did, had she acknowledged his presence in the audience when she first noticed him. Because she had noticed him, and she had tried her utmost to ignore him. The audience at these places always brought a lot of fanatics out, and she was quite good at judging who she could smile at, and who she would need to get moved on by the burly Jacques le Brun, the lovely yet terrifying-looking man who was protector to all the girls in the troupe. Jacques was often quite polite when he suggested that the stage-struck admirers should stop bothering Lily, but on one memorable occasion, he had needed to knock out a particularly excitable gent with a well-placed left hook in the alley by the stage door.

Lily had never felt threatened by Edwin. Indeed, it had come to the point where she had begun to seek him out. She was sad when he wasn't there and happy when he was. When they had eventually met and he had presented her with those lilies, she had been struck by how kind and thoughtful he was, but there was definitely a veneer to him. He sometimes seemed distant, and she saw his gaze drift off and take him elsewhere at times; then she would gently touch his arm and he would blink and come back to her with a smile.

However, she was the first to admit she had used him to get away from Paris when the opportunity arose. She felt horribly guilty about that now, but she had known it was the only way. The only way she could keep her reputation and the only way she could escape fully.

And today, in the sun-drenched gardens of Pencradoc, she could almost believe she had got away with it. But there was always that nagging feeling within her.

He had found her once. And *he* might find her again.

And that gunshot had unsettled her, especially when she saw the man standing across the river in the shadows of the trees watching them.

Although it was beyond comprehension that *he* could find her here in deepest Cornwall.

She gave herself a metaphorical shake and held the ladder a little more steady. She had practically retired from public life. Nobody knew where she was. It was a gamekeeper. Nobody more, nobody less.

Surely she was safe at Pencradoc?

Present Day

Cordy's heart was pounding so hard she thought it might be heard on Bodmin Moor itself. She looked around, her eyes wide, trying to establish what might have made the image appear to her. It wasn't real. It couldn't be real – it had to be … it had to be … what could it be?

'Aha!' Her gaze alighted, almost thankfully, on the shady

greenery around her, the leaves rustling above her and the glints of light through the canopy of summer blossom.

That was it – a trick of the light. The refraction of afternoon sunshine rays – green and white. Of course. And the rustling – why, that was definitely the sound of the wind whispering through the branches merged with the rushing of the water behind her.

The explanation satisfied her for as long as it took to scramble to her feet and hurry away from the stage as fast as she could. And it seemed as if she was just in time, because a family was walking along the pathway towards it, and Cordy gradually became aware of other people in the grounds of the Arts Centre. Of course, didn't they have a visitors' trail set up? And of course, that would head past the stage, wouldn't it? The thought didn't stop her shivering though, despite the sunny weather. For the time she'd been there, she'd been completely alone; almost in a bubble, hidden away from everyone and everything in the twenty-first century.

Almost, she thought with another shiver, as if something had deliberately made that bubble and an invisible boundary had been set up, preventing casual visitors from straying too close to the stage. Preventing modern-day people from being there when Lily Valentine was paying a visit …

'Oh Goddddddd!' she yelped, and picked up speed as she ran towards the house and the safety of her little attic bedroom. Suddenly, seeing what Lily Valentine did best wasn't so appealing after all.

The problem with Pencradoc itself, was there were just so many damn stairs. Then Matt checked himself, trying not to be grumpy. He usually had a bit of a hand with setting these workshops up, but Kit was nowhere to be seen, and Coren had greeted him vaguely yet pleasantly in the corridor, simultaneously texting someone and dangling his car keys from his little finger as he dashed off somewhere.

Coren thrived on that sort of stuff and, yes, Matt was happy to be busy. He wasn't afraid of hard work, but the idea of trying to run a business on the scale of Pencradoc Arts Centre was not his idea of fun. Everyone had to admit that Coren had done great things with the place, but Coren himself was the first to admit that the place wouldn't be where it was at all without the backing of Kit and Merryn and, yes, Sybill. Matt grinned at the idea of Coren ever slowing down enough to have a relationship with anyone at all, never mind Sybill – he'd had his flings, as they all knew, but work came first, especially now he had this place to look after.

So it meant that Matt was trawling up and down stairs lugging materials back and forth from his room and locating the other things he needed from the cupboards and stockrooms of the Arts Centre, not to mention setting the room out to take advantage of the way the light would be at the time he was running his course. It all had to be just so – otherwise it wouldn't work.

Just as he had taken a chair from a stack in the corner and was half way across the room to set it out by an easel, there was an almighty crash and a rush of wind, then the sense of someone running past him, smelling of earth and sweat and dirt.

'What the …' He spun around, still clutching the chair, to see the rest of the stack tumbled into a heap on the floor. 'Well, thanks a bunch, whoever was in here last!' he growled to nobody in particular. 'You clearly didn't think to put the chairs back in a *safe* way, did you?' His heart was hammering and he glared at the pile of chairs, swearing roundly as he scanned the mess around the fallen chairs, hoping that nothing had been broken by the avalanche.

There was another clash behind him and he jumped again, spinning around the other way, but what he saw wasn't another pile of furniture – it was Cordelia Beaumont standing in the doorway where she had thrown it open to the hallway, her eyes round and a shocked expression on her face.

They stared at each other for a moment as recognition dawned on each of them, then she spoke. 'Is everything okay? I heard a noise. And I thought there was someone ...' She didn't finish the sentence.

'Hello again. That pile of chairs just collapsed. I'm trying to sort the room out and someone put them away wrong.' He was clutching the chair until his knuckles whitened for some reason, and he forced himself to put the thing down loudly on the wooden floorboards. 'They put them away wrong.' He gestured vaguely to the mess behind him. 'Nobody in here except me.'

'Just you?' She blinked at him, her hand still on the door handle. 'Nobody else?'

'Nobody else.'

'Oh. Just I ...' she cast a glance a little nervously down the corridor, then took a deep breath and stepped inside the room, closing the door gently behind her. 'I thought I saw someone running down the corridor. A man.'

'No men here except me. Coren's away doing business things, I presume, and I expect Kit is still in the gardens. Nobody else should be in here. This floor isn't open access. It's only for workshops and events.'

'So nobody would have been coming along the corridor then?'

'No. Unless you saw someone who was having a sneaky look up here. Maybe a couple of the retreat rooms are being used – but they're on the floor below us.'

'Ah. Yes. Merryn did say they were saving the retreat rooms for proper guests. Don't look at me like that – apparently I'm *also* not a proper guest.'

She didn't seem to want to go back out into the corridor, and that sense of awkwardness was back – but if she felt it too, which he believed she did, due to her body language, then why was it preferable to be in here with him than back out there?

'Well, this is me trying to set a workshop up. On my own, because everybody else seems to have vanished.'

'Ah. Okay.' She shrugged and folded her arms even tighter.

'This is a bit weird, if you don't mind me saying so,' said Matt. 'We've been in a cellar together. We've met before now under peculiar circumstances. And we're kind of dancing around each other with small talk.'

'It's a *bit* weird,' she conceded. She looked back at the door. 'But the truth is I don't want to go back out there until that fellow has gone. He was just sort of stomping down the corridor after he barged out of here, and I really didn't want to get in his way. He was a bit ... purposeful. And this *place* is weird. If I'm honest.'

'Hmm. Well, firstly there was nobody in here with me to stomp out.'

'But he came out after the crash.'

'Maybe he did, but I guarantee I was on my own – so maybe you saw him come out of a different room?'

'Maybe.' She was silent for a moment, 'But I was sure it was here. Never mind, I was a bit further along the corridor when it happened.' She shrugged, but he wasn't sure she was particularly convinced. Unaccountably, he shivered as he recalled the rush of wind and the sense someone had come past him at a rate of knots.

'And.' She frowned and looked at the floor. 'I imagined some other ... stuff ... at the stage area, so I'm feeling a bit fragile.'

'I see.' Matt looked at her and suddenly felt sorry for her. 'Look – I'm guessing if you travelled up here this morning, you probably haven't eaten for a while?'

'Not since breakfast.'

'So maybe you just need some food to stop you imagining ... stuff?'

She laughed and that spark he'd seen before was back. 'It's not something I hadn't considered, to be honest.'

'Great – well, why don't you help me sort this out, then

we'll go out to the village and find some food. I hear there's a really nice Italian place there.'

'Really?' She grinned. 'Show me what to do and we'll get food quicker – because that's literally the best offer I've had today!'

Matt grinned back, hardly believing he'd invited this girl out for something to eat, when only a few hours ago they'd been simmering at each other in the hallway after they'd had an unfortunate incident with their luggage.

'Come on. I'll show you. But first …' He scowled a little. 'Let me just check the corridor. I don't like to think of anyone prowling around up here where they shouldn't be.'

'Sure.' Cordy nodded and moved towards the chairs. She righted one of them. 'I'll start sorting these out.'

'Thanks.' Matt headed over to the door and peered out along the corridor, left and right. There was nobody there. 'All clear,' he shouted back over his shoulder. 'I'll just have a walk along though, to make sure.'

He stepped into the corridor and had a good look around. He was right – nobody was lurking there, thankfully, so whoever it was must have found their way back downstairs.

He went back into the room and closed the door behind him, assuring Cordy that all was well.

He didn't see the damp footprints appearing on the carpet, following in his wake, whichever direction he turned, whichever room he looked into.

He didn't see them appear at the doorway then stop, as if they were pausing before they came in after him; then they faded away into nothing, leaving no trace that they'd ever been there.

1895

They had no idea. No idea at all. He stood on the opposite bank, watching them together, watching them on that wooden contraption they were working on.. She had brought a basket with her, and his lips curled in distaste as he saw them eat and drink.

He raised his gun and pointed it in their direction. He wondered if the bullet would find its mark should he fire it. He pointed it first at her, then him, then her again. Then he lowered it, still staring at her.

No. How many times did he have to keep telling himself he needed her alive? But there was no harm in just letting them know he was here.

So he raised the gun, aimed it over the treetops and fired.

He smiled as he saw them jump, saw her look around as the birds cawed and shrieked around him.

'That one, Lily Valentine, is for you,' he murmured.

He waited until the man looked at him, looked right in his direction, then waited a moment more. Then he turned around and walked back into the woods where he could, quite easily, disappear again.

She wasn't safe anywhere. He would find her, and he would keep on finding her.

When would she ever learn?

Chapter Eight

Present Day

The restaurant was gorgeous. It was one of those bijou family-run Italians, with checked tablecloths and Chianti bottles with melted candle wax down the sides of them. Only, Cordy realised with a smile, that upon closer inspection, the bottles were gin bottles and so much prettier than the old-style ones.

They shared a plate of dough balls, dripping in garlic butter, and a bowl of juicy olives as they waited for their meals. Away from Pencradoc, Cordy found Matt surprisingly easy to talk to. There wasn't the tension there had been at the Mill House, or the uncertainty caused by an unwelcome visitor in the corridor, so she could fully focus her attention on him and he on her.

But despite her resolutions not to obsess over the items she had found in the cellar, she desperately wanted to talk more about that mysterious wedding certificate with him. It seemed as if he should know, if that made sense – but she was halfway down a glass of red wine and she was certain that not much would make sense for much longer if she kept drinking. It really was very delicious red wine.

Matt, however, made it easy for her to mention her secret stash by asking a genuine question. 'So come on – let's talk about what you found in the Mill House cellar. Have you had a better look at it all? And have you told Merryn yet?'

'I haven't told Merryn yet.' She risked a smile. 'She's a very busy lady, you know …'

'Sure!' Matt laughed. 'But I bet the answer to that other question I asked was yes. I bet you've managed to have a good old look.'

'Now that I may have done. The photos and little programme are beautiful – real Lily Valentine treasures. But

I'm not sure what to make of the note from the church. It looks like marriage lines, but who knows?'

'Marriage lines? What were the names again?'

'Evelyn Sullivan and Francis O'Hara. From Ireland.'

A strange look passed over Matt's face, then was gone. 'Irish. Right.' He suddenly seemed very interested in his glass.

'What's wrong with Irish?'

'Nothing! Nothing at all – it's just ...'

His voice trailed away and Cordy leaned forward. 'Just what?'

'You'll think I've lost the plot if I tell you. It doesn't matter.' He looked at her and smiled.

But Cordy wasn't going to let him wiggle out of that one quite so easily, despite the fact that his smile was rather incredible. 'Tell me.' She stared at him. 'And then I can tell you something that'll make you think I've lost the plot as well.' She indicated the olives and dough balls. 'The theme of the evening is sharing, is it not?'

'I thought the theme was more one of hunger and alcohol consumption – but if you say so.'

'I say so. Come on. Tell me.' She was almost hoping he'd say something that would make her little daydream on the stage less bonkers and more rational.

'Okay.' He sighed and refilled the glasses. 'I thought I heard someone speak to me in an Irish accent. When I was in the garden, after we'd – you'd – found the programme and things, I got a bit lost and couldn't see the shortcut I'd taken to get to the Mill House. It was like a woman said there was nothing logical about Pencradoc, and I thought – I think – that it's because of that marriage thing. It's the only explanation.'

'Explanation?' She smiled. 'We just agreed there's nothing logical about this place, which means it's unlikely we can have an explanation for that. Unless, because it was warm and sunny and quite still, a visitor with that sort of accent was nearby and you heard her talking? Maybe her voice carried?

I'd be happy to tell myself that one, I think. Rather than any—' she dipped her head down momentarily, blushing '—illogical explanations.'

'Illogical. Come on then, your turn. You're blushing so you must feel a bit silly as well, with whatever you want to say.'

It was an attempt at humour, and she was grateful. 'Okay. Mine is more than even silly. I was on the stage, and I was imagining myself as being Lily – you know, thinking about her, getting into character, because of the performance piece I'm basing on her. I imagined it so well that I thought I saw a little girl next to me, and she was asking if it was time for her to stand on the stage with me, and complaining at the fact she was Mustardseed.' She pulled a face. 'She had a little green tunic on, and a yellow sash. I've no idea who bloody Mustardseed is. Anyway, that shook me, so I sat down, and then, I swear, someone walked through me. *Through* me, Matt! Like – she was all swishy. And I saw her shoes and everything.'

'Good grief.' Matt was staring at her. He was silent for a moment, apparently processing the information. The moment stretched out until Cordy felt as if she was as scarlet as the pasta sauce she was about to enjoy, and started to wish she'd never breathed a word about the damn swishy woman. Then Matt startled her by speaking. 'Well, I actually think your explanation goes something like this – you found that programme, yes? And there was a list of characters inside it – am I right?'

'Probably. I didn't read it, I just glanced at it. Elsie's writing is a little bit … tiny. I need to study it a bit more.'

'Ah, but the word I'm looking for there is "probably".' He nodded. 'For my sins, I have to help out with drama at the school I work in. One of the plays we did a couple of years ago was *A Midsummer Night's Dream*. There's a fairy in there called Mustardseed. I remember because one of the kids kicked off because they said they wouldn't play Bottom because they'd get it ripped out of them for the name, and we started on a debate on the craziest fairy name in the play. I can't recall which one won, but Mustardseed was definitely up there.'

'Probably Bottom,' replied Cordy wryly. 'Bottom is the craziest name. I'd not like it either. But you think that's it, then?

'Yes. You've seen the name subconsciously, and because you were concentrating on the character and thinking about what she would do, you magicked up that image.'

'That sounds plausible.' Cordy nodded. Then her stomach lurched a little. 'But that doesn't explain the swishiness. The dress. The woman walking through me.'

'No. That,' said Matt, deadly serious, 'was good old hunger.'

Cordy stared at him for a moment, then suddenly burst out laughing. 'Of course. You're right. It's all rational. Let's not say logical – but rational is good.'

'Rational is very good. Now – that wine looks like it might evaporate if we don't finish it, and the meals are looking pretty tasty. What say we finish up here, and head back? Hey. I can offer to walk you back home and not sound as if I'm trying it on with you.'

'Ha! You can. Walk me back home that is ...' Feeling a lot better, and happy with the explanations Matt had come up with, Cordy grinned and raised her glass. '*Not* try it on with me.'

'Damn.' But he raised his glass to match hers, and there was a smile in his voice, and a teasing light in his eyes and she knew it was just a joke.

But a teeny, tiny part of her went *damn* as well – all of its own accord. She'd had worse people than Matt Harker try it on with her. But starting a relationship with anyone at all was not on her agenda for this couple of weeks. Toby had wrung her out and she just wanted some time to relax and not think about men.

But still: *damn* indeed!

*

Matt walked Cordy back as planned – they said a very decorous 'goodnight' at the bottom of the grand staircase, overlooked by the portrait of the beautiful Duchess Rose; then there was another sort of awkward moment as they both began to head up the stairs together.

Cordy, seemingly slightly tipsy, giggled. 'We're going to be in adjoining rooms, aren't we? We're going to have to walk up here and along the corridor and make polite conversation until we reach our doors.'

Matt laughed. 'That would be kind of typical. Okay – before we do that, let's just stop here and see where each other is.'

They paused on a little half-landing and Cordy looked around. She pointed up and to the left. 'All the way up – in *that* wing. At the far end.'

'Good. I'm *that* way. The other wing. Also at the far end.'

'Excellent. No awkwardness then. That's good.' She nodded seriously. 'Okay. Well, I think I'm starting in the Tower Tea-Room tomorrow.' She screwed her nose up. 'It can't be too much different to the other places I've worked like that. And I've got a kettle in my bedroom, I believe, so I should be good for breakfast until I get there. Don't you think they should do bed and breakfast here?'

'Perhaps. But they are good enough to provide a fridge and a toaster and a microwave and a kettle in the rooms – it's a start. Because having staff to do B&B is more expense, and there is the tea-room after all.' He smiled to take the edge off his words. He had the impression that Cordy was used to London, and a big city and a place for breakfast on every corner, twenty steps away from wherever she was at the time. 'Plus there's the village. Maybe they've got somewhere.'

'Maybe. I know I probably sound a little food-obsessed, but the thing is, if I was imagining swishy woman because of a lack of food, I need to get fed and watered, don't I?' She frowned a little as she apparently considered it. She also swayed a bit. Okay. Maybe she was more than a little tipsy. Matt hid another smile and took hold of her arm, about to suggest he lead her up to the top floor for safety, when one of those odd little tingles of electricity shot up through his fingers as they connected with her. She stared at him for a split second ... then she seemed to shake it off.

'Perhaps,' he said, trying to get back to the original question of Cordy being fed and watered. 'Come on. We'll escort each other to the top of the stairs then split off our separate ways.'

'Mmm.' She seemed to be agreeing with him, her eyes darting around, even as she moved a little closer to him. 'Yes. Good idea. But – and don't take this the wrong way – but it felt more as if I should be staying at the Mill House, rather than here in Pencradoc. Do you know what I mean?'

There was a beat. 'Yes. Yes, I know what you mean.' And it was odd, because it really did feel like that – as if they were more anchored to that part of the estate, rather than being here, in the Hall – which was extremely weird. Before he'd encountered Cordy, he'd never felt out of place in the main house. Never felt as if he should be somewhere else. But at that moment, with his fingers still gently holding onto her arm, it felt as if they had done this before; that he had walked up the stairs before, escorted her before – but not, he felt, for the right reasons ... and besides that, getting into a relationship was definitely not on his agenda for his summer.

At all.

Cordy bid Matt farewell at the top of the corridor, without the embarrassment of a sort-of kiss, or a limp type of hug. Rather, they just said their goodnights, thanked each other for the company and headed along their respective passageways.

She changed into her pyjamas because it was almost ten o'clock by now, and even though a twilight wander around the estate was very appealing on some levels, on a more practical level, she was dead on her feet. She'd travelled there from London, got stuck in the floor, kind of fell into a cellar, imagined someone down there with her, further imagined someone swishing past her on the stage – as well as conjuring up a small, indignant Mustardseed person – moved furniture around and been out for a meal. Good grief. London life was full-on at times, and the sort of career she was aiming for had very little respite in it, but she'd imagined a slightly slower pace of life in Cornwall.

It was as she pondered this phenomenon that her eyes alighted on the notebook and pencil she had bought at the Tower. She'd put them on the desk in the corner of the room when she came back from the Mill House, intending to do a little work on the show she was planning.

Inspiration had kind of struck in tidal waves as soon as she had opened that envelope in the cellar – but bizarrely, she had no inclination now to write anything down.

'My dear, I've hit the wall,' she announced to the empty room. She crawled into bed and flicked the light off. She was asleep almost as soon as her head hit the pillow, but her dreams didn't seem to be her own, and neither were they very pleasant ...

She was on a boat, being tossed on the waves, glimpses of another life just within her grasp. She had left everything she had ever known – left to make a new life for herself. A new life where nobody would ever find her again. For all her bravado, deep down she was terrified. She did what she had to do, when she had to do it, and now, now she was here – at Pencradoc ...

Cordy started awake with a gasp. Her head was thumping, her heart was pounding and she felt like she had a three day old mouse-corpse in her mouth.

'Good God.' She sat up and stared around the room. It wasn't yet daylight – a strange milky light was evident in the gap between the curtains, and she saw a faint, blurred outline of a woman wearing a long, green dress fading away by the desk in the corner. 'What the—' She scrambled to her knees and focused on the spot, blinking in astonishment. The dream had been weird – sort of her life, yet sort of ... *not*.

Her mind was absolutely boggled. Of course there was nobody in her room – of *course* there wasn't. Just a fleeting shadow, something left over from that odd dream.

Yes, she had moved to London to take up a new life; yes, she was here at Pencradoc – but she hadn't travelled here by boat and she had certainly never done anything she was ashamed of. Well, apart from that one time she had been papped with Toby Fowler, falling out of the 'Libertine by Chinawhite' club in Fitzrovia. She was definitely drunk and dishevelled, and had definitely had a wardrobe malfunction ... but that was a while ago now, and she had learned from that. Don't wear a buttoned-up top and don't drink two bottles of champagne, even if someone else is paying.

'Urk'. She shook her head, painfully, trying to rid herself of the memories. Maybe the boat was a subliminal dream thing – it meant that she had taken an unsettling journey – some of which had been out of her control, like the flood ... 'Of course!' She opened her eyes wide. *That* was where the water came in. Good God.

Sitting in her bed, she looked around, trying to orientate herself a little more. The notebook was open and the pencil lay on top of it, inviting, almost. She had been fairly drunk last night, but was quite sure she had just laid them there, the book closed, the pencil neatly beside it, ready to use. But no – she shuffled down the bed on her knees, her heart thumping, almost reluctant to touch them, but her hand reaching out anyway.

The page was open at her notes and ideas about the stage show – she'd jotted down the words Titania and Music Hall songs and had begun creating bullet points as to what she could do in each section – and she shook her head and flipped the book shut. There was no way she was going to work on it before dawn. But she couldn't for the life of her remember opening it.

Then she caught a glance of the envelope from the Mill House she'd left on the desk and thought about that marriage certificate again. 'Evelyn O'Hara. That would be your married name, wouldn't it? What sort of life did *you* have, I wonder? Were you friends with Lily Valentine? Is that why your papers are here with her pictures?'

The voice was forceful, bitter, when it came; louder this time, the Irish lilt harsher. And it wasn't in her head. It was right in her ear: '*You can't let him find you. Let him die with Evelyn.*'

Cordy cried out. 'Bloody hell!' She jumped up and shrugged on a pair of joggers and a sweatshirt. She burst out of the bedroom, and, despite, the early hour, she scurried down the corridor towards Matt's room at the far end of the corridor in the other wing.

Matt woke up, startled, to a persistent knocking on his door. It took a moment to remember where he was. In his dream he had been on a battlefield somewhere, and it had been pretty hideous, he had to say.

His hair was damp, his heart was hammering in his chest and the knocking was echoing like gun shots as if the world around him was on fire. He could feel the left-hand side of his body burning and the pain was indescribable as he felt red hot bullets ripping into him—

He swore, more at the images in his head than the knocking on the door.

'Matt? Matt … I'm sorry. I'm sorry. Let me in. Please! Let me in …' It was, he realised, Cordy. Her voice was strangled, upset and probably the most welcome and down-to-earth thing he could have hoped for at that point. Suddenly it was the best idea in the world to jump out of bed and open that door.

He made to get out and his left leg collapsed under him momentarily. He swore again, steadied himself and limped to the door. He'd obviously been in a really stupid sleeping position and cut off his circulation. That explained a lot.

'Coming – coming,' he called. Then he grabbed the door, wrestled with the lock and flung it open.

She stood there with her fist in the air, ready to rap on the door again. 'Matt! Again. I'm so sorry. Can I …?' She gestured and he stepped back, indicating she could come in.

Cordy hurried into the room and turned to face him, her eyes wide. 'This place is weird. It's illogical and it's *weird.*'

'Do you want a coffee?' Matt didn't really know what else to say. He waved his hand in the direction of the kettle.

Cordy followed the direction of his hand and nodded. 'Yes. Yes please. God, my head is thumping.' She sat down, perched almost, on the edge of the bed. 'I – I just thought I saw a figure in my room. Then it disappeared. And I thought she'd really gone, and I imagined it, but then she spoke to me – something about dying. Ugh.'

Matt raised his eyebrows. With Cordy, it seemed that pragmatic and direct was the way to go. 'That *is* quite weird. I was having a weird dream, to be honest, so I'm kind of pleased you barged in like this.' He ran his hand through his hair. It wasn't often he had a visitor this early in the morning, and he was still trying to make sense of things in his semi-awake state. The news that Cordy had apparently seen a woman in her room was something he hadn't considered he'd be – well – *considering* at dawn.

He turned and headed towards the kettle, still limping a bit as he went. He cursed again under his breath and rubbed his leg as he waited for the kettle to boil.

'Are you okay?' Cordy asked.

'Just lay on it funny, I think.' He turned and smiled, surprised in a nice way that she'd thought to ask when she was the one who had run to him seeking comfort and solace … *hang on*

– what the hell? Where did that old-fashioned phrase come from? He shook the thought away, dismissing it as the product of being awake too early in the morning and a distinct lack of caffeine. 'Just as well there's nobody lurking in my room, or I think they might catch me if I tried to run. It'll be fine when the circulation's come back into it. Milk? Sugar?'

'Just milk, thanks. It's kind of you to make it. I'll have to return the favour because I'll be doing this sort of thing in the tea-room tomorrow – today, even.' She shook her head. This was really ridiculously early.

'Ah yes. Kit was telling me they had to get some help from the village. I think the kids are going to be back at college on Monday. Just weekend staff, apparently. I'm going to be busy tomorrow too. We've got twenty ladies booked in for a "Back to Nature" sketching session.'

Cordy raised her eyebrows. 'Back to Nature?'

'As in flowers. Plants. Not nudes.' He grinned at her.

'That's good to know – I don't want to be worrying what I'll find around the estate tomorrow in that respect. Well, my fellow baristas are very enthusiastic so that's a good start, I think.' Cordy was sitting on her hands, the conversation light, but Matt knew that was to take her mind of the alleged weirdness of Pencradoc. 'There was something else,' she suddenly said. 'And you'll probably toss me out that window once you hear it. That lady in my room. She said all that weird stuff about dying just after I mentioned Evelyn. The lady on the marriage certificate. I talked out loud, which was also quite crazy, thinking about it.' She was silent for a moment and glanced down at the floor. 'Maybe whoever it is really hates Lily and she's out to get me for – I don't know – bringing her back to life. But then – she might even have been Lily, because she told me Evelyn had died. But if she was a ghost, then she could have been Evelyn. As in dead. As in a dead ghost. Ugh.'

'Okay.' Matt half-smiled. 'I don't think ghosts can be alive or dead – by definition, they're already dead. But, given your experience of swishy dresses, and ladies in your room and disembodied voices, I have to ask … was the voice Irish?'

'Yes. Just like the voice you said you heard.' It was a statement, not a question.

'Hmmm.' There wasn't much else he could say really. Cordy stood up and came over to the little table with the kettle on. She took her mug and sipped at it gratefully.

Wrapping her hands around it, she smiled a little wryly at him. 'At least we're both weird together. And this coffee might make me feel a little more human.'

'It might be worth asking if anyone has ever heard of this Evelyn lady? Kit or Merryn or Coren might know.'

'I could maybe have a look on the computer. Do a search on some genealogy sites for her. Maybe it's just my imagination – and I certainly don't want those guys to think that they've got even more ghosts roaming around the place. I tease Merryn enough about Duchess Rose.'

Matt flashed a look at her. 'Duchess Rose? You know about her?' Snatches of conversations he'd had with Kit and Coren over the last couple of years hinting at odd things at Pencradoc, their tongues loosened by local cider and ale, played about his mind. Clearly Merryn had spoken to Cordy about similar things.

'Yes. She was supposed to wander around by the waterfall, but nobody's seen her for ages. Hey, perhaps Evelyn has moved into the breach, so to speak?'

'Pencradoc is a big house. I'm sure it's got room for several ghosts.'

'I'm sure it has.' She took another sip of her coffee. 'But we think that Evelyn was real, yes? Because we have the marriage lines.'

'Evelyn and Francis, yes—'

The conversation was interrupted by a crash from outside in the corridor as if something had been hit against the door, and they both stared at one another, Cordy's coffee slopping over the side of her mug and splashing down her soft sweatshirt. She seemed not to notice; rather she stared at the door, her eyes wide.

'I'll check.' For some reason, Matt lowered his voice. He went over to the door, glad to realise that the circulation must have come back into his leg, his usual long strides carrying him the short distance quickly. He threw open the door, ready to challenge anyone that was lurking outside. But the corridor was devoid of people.

He honestly didn't think it could have been anyone else at this time in the morning. He knew Coren lived on-site, but his flat was pretty much self-contained and on the floor below, and he didn't think he'd be patrolling the corridors before dawn for any reason. It was also way too early for any cleaners – or, he reasoned, any guests – apart from Cordy, obviously. There was no reason for anybody to be out there.

The only thing he could see was a silver cane, topped with a hornbill, lying by the window a little further along. The window, however, was wide open, and the flimsy curtains flapped around in the wind that blew through it.

Matt swore under his breath and hurried along the corridor, closing the window firmly and picking up the cane. He recognised it as being one that was usually displayed in an old-fashioned umbrella stand at the bottom of the stairs. The reason it was there was a mystery – he could explain the window coming open; a dodgy catch, a strong gust of wind – but why the cane was there, he didn't know. Unless one of the other guests had picked it up and brought it upstairs. They might, he thought, have lain it on the windowsill, and the fact the window itself had flung open might have propelled it across the room.

He felt Cordy come up behind him, her fingers grasping his arm and her soft breath on his neck as she peered over his shoulder.

'What was it?' Her voice broke into his thoughts, but it

came from the doorway of the room – not from behind him, where he stood by the window.

She was nowhere near him, yet the impression of someone holding his arm lingered for a brief moment, then faded as the sun broke over the horizon.

Chapter Nine

1895

Elsie was happy with the way the Pageant was taking shape. They had all come to the conclusion that it would be good for Lily Valentine to do Titania's speech, then to sing 'Daisy Bell'. Every time Miss Valentine stood on the stage to practice, a crowd of delighted spectators would cluster around; be it the gardeners, or the estate workers, or even the family itself. Miss Valentine laughed and smiled at everyone, and always curtsied beautifully at the end of her performance. Elsie was trying to copy those curtsies, but only on her own in the privacy of her bedroom.

She was also working on some very special programmes. When she had a moment in her busy schedule, she would take herself out to the rose garden or the wilderness area where she could hide away a little, and carefully draw and paint the covers. She was doing some very splendid pictures of Lily Valentine and was writing the wording as far as she could – she did want to leave some of the fun for her cousins, but also wanted to make sure the programmes were as good as they could be before they got their hands on them.

It was on one of her expeditions that she saw a figure in the woods. It was one of the workmen, and he was at the edge of a coppice, chopping some logs. He paused and stood up, apparently unaware that she was there, and looked across the estate to the Mill House. He seemed to freeze and didn't move for some time.

Elsie followed his gaze, and she saw what he saw: Lily Valentine in the garden. She was moving around the area, snipping flowers and making a beautiful bunch of them, probably to display in a vase in the Mill House. She stood up and stretched, then pushed her hands into the small of her back. Then, after a moment, she went back to her snipping.

When the bouquet was complete, she went back in the house and closed the door. The man watched her a minute longer, then went back to his work.

Elsie smiled, a little smugly, as she continued to her destination. Lily was *her* friend and she was visiting *her* house and she would be in *her* pageant. Elsie knew she was a very lucky girl and was glad that Lily was in her life this summer. Even the workers had heard of her, because a lot of them came to see her rehearse; that man in the coppice was as much in awe of her as any audience ever was. She felt proud of Lily for being able to command attention at such a distance. One day, she too would be able to do that – to make people stand up and stare at her artwork. It was a very exciting prospect.

Yes. Elsie thought that it was a *very* good time to be Lady Elsie Pencradoc.

Most definitely.

Present Day

'Everything all right in here?' Coren popped his head into the Tower Tea-Room. Cordy had waved off Steph and Josh about an hour ago, happy to take charge of the place now she knew how the machines all worked.

Cordy looked up as Coren came in and smiled at him. 'It's all good. I'm not sure whether Matt was trying to catch you. There was a problem with a window latch in the corridor by his room this morning. It made a hell of a bang when it flew open. It was quite scary at 4 a.m.'

Coren raised his eyebrows in amusement. 'And may I ask what you were doing in Matt's room at 4 a.m.?'

'God! Yes, that sounds bad, doesn't it?' Cordy, unfazed, laughed, and came around the front of the counter to speak to him. She lowered her voice. '*Not* making a hell of a bang with him, let's just make that clear.' She grinned. 'It's a bit stupid, saying it here in daylight, but I had a bad dream and scared myself silly. We'd been out for dinner – no, stop looking like that, Coren, it was as friends! – and I had too much to drink. I can't handle it the way I used to. And, well … I thought I saw something in my room.' She ducked her head, feeling herself grow hot with embarrassment.

'Something in your room?' Coren knew all about Duchess Rose, and also knew how Cordy teased Merryn about her. 'It wasn't Rose again, was it?'

'No idea. She had a green dress on. Merryn says Rose favours white. Sorry. That sounds ridiculous, doesn't it? As Scrooge said, there's "more of gravy than of grave" in that one. I had eaten quite a bit as well as drunk quite a bit.' She frowned. 'Okay. So, to go back to your original question – yes. Everything is fine in here. Hurrah.'

'Good. But maybe not so good on the top floor with the window latches. I'll have a look and see what we can do about it. Are you all okay in here then? I'll leave you all to get on with it if you are, but it looks as if you're under control.'

'I think we are. One thing – can I ask you a favour, though?'

'A favour? Sure.'

'Thanks. I'm just wondering if there's a computer somewhere I can use? Did Merryn tell you I'm working on a play focused on Lily Valentine?' She felt her cheeks flush as she knew she wasn't *quite* going to tell him the real reason she wanted a big screen and faster internet access than her phone could deliver.

'Yes! She did mention it. It sounds really exciting, and exactly the sort of thing we're trying to encourage at the Arts Centre.'

'Well, I think it would be a bit easier to research her and her life on a computer.' It wasn't a lie.

'I agree. Yes – you know where the office is, don't you? Along from the classrooms Matt will be using?'

Cordy tried very hard not to blush even more furiously; she certainly didn't miss the cheeky twinkle in Coren's eyes when he said Matt's name. Coren wasn't a man who did cheeky very often, so he must have found something highly amusing in the conversation. 'Yes. I know the office.'

'Well there's a spare desk in there – Merryn sometimes uses it when she's around, but she's in Marazion for the beginning of this week, so you're good to go.'

'Fabulous. Thank you. And—' she hesitated to ask yet another favour of Coren, but battered down the doubt and did so anyway. '—is it okay if I go in there at odd hours? Like this evening, perhaps, when we've finished.' She desperately wanted to get on and find out about Evelyn and Francis, but she knew the primary reason she was here was to help her friend out in the tea-room.

Coren laughed. 'Of course it is. I'll make sure I give you the key and you can nip in and out whenever you fancy it.'

'Thank you! I'd hug you, but it's a bit inappropriate to hug the boss.'

'Don't be silly.' Coren grinned and hugged her briefly. 'It's good to see you. Sybill was saying she might pop up today, so I'll tell her to come and say hello as well.'

'Sybill. Nice.' She winked, then turned her back on her boss before he could answer her or deny anything. There were other, equally important, things to do – like learn to froth milk.

But deep inside, she couldn't help a squiggle of excitement. She'd hopefully find herself a bit closer to Evelyn and Francis after some online research. She couldn't wait to get started.

Matt was well into his work already. His group of Women's Institute ladies had turned up and spilled out of their coach in a flurry of cotton frocks and floral perfumes.

He'd decided that the weather was perfect enough for them to sketch outside, which was always better than sitting indoors as far as he was concerned. He'd therefore set them off around the formal gardens, telling them to find a comfortable place to sit and to just enjoy the process of creating, rather than worrying what the end result would look like.

'It's not a competition,' he told them. 'You're here to have fun and relax.'

He took the opportunity to sit with them and chat, offering advice and encouragement, and also to work on something himself. He found a nook next to a bower of roses, just on the cusp of Rose's Garden. The ladies were all enjoying sketching out the geometric beauty and riotous colours of the borders and beds, marked out by well-worn pathways, but Matt wanted to break with that formality. He was happier sitting by the knots of ivy and bright blooms of Old English roses, the broken edges of the follies and tree stumps peeking out of the foliage, just through the thorny screen.

He gazed into the distance, his eyes travelling across the landscape, picking out things that would look good in a picture – Pencradoc house itself, mellow in the sunlight; the way a rose stem bent with the weight of the blooms; the tight buds and the full-blown blossoms; the rich green canopy of trees; the twisted and gnarled tree stumps, half-buried in the ground; the rocks covered with lichen; the pathway winding into the Wilderness Gardens.

He followed the direction of one of the pathways, knowing that the Tower Tea-Room was at the end of it. Knowing, also, that Cordy was more than likely in there, frothing her milk and smiling that wide, confident smile at the visitors. He guessed that the day, for her, wouldn't just stop at observing and training, even if she was in a new place. No, she seemed the sort of woman who'd be straight in there, getting directly on with the task in hand. He knew when the ladies in his workshop had their tea break, they'd all stampede towards the Folly, and he might, just might, have to have a trip along there with them.

Almost unconsciously, smiling at the thought of Cordy's

cheerful presence and lulled by the gentle buzzing of the bees and the warmth of the day, Matt began to loosely sketch the outline of a figure. His fingers held the pencil comfortably, making confident strokes on the page, building the image up until the clock in the village struck ten-thirty and brought him back to reality. He realised he'd sketched the image of the woman he'd seen drifting through the gardens. She – or maybe Cordy – was obviously on his mind for some reason, and he closed the sketchbook hurriedly in case anyone started asking questions he couldn't answer.

But it was time for tea and he stood up, looking around at his class. 'Let's take a break!' he called. 'Say, half an hour? Then we'll reconvene and see how everyone's doing. And we can maybe play with pastels or chalks. Or water-soluble pencils. How does that sound?'

'I've tried to put some colour on already,' said one lady apologetically. 'It just looked as if it needed it. But I'm not quite sure how these water pencils work.'

Matt smiled at her. 'There aren't any rules about the pencils. It's your picture. It's up to you what you do with it.'

'I thought I might get into trouble,' she said with a cheeky grin. 'I'm always trying to get ahead. I have no patience.'

'Like I always say, there's no right or wrong in my classes. I'll take a look after our break and see if we can try out some techniques with your pencils, yes? There's more you can do with them than you think.'

'I look forward to it!' The lady grinned again and pointed towards the Folly. 'Is that the tea-room over there?'

'It is. I'll be joining you in just a second. But it's straight along that path. You can't miss it. I'm just going to have a quick look at everyone's work while I have the chance.'

The lady nodded and hurried off to join her friends. Matt had a quick peek at her work and was pleasantly surprised at how good it was – and he was certain that he could give her some tips to improve it even more.

'You've got a nice group today,' came a cheerful voice, thick with a beautiful Cornish accent.

'Sybill! Good to see you.' Matt smiled down at the woman who had been so helpful to the Penhaligon brothers over the last couple of years. Over her arm she had a ream of green fabric. Upon closer inspection, it seemed to be a dress of some description on a clothes hanger.

'Good to see you too, Matty.' She leaned in and gave him an awkward air kiss, hampered as she was by fabric. 'I'm looking for Cordy. I have something she might like.' She raised her arms and nodded to indicate the dress. 'It's one we had in storage from a few years ago when there was a costume display at Wheal Mount. This one was our Arts and Crafts one. We'd matched them all to different styles of art and displayed them around the downstairs rooms with various pieces of the same era.' She smiled, remembering.

Matt knew that part of the bottom floor of Wheal Mount was open to the public, the walls hung with pictures by the famous Ruan Teague and even some by the redoubtable Lady Elsie Pencradoc.

'I bet that was a good exhibition,' he told Sybill. 'It's a shame they can't do something similar here.'

'Oh they can.' Sybill's smile was mischievous. 'I just need to make Coren think it's his idea first. Give me time. We have plenty of costumes they can use!'

'Were they original?' Matt reached out and ran the green fabric through his fingers. It felt like cotton.

'No, they were made by a local designer based on patterns she'd sourced over the years. We had the most incredible fairytale princess one. Well – vampire princess, maybe. Beautiful.' She smiled her cheeky grin again. 'It went down well in the Gothic display.'

'I'm sure it did. So you said this one was for Cordy?'

'Yes. Coren said she was doing a play or a pageant or something to do with Lily Valentine. From the couple of pictures we have of her visit here, it seems she liked this style.'

'And this is a costume for Cordy. I get it now!'

'It is indeed. She can customise it, of course. It might not be exactly what she wants, but it's a basis. I just need to find Cordy to explain all that. Oh – I've got a key for her as well. Coren said she wanted one for the offices.'

'I can do all that.' Matt swept the ream of fabric out of a surprised Sybill's arms and held out a hand for the key. She paused for a second then dropped it into his palm. 'Coren's still around somewhere.' He nodded over to the house. 'You might be lucky and get a coffee out of him, now I've given you some extra time to play with.'

'Hmm. We'll see. Okay – I'll go and look for him, see if he's where I left him which would be unusual. That man slopes off whenever he thinks I want to spend some extra time with him. Anyway, are you sure you don't mind?' She pointed at the dress.

'I don't mind at all. Cordy is in the tea-room, and I was just heading there.' *It wasn't a lie.*

But even if he hadn't have been heading there, he might have just used the dress as an excellent excuse to go there.

'Lovely. Thanks so much.' Sybill smiled and turned on her heel, walking purposefully to the hall.

And Matt turned purposefully in the other direction, grinning to himself at the fact he now had a genuine excuse to chat to Cordy, beyond ordering a coffee from her.

Today was a good day.

1895

Today was a good day – Lily was amazing, the scenery was incredible and the little *troupe* of Pencradoc girls had eventually decided which child would be which fairy. Elsie was determined to have her *tableau*, and it was all looking wonderful. Alys and Jago were with them in the garden, and they'd received a letter from Zennor that morning, confirming Elsie's suspicions that she would be getting a new brother or sister soon. Everyone was happy and cheerful and enjoying one of those idyllic Cornish summer days.

But Edwin knew what would make it even more special. He beckoned Elsie over from where she was sketching Biscuit, and the little girl came hurrying across the lawn, a big smile on her face.

'Elsie, I'm thinking about your pageant. Have you given any thought to professional photographs, just like they do in the big shows?'

'Just like the pictures in my scrapbook?'

'Exactly like the ones in your scrapbook.'

'I haven't thought about it, but I think it would be a very good thing to do, really.'

'I do too. So I'm happy to take some pictures of you all, but if you would like to use my portable camera to try it yourself, I'm happy to help you.'

'*Would* you? Oh thank you Mr Griffiths!'

'It's my pleasure. Let me just get it ready for you. You can have a think about what you would like to have in the pictures.'

'I'd definitely like one of Miss Valentine. And one of Biscuit. And we need some of my cousins, so they can see what they look like on the stage. That would be very good.'

'And we need one of you as well, I think,' said Lily, coming up behind them. She'd been lazing on a daybed, reading a book, but had clearly tired of doing nothing. 'Because it's your pageant after all.'

'Really?' Elsie looked embarrassed and delighted. 'I thought with me being behind the scenes that I wouldn't count.'

'I think you will count. Look. Stand there and let Mr Griffiths frame the shot.'

Lily indicated a position in front of the camera, but

surprisingly Elsie shook her head. 'No. I think I need to see you do it first. Just so I know what to do.'

'It's really not difficult. Stand there and I shall direct you.'

'All right. If you say so, Miss Valentine.'

Edwin was amused. It hadn't taken Elsie long to change her opinion.

'Very good. Now – arms like this. Head like this – no this. That's right. Stand a little more to the left, shoulders back. Look at the camera. Be ready to smile when Mr Griffiths asks you. No, stop fidgeting. Just stand still. Shoulders back again, you're slumping ... perfect! Absolutely perfect. Edwin? Now.'

Edwin pressed the shutter, and the picture was taken.

Elsie blinked and looked at Lily. 'My goodness, Miss Valentine. That was very easy.'

'It *is* easy.'

'Would you like to take one of Lily now?' Edwin asked.

'I shall try,' said Elsie and came up to him. 'Do I need to tell her how to stand?'

'No, she'll know.' Edwin caught Lily's eye and Lily winked. She took her place in front of the camera and assumed a wonderfully professional pose. She was wearing the green dress again and had her sunhat on. Even Edwin could see that this might be one of the best pictures of Lily he'd ever see. It would be natural and she looked relaxed – but also extremely beautiful.

'Perfect,' he murmured.

'Thank you.' Elsie nodded, clearly thinking that he meant the way she was handling the bulky piece of equipment. Lily looked at him, and her smile grew. It seemed that she knew exactly what he was really thinking, and that was that Lily Valentine was beyond compare.

Lily enjoyed that afternoon in the gardens. Elsie soon took charge of the photographic session, and had her cousins and even her dog posing dramatically for the pictures. She also took one or two quite candid shots where the little ones weren't quite ready for the picture, but Lily could tell, even by seeing the positions they were in, that the pictures would be delightful.

Alys and Jago were laughing over a game of croquet which Jago was, truth be told, appalling at, and soon their two eldest girls had drifted off to help their papa. The little ones were trying to encourage Biscuit onto his back legs by waving sandwiches at him, and Elsie and Edwin had their heads together looking at the innards of the camera.

The only thing that marred it slightly was the fact that she couldn't quite shake the feeling that they were being watched. Her gaze kept drifting towards the river, and at one point she thought she saw a figure on the opposite bank. For a moment, his build and his stature looked far too familiar and her stomach lurched.

He couldn't be here. Of course he couldn't be here.

'Don't be stupid, Lily,' she scolded herself and looked back over the water. The man had gone. Silly, silly tricks of the light. It was, she reasoned, because she couldn't allow herself to be happy or to forget all about her other life. She was too scared that something would happen to ruin it all.

Her hand crept almost unconsciously to her stomach.

This was Edwin's baby. Hers and Edwin's, and she must never forget that, no matter how many tricks of the light she encountered.

Chapter Ten

Present Day

Cordy was willing the trained actress in her to keep a smile on her face whilst the woman she was serving asked for a half-caff, skinny soy latte at the same time she was ordering one babyccino to share between two of her children; the third child was strapped, papoose-like, to her front, and occasionally she cradled the baby's bottom as if she had really, really loved being pregnant and missed a great big weighty bump there, and now relished having a great big weighty person there, still making her waddle in an awkward fashion and tilting her centre off balance.

And what would she do if she tripped over one of her very long, trailing scarves and that poor baby got squashed?

It didn't bear thinking about.

Cordy was also wondering how the woman could even control three children, considering the way the eldest two were rampaging through the small tea-room – and could you even *get* skinny soy milk?

She turned to the fridge behind her to have a rummage, scowling as the woman's reedy tones filled the room: 'Rupert! Arabella! Sit nicely, or this poor waitress won't be able to serve you.'

'Is she our servant then?' That was Arabella.

'Can we tell her what to do?' That was Rupert.

For God's sake.

'Please just take a seat,' Cordy said between gritted teeth. 'I'll be with you shortly.'

It was worth a try.

'Need a hand?' Matt's soft voice was full of amusement, and Cordy flushed as he squeezed in behind the counter with her. 'I'll take the tray over. You stay there and count to 'ten.' He put something carefully down on a shelf behind the counter. It looked like a ream of green fabric. There was a soft *clink* as he placed a key next to it. 'That's from Coren, apparently.'

'Super. But can you *get* bloody skinny soy milk?' she muttered.

'No idea, but I won't tell her if you won't. Anyway.' He shrugged and nodded to the table where the family had sat. The woman had opened up a plastic box full of cakes and sandwiches and was putting snacks out in front of the children. Apart from the cakes. She was snaffling those for herself, greedily tucking into them when she thought nobody was watching. 'What difference will it make? She'll probably have the kids' hot chocolate instead.'

'Babyccino. Basically hot frothy milk. One between them. So she won't have much to greed from them.' Cordy was whooshing the milk as she spoke, but soon she was finished and, good as his word, Matt took the tray to the family and Cordy let her temper subside.

Most customers were a pleasure – but some of them ... grrr. That was why, she reflected, she'd never stuck at café work for very long. Oh well. Soon Sorcha would return, Cordy would be back in London and no doubt temping in an office somewhere, because goodness knew her acting career wasn't particularly brilliant. She had to try and enjoy Pencradoc while she was here.

Matt returned, grinning. 'They asked me if I was their butler. I said no. I told them I was the best friend of the Duke and was helping out the Duchess's best friend because they were in London visiting the Queen today and had left the place in our care.'

'Nice one.' Cordy nodded, impressed, and pulled herself up into a much more regal stance, channelling her *Downton Abbey* persona.

Rupert and Arabella, she noticed, were staring in awe at

the pair of them now, and Mummy was indeed snaffling the babyccino whilst they were otherwise occupied.

'I thought so.' Matt dipped down and picked up what he'd put there earlier. It was green fabric, as Cordy had spotted, but now he held it up, she saw it for what it was.

'A dress! How lovely.' She couldn't help herself; she reached out and fingered the fabric gently. It was a sort of cotton, she thought – something quite simple and lightweight.

'It's from Wheal Mount. Sybill brought it for you. She says you can customise it for a costume. I took over the job and sent her to find Coren.' Matt grinned.

Cordy shook her head. 'That man is unbelievable. They're perfect for one another – why doesn't either one of them do anything about it?'

'Who knows? Anyway, Sybill suggested it was from an exhibition where they'd displayed some Arts and Crafts items. And as we think it's the sort of thing Lily Valentine favoured, she thought it might be useful for you. For your play.'

'Ooh. Yes. Those photographs ...' She checked herself and lowered her voice. 'Those photographs we found – she's wearing something similar in those. Nice and spacious, I guess, if she was in an interesting condition.' She allowed herself a small smile. 'It'll be perfect for my "Lily" character – I've also got some good ideas about including the audience. We can make it a bit more interactive for the children, otherwise they'll just get bored listening to Shakespeare. I've got until the tenth to sort it out. That was the original date, which is quite nice to know.'

'At least you've got that programme to refer to. It's a pretty concise record of the original pageant.' It was Matt's turn to lower his voice. He leaned down towards her and her heart stuttered. His eyes, very close up, were the most curious colour – the sort of swirly dark brown you get when you're stirring a very rich hot chocolate. 'Elsie would have had it all sorted – you only have to listen to her.'

'Listen to her. Ha!' It was very difficult to breathe, to be fair. Difficult to breathe and concentrate on anything more than those eyes. 'I hope she doesn't start talking to me. Like, for real.'

Matt drew back. 'Yes. That might be a bit strange. Listen, Cordy, I—'

'—Cordelia? *Cordelia*! There you are! I've looked *everywhere* for you! What on earth are you doing *here*?' The voice boomed out from the doorway to the little tea-room, and Cordy looked up, startled.

'Toby? I could ask you the same thing!'

Matt spun around to face the door, equally startled. It was indeed Toby Fowler, standing in the doorway. He was silhouetted against the bright sunlight outside. The man sure knew how to make an entrance. He flung himself over to the counter, neatly stepping in front of Matt, and flung his arms around Cordy who looked, it had to be said, as stiff as a board within them.

Toby Fowler did a lot of flinging.

'Toby – get off me.' Cordy wriggled out of the embrace, but Toby then grabbed her face in his hands and planted a huge kiss on her lips.

From the corner of the tea-room came a flash as a camera went off. Matt looked over, and saw a man sitting, a black coffee in front of him, his camera pointed directly at Toby and Cordy.

'God, babes. You had me worried – running off like that.' Toby's voice carried around the room, bouncing off the curved, pastel-painted walls. Here was a man who clearly liked an audience and knew how acoustics worked. 'And here you are, hidden away in this quaint little village – home of your childhood friend, Merryn, who's married to the Duke of Trecarrow—' *Pause for effect*, thought Matt. 'Look – I told you, it doesn't matter if the parts aren't coming your way.

I've got a leading role in a new show at the Royal Queens, on Shaftesbury Avenue, and I start rehearsals next month. You, babes, are standing with the Gypsy King, from the musical revamp version of *The Black Rose*. You know – the one Lily Valentine was in?' He stared around the tea-room triumphantly and flung his arms out again. *More flinging*, thought Matt, feeling his hands curl into fists. God, the man needed a punch on the face to shut him up. 'In this special exhibition,' bellowed Toby Fowler, 'celebrating Lily Valentine's visit to Pencradoc, it's *quite* the perfect location to research the part. To live the brand, as it were.' A self-effacing little laugh, which was more of a smirky little giggle in Matt's opinion. 'You, my darling, are my Rosalee.'

Good God. This fellow was unreal!

'How the hell did you find me?' That was Cordy, muttering under her breath, casting a glance at the man in the corner who was, it seemed, recording everything Toby Fowler said, judging by the way his smartphone was blinking and the odd angle it was placed on the table – directed right at Toby.

'What do you mean, my love?' Toby clutched Cordy's shoulders, then ran his hands down her arms so he was holding her hands tightly, his face creased in a puzzled, brooding expression. 'You ran off after our silly little misunderstanding. I *told* you it doesn't matter if you aren't doing as well as I am. I love you anyway. So I spoke to our friends and managed to find you—'

'—Friends?' exploded Cordy, shaking herself out of his grasp. 'We have no mutual friends! If by "friends" you mean Ash and Paul, I'm going to kill them! I really am. How did you track me there? Roland, I bet? *Was* it bloody Roland? Oh, wait until I get my hands on him!'

Cordy was raging, and even Toby looked a little stunned. He recovered himself, though, but Matt didn't miss the quick glance he shot the chap with the black coffee before he started trying to soothe Cordy again, and the slight alteration to the angle they were standing at so he was more in the direct line of the man and his camera, should he choose to bring it out again. Ah. Of course. It was set-up. A total set-up. A reporter getting a scoop, no doubt – not just a fan taking a quick photo. Well, it might have been nice if Toby had his facts right first. Merryn married to the Duke? Matt felt his lips curl into a smirk. Cordy had this, he was sure, but he could help. Oh yes, he could help.

'Hey.' He walked over to the man with the black coffee and nodded at the mobile phone. 'Pretty sure that's illegal. Recording someone's conversation. But so long as you're doing it, can I add to it?' Uninvited, he sat down next to the mobile phone and leaned in towards it. 'Hello, everyone. Not sure which paper this is for, but hello anyway.' He cast a glance up to the man and grinned. They both knew the reporter was in an awkward position. If he complained or picked the phone up, it was an admission of guilt. If he just sat there – as he was doing – the phone would record everything Matt said. And yes, it might not make it to the paper, but he had that covered as well. Matt put his own phone carefully next to him. 'It's already on. Don't worry. I can send the recording to the paper if you don't use my quotes.' He leaned back in the seat and crossed his legs. 'First of all, welcome to Pencradoc Arts Centre. I'm sure you know where it is, as Toby Fowler will have told you when he set this nice little meeting up.'

'Now just wait a minute ...' Finally, the reporter found his voice and lost the stunned look he'd had since Matt joined him.

'Oh no, this won't take too long.' Matt smiled again. 'I'll give you a brief history of the place we're in – the Tower Tea-Room was built as a folly in the nineteenth century, and the story goes that a previous Duchess – that's Rose, her portrait is in the hallway – died in here by falling down the stairs. After the Duke died, his second wife, Zennor, had Ellory's posthumous daughter, Lady Elsie – then married the artist Ruan Teague. Pencradoc was inherited by the Duke's younger brother, Jago. And as he and his wife Alys only had daughters, the title lost its way a little. In fact, I'm pretty sure the title ended. However, Coren and Kit, my good friends, now own the property, courtesy of their direct descent from Elsie's family. Are you keeping up with me? Good. Now, Merryn, who Mr Fowler mentioned earlier, may be Cordelia Beaumont's – Cordelia Beaumont – remember the name, please – best friend, but she isn't married to a Duke. She's living with Kit Penhaligon. Can you make sure that's reported correctly, please? I'd hate to confuse your readers.' He shifted position and crossed his legs the other way, steepling his fingers thoughtfully. 'Now, the reason Cordy is here, is because she's actually looking to enhance the Lily Valentine Exhibition by writing and performing a show, based on an extant pageant programme found in a secret location on the estate, which was written and illustrated by Lady Elsie herself. So, I believe the day scheduled for this is the 10th August. The original date of the Lily Valentine Pageant.'

He cast a glance at the reporter – who actually looked quite interested. 'I say,' said Matt suddenly, feigning realisation hitting him. 'Are you the Arts and Culture reporter for …?'

'Yes, that's right.' The man suddenly held out a hand. 'Rick Hoffman. For *The Sunday Stage*.' The paper or magazine or whatever it was, wasn't one Matt had ever heard of, but he nodded thoughtfully, as if he knew all about it. His risk had paid off. 'I thought so. Okay. I really must go now. Cordy needs to regroup. She was helping me in here while I looked after a group of lady artists who needed a little extra attention.' He smiled, disarmingly, he hoped, at Rick Hoffman, and stood up. His leg gave a little under him, but he managed to steady himself. He really should stop crossing his legs. 'And that, Mr Hoffman, was an exclusive. You managed a coup, there, sir. It would be most appreciated if you could give us a little mention in the article. Coren and Kit would be very grateful.

And have a refill.' He nodded at the black coffee which now had a shiny sort of scum on the top as it grew cold. 'On us.'

He turned and walked back to the counter where Cordy was still having a heated discussion with an indignant Toby, who had one eye on her and one on Rick Hoffman. Yes, she definitely had this one, but still ...

'Excuse me.' Matt put his hand on Toby's arm and made his face deliberately blank as if he had no clue who this chap was. 'I can't allow you behind the counter.' He grimaced and looked the man up and down. 'It's unhygienic. Sorry, mate. You have to leave.' Gently but firmly, he steered Toby, still protesting undying love for Cordy, out of the space behind the counter and towards the door. 'Can't have you manhandling my staff either, sir,' he said in a low, dangerous voice. Toby blinked and seemed to quail a little. *Good*. 'We can do this nicely and you can sod off, or I can call the police and have you removed from the estate. I've also called your pet reporter off. But I can get him back for another exclusive if you really want him to photograph you being escorted away. And next time you want to use one of my colleagues as bait for your self-serving theatricals, I suggest you think again. Or I won't be as amenable.' He squeezed Toby's shoulder, just enough to make the man blink again.

'I was trying to get my girlfriend back!' Toby scowled. 'That's all it was.'

'It wasn't, and we both know that. Now please. Leave.'

'Fine.' Toby turned and walked with as much dignity as he could apparently muster out of the tea-room. He couldn't resist though: 'Well, if you want me in the future, I shall be playing Vadim, the Gypsy King, at the Royal Queen's—'

'—Get *out*!' A takeaway cup came flying through the air and bounced off Toby's chest. 'And *stay* out.' Matt turned and saw Cordy standing there with her hands on her hips. A glint of sunlight came through one of the high, narrow windows and struck her hair with shades of auburn and red. Her eyes sparked green instead of their usual blue, and it was his turn to blink. She looked … different. Then a cloud must have come across the sky, and the sunlight faded and she was Cordy again. A furious, scowling Cordy.

'He's bloody lucky,' growled Cordy, stomping up to Matt and standing beside him, possibly checking that the coast really was clear of Toby Fowler. 'My first choice of weapon was a china cup.'

'Perhaps best that you didn't use that,' Matt murmured, turning back to the door and making sure that Toby had strutted off and wasn't going to try to do a curtain call.

But it seemed as if he had gone.

'And that, my friends, is the end of the show.' Suddenly, Cordy's voice was amused, but firm. He turned back to comment and saw her curtseying deeply to a surprising round of applause from the clientele in the tea-room – largely made up of Matt's WI ladies. He couldn't help but smile and join in the applause.

That's my girl, he thought. Then he stopped that thought right in its tracks. They barely knew each other. She certainly wasn't 'his' girl.

Was she?

'I'm so sorry you had to witness that.' Cordy was still annoyed at Toby. It was amusing, in some ways, however, that he had blustered on so dreadfully, and been so very wrong about so many things. She couldn't help a sly smile. 'I'll tell Merryn she's supposed to be married to the Duke. Perhaps I should start calling her "Your Grace".'

'I'd like to see her reaction to that.' Matt smiled. 'I have to go now – the entertainment and the workshop break is over. Your Yummy Mummy has finished snacking on her kids' food, and you've got a write-up to look forward to in *The Sunday Stage* magazine. I therefore bid you farewell.'

He did a little mock bow and Cordy laughed. 'Thanks again.

I'm looking forward to seeing what *The Sunday Stage* come up with. I suspect I need to do a little more work on the pageant thing now though.' She frowned. 'Not a proper pageant. A performance. I can't magic up puppies in wheelbarrows and sprites and fairies.'

'Puppies in wheelbarrows?' Matt looked amused.

'Yes. You know. Being pushed on stage while I sing "Daisy Bell" … oh!' Cordy brought herself up short. '"Daisy Bell". Yes. Of course. I can do that.'

'But where did the idea of the puppy come from?'

'I don't know.' Cordy shrugged. It's the sort of thing I imagine Elsie would have done. Especially having seen that photograph of her dog. He looks like the sort of dog you could put a ruffle on and stick in a wheelbarrow …' She stopped again. 'Okay. I'm getting truly carried away now. I almost – no. I can't say.' She dipped her head down and began stacking cups and saucers neatly on the shelves.

'Can't say what?' Matt persisted.

'Can't say that I actually *saw* that in my head just then. Just a flash – just a quick image. I've got waaaaay too much imagination. Ah well.' She looked up and flashed a quick smile at Matt. 'The show should be good. It's maybe starting to come together a bit. Hurrah. Toby must have brought some West End inspiration to the West Country.' She lifted her hands, a tea towel in one of them, and did a little jazz-hands movement. 'We must be thankful for small mercies.'

'Great. Right. I'll … see you later? Perhaps?'

Matt almost looked hopeful, and Cordy smiled at him again. 'Perhaps. I need to get this stuff written down before I forget, though.'

'Ah. Okay. Well. Whenever.' He shrugged and made to turn away.

Cordy reached out and touched his shoulder, a little *zing* of electricity taking her by surprise as her hand connected with his body. 'But I'll be free about seven, I think. If you are?'

'I can be.' He smiled again, slowly, and Cordy was surprised that her knees didn't give way.

'Good.' She cleared her throat and went back to her crockery. 'I'll probably take my notebook to Rose's Garden after I've done some work on the computer – now I've got that key. Meet me in the garden?' She knew that he had just as much right to want to check up on Evelyn and Francis as she had, but she wanted to keep it quite private for them just now, because ... because of what? She paused, getting that weird feeling again; the one she'd had about the dog—

Biscuit. The soft Irish voice was amused and Cordy felt her eyes widen. *He's called Biscuit.*

'Absolutely.'

The real voice of Matt startled her out of the strange little bubble she was suddenly in, and she nodded. 'Good. See you then.'

And this time, he really did turn and leave, but not before dropping a kiss on her forehead. Which made Cordy hang onto the counter, positive, this time, that she would collapse in a heap. But whether it was due to Matt's kiss or the potential dog name she had just conjured up, she wasn't quite sure.

'Oh!' Her gaze landed on the green fabric, still folded up under the counter. And *that* needed to be moved before it got coffee spilled on it, or clotted cream dribbled down it.

'Miss Beaumont?'

Cordy looked up, still reeling a bit. 'Yes?'

The man who had been sitting in the corner of the tea-room, the one Matt had been speaking to, was standing in front of her, holding his hand out.

'It's Cordy.' She reached out and shook his hand, still puzzled.

'Cordy. Thanks.' The man smiled and behind the shifty sort of look he'd had, there was a flash of a genuinely good-looking man, a little rugged and tough around the edges, perhaps, but with nice blue eyes which crinkled at the corners when he smiled. 'I'm Rick Hoffman from *The Sunday Stage*. Sorry I got dragged into all this with Mr Fowler. But. You know.' Rick looked out of the door and frowned. 'Yeah. Sorry again. I'll be sure to mention your performance in the magazine. Good luck with it.' He let go of her hand.

'Oh – thanks. Yes. Toby and I are well finished. He had no right to come down here. And my friends had no right to tell him where I was either.'

'I agree. It's the part of the job I dislike the most – the celebrity stalking. That kind of thing.'

'Well, I'd hardly say I was a celebrity or that he was stalking me.'

'Yes, but your privacy should really have been respected. Sorry again.' Rick looked contrite.

'There's no need to keep apologising.' Cordy grinned. 'It's just annoying he found me. Oh well. We told him the score, if you'll pardon the pun.' Rick frowned slightly, not understanding. 'The music score? He's in musicals? Yeah?'

'Oh! God. Of course. Sorry, that's guilt addling my brain. Sorry! For apologising. Yet again.'

'Forget it. Now, if you'll excuse me, I really need to get back to work.' A seemingly curious bevy of WI ladies were queuing up behind Rick, possibly eager for some more gossip – or perhaps just for more takeaway tea to see them through the rest of the morning.

'Sure. I understand. Here.' Rick opened his wallet and handed a card over to Cordy. 'That's my number – call me once you have the details of the Pageant. We'll see if we can get you some coverage.'

'It's really not a pageant.' Cordy went hot and cold all over, even as she accepted the business card. A 'pageant' sounded like a massive undertaking, when all she was planning to do was sing a song, talk a bit about Lily, get some kids up on the stage and do a Shakespearean monologue from *A Midsummer Night's Dream*. That, she realised now, was all she realistically had time to do. But it would be fun. Especially if she could wear that dress.

'Well. Call me whatever you decide to do. We'll still get you some coverage. Ummm – your boyfriend said I could get a coffee refill, because that one went cold?' He grinned, hopefully.

'Actually, he's not my boyfriend, but yes, you can have one. Here.' She poured a filter coffee into a takeaway cup and pushed it across the counter to him. 'Enjoy the rest of your day.'

'Oh – well if he's not your boyfriend, perhaps you could call me anyway, and we can get a drink sometime?'

'Oh! Right – ummmm …' Her voice trailed off even as she glanced across at Matt, standing just outside waiting for his class.

'Okay, so he's *not* your boyfriend, but you'd like it to be that way. I understand.' Rick shrugged. 'It was worth a try – I get that actresses don't want to get involved with reporters. If you change your mind, you have my details. Thanks for the refill. I think I'll take a wander through the estate – see if I can get some nice photographs for the article. The new version of the article – don't worry.' He took the cup and raised it to her. 'Cheers.' Then he left the tea-room and stood in the doorway for a second. He looked curiously around him, but then Cordy's attention was taken up by several ladies wanting service, so she smiled and did exactly as they wished.

What a morning it had turned into! And she hadn't even *considered* Matt in the role of a boyfriend. It wasn't what she was looking for. She certainly hadn't come here to Pencradoc with that in mind at all.

But even as she served them coffee and tea and snacks and cakes, a little part of her couldn't help but wonder … *what if?*

After the excitement of Toby Fowler landing in the Tower Tea-Room, the WI ladies were quite difficult to settle down.

'Do you know that young lady well?' asked the woman who had jumped ahead with the colours. She was called Betty. Matt was sitting with her, showing her how to cross-hatch and shade with a couple of different shades of green to reflect the colours in the foliage.

'Who? Cordy? We only just met, really.' He put a forest-green pencil down and smiled at Betty. 'We have mutual friends though. I'm surprised in some ways our paths haven't crossed before.'

'She seems very nice – too nice for that silly actor man.' Betty scowled and scrubbed unnecessarily hard at a rogue pencil line with an eraser. 'The cheek of him! Fancy stalking the girl to her job. With a *reporter* in tow!'

'It's a bit out of line,' admitted Matt. 'But I think Cordy can hold her own somehow.'

'Hmm. She'd have to be able to in that business. She's an actress, you say? "Resting" no doubt.' She nodded sagely.

'Perhaps. But she had a flood in her flat, which is why she's here. Or we maybe wouldn't have met at all.'

'But you're pleased you met, aren't you lovely?' Betty grinned.

'I suppose so.' Matt laughed, then stood up. Nice as Betty was, he guessed she was quite the chatterbox and would love nothing better than a bit of gossip to take back to the meetings with her. 'I'd best see how everyone else is getting on. You're doing splendidly.'

'Thank you.' Betty positively glowed. 'We're going to exhibit the work in a local café, perhaps mount them with some cheap frames and sell them if we can.'

'Good luck. Well, you know I'm always willing to come and do sessions at the meetings – and who knows? You could branch out so you have yourselves a nice little art club. Maybe have an exhibition here.'

Betty's eyes widened. Matt could see she was putting herself in charge of that as well. It was probably a good time to slip away and see the rest of his pupils. He had to say, they were a nice crowd and he'd be sorry to wave them off soon. Hopefully they'd come back again for another session.

And anyway, once they were gone, and things had settled back down, he'd be able to do a little stalking of an actress himself.

Chapter Eleven

1895

'Miss Valentine!' Lily turned and saw Elsie running through the rose garden towards her, an envelope clasped in her hand. 'I'm very pleased I have seen you. What a surprise!'

Lily raised her eyebrows. 'Indeed it is a surprise. I thought I'd take a turn in the rose garden. Perhaps read a book for a little while.' She hid a smile. 'Or study my script. I know it is important that I am absolutely word perfect for the Pageant.'

She felt a little lost without Edwin around, hence the fact she was wandering Pencradoc like a lost soul. Edwin had gone into town with Jago to meet an old friend of theirs, and Alys was busy with correspondence relating to Wheal Mount. Lily had pleaded fatigue and dear Alys had fussed her like a Mother Hen, until she had kindly told her she just needed to rest for a while in peace and quiet.

The peace and quiet idea had been lovely, but she soon became restless and cross with herself for missing Edwin, and the truth was, there was a strange feeling about the Mill House today. It was far better to be out here than in there.

But now, her contrary body really was exhausted and she did desperately want to get back to the Mill House to sleep for a little while. Carrying a baby could be a terrible, tiring thing she reflected, and she longed for the time when she would feel more like herself.

But how could one feel lost or lonely or grumpy when Lady Elsie Pencradoc was in the vicinity? She smiled at the little girl encouragingly, but Elsie's face became quite concerned.

Then the little girl sighed. 'Perhaps "pageant" may be too grand a word for it. But I do think it is more than just a show, isn't it? More than just a piece of stagecraft.'

'Stagecraft? My goodness, you *have* been studying the business well.'

'I have.' The little girl nodded seriously. 'As you would have seen in my scrapbook.'

'Oh yes. It's a beautiful scrapbook. You have pictures of some very famous people in there.' They had gone through the book together several times by now.

'Yes. Marie Studholme. Mrs Patrick Campbell. Ellen Terry. Sarah Bernhardt. Lillie Langtry.' The little girl's eyes sparked with interest. 'Lille Langtry had a baby as well and it was terribly scandalous. Do you know she had her photograph taken while she was expecting it? Some people think that was very wrong but I don't.' Elsie's gaze scanned her thoughtfully, and Lily flushed. She just knew the girl was imagining a similar sort of photograph of her, probably taken by Elsie herself on Edwin's camera and pasted into the scrapbook in pride of place. Suddenly she wanted to burst out laughing, and then bit her lip. Scandalous. Quite. But Elsie was so damn serious, and yet so damn delightful at the same time, how could one fail to be cheered by her presence? She was a wonderful child. 'Miss Langtry's baby's Papa may be royalty. Do you actually *know* Miss Langtry?' Elsie planted herself firmly in front of Lily, gazing up at her, hopeful, clearly, for some gossip about that good actress.

'No! No I don't know Miss Langtry. Although I'm sure she is a lovely lady.'

'And very beautiful. But not quite as beautiful as you, if you don't mind me saying.'

'Well now. Thank you.'

'It is most clever how you are both called Lily and how you are both actresses. But I do think "Valentine" is a much prettier name.'

'Thank you again. I quite like it.' Lily had, to be fair, always admired Lillie Langtry. Even before she went on the stage herself.

'Oh! *This* is what I meant to be finding you for.' Elsie looked at the envelope in her hand in some surprise, as if she had forgotten she was holding it. Her mind had, clearly, been on the stage somewhere, probably as she held court amidst a flurry of famous actresses. 'It's a programme for the Pageant, which I designed especially. And some photographs. The ones I took of you and some of all of us from the day we were rehearsing. Mr Griffiths said I can experiment a little more with the camera if I need to. I think it would be most marvellous to. But for now, you can have these. Uncle Jago brought them back from the town today.'

'Uncle Jago? Are they back, then?'

'Uncle Jago was. But I haven't seen Mr Griffiths.' Elsie frowned. 'If I see him, I will tell him you are looking for him.'

'Oh. No need. Really.'

'No, I will tell him. I really will. Anyway, I must go back. My art tutor is coming soon, and although I do not think I really *need* him, it is good to have him.' The little girl smiled and bobbed a curtsey, then hurried back the way she had come, leaving Lily standing in the rose garden, clutching an envelope, and wondering whether she should hurry back to the Mill House just in case Edwin went straight there, or continue her walk.

She hurried back to the Mill House.

'Edwin?'

Lily's voice came through the hall as he moved around the sunlit, airy lounge, rearranging small items, moving a letter-opener from one side of the desk to another, pulling some books off the shelves and stacking them on the side-table, twitching at the curtains so they were more closed than open, collecting small handfuls of loose change …

She was home.

Why the hell had she not stayed out longer, playing at being a Lady and being friends with a damn Duke and Duchess? Who did she think she was?

'Edwin?' Her voice was coming closer. 'I've just seen Elsie. She gave me something. I've had a little look – some photographs and a programme for the play! Just imagine that!'

The door opened and he ducked behind the curtains, his heart pounding, inches away from her as her footsteps came closer and her scent drifted towards him like the dust motes he'd disturbed, dancing in the sunbeams.

He could reach out. Just grab her as she came past. Put his hands around her neck and—

But what use would that be? He needed her alive. He needed the money she could give him. The coins in his palm felt cold and heavy. It was enough for now, but it wouldn't last.

'Edwin? I thought you were in here? I thought I heard you.' There was a soft noise as she apparently tossed something onto the desk and he pressed himself further against the window, feeling behind him for the latch. He took hold of it, turned it gently, ready to push the window open and escape, when there was another noise. The front door opening again.

It had to be him – that idiot she'd married. No, not married. Ensnared. His lips twisted in a smile and he momentarily loosened his hold on the latch.

'Lily?' His voice, the idiot's voice, carried through the house. 'I saw you heading over here. Sorry – I came back from the carriage house and couldn't reach you in time.'

'Edwin? I thought you were in the lounge!' A rustle of skirts as she hurried off in the other direction, towards the door. 'Come here – come and see what Elsie gave me!'

They were both heading this way now. He swore again, his palms feeling sweaty and his heart pounding fit to burst.

'Look – isn't it sweet? I think Elsie painted it herself.'

Peering out from a gap in the curtain, he saw Lily bending over the desk, taking some papers out of an envelope. He saw a painted picture of the woman, on a piece of paper otherwise filled with words. He saw several black and white prints – photographs of rich little brats, too full of themselves for words, and pictures of her: Lily Valentine. Ha! Lily Valentine.

'I knew those photographs would capture everything she wanted them to. She did well.'

'I still can't believe you let her use your camera.' Lily laughed. 'But I suppose you had no other option.'

'Not really.'

They talked a little longer about inane things that held no interest for Francis, until they eventually, thank God, left the room, but not before slipping the envelope into the desk drawer 'for safe-keeping,' she'd said, with a stupid little laugh that made him want to punch her.

He clenched his fists and closed his eyes. He couldn't. He had to control himself. This was not the time or place.

He waited for a few moments, just to be sure they'd gone and stepped out from behind the curtains. He toyed with the idea that he could empty the drawers completely, overturn the desk, cause more chaos …

But then he thought he needed to be subtle. Gentle. So nobody suspected him.

He opened the drawer and took the envelope, then he closed the drawer carefully and slipped back behind the curtain.

Lifting the latch again, he climbed out. Then he hurried through the tiered garden, winding his way down to the riverbank, and removed the planks of wood that led into the cellar of the Mill House.

He slipped his most precious document, the one he had brought with him from Ireland, into the envelope, and tucked it up behind the mechanism for the water-wheel.

Then he picked up his tool bag, put the coins in his money pouch and stepped back outside.

It was time to go to work on Pencradoc estate. And nobody had any idea at all that he had found his own lodgings, right in the cellar of the Mill House.

There were worse places to live, for sure. And places that weren't quite so close to Lily Valentine.

Which were absolutely no good to him at all.

Present Day

Cordy locked up the tea-room, exhausted from being on her feet all day. It was tiring in a different way from being on the stage – plus she had to try and remember things that she hadn't done for a while.

But she had plenty of time to get into the swing of things so she wasn't going to worry. And now she had the key for the office as well ... her stomach gave a little flip of excitement at the thought. Evelyn Sullivan couldn't hide away forever – and Cordy wanted to know if Evelyn was in any way related to the strange dreams she'd had. It all seemed as if it was joined together somehow. Unless, of course, she just had a gigantic imagination and Lily Valentine's story was consuming her.

What she *really* wanted to know, of course, was why there were photos of Lily and a programme for the Pageant and that marriage certificate.

Perhaps they had all been gathered together as a drawer was cleared out, or a guest had left the paperwork behind and it had been forgotten about, bundled up and never sent on to the owner. It was a mystery, but hopefully the computer in the office would help out.

She headed up to her room to drop off the dress, and came back down to where Coren had directed her. The office was just along the corridor, and as she put the key in the lock she felt a little thrill of anticipation. It was only a few minutes before she had found the computer and switched it on. There was a note in Coren's handwriting next to it with a password on and instructions as to where the tea and coffee could be found, and she typed the password in, happy to see the home screen flash up. A moment later and she was connected to the internet, and the connection was far better than the one she had on her phone; not to mention the screen was a lot bigger.

'Evelyn Sullivan and Francis O'Hara – you can't hide forever. Here we go.'

Cordy worked for a good hour or so, and it was, she reflected later, the most frustrating hour she'd experienced in quite some time.

Sure enough, she had found Evelyn and Francis – married, just as the document said, at a church in County Meath, in November 1887. However, there was nothing else about them at all – nothing in any of the census records she could find. She could find several Francis O'Haras in Ireland, which wasn't surprising, but none of them were married to a lady called Evelyn. Most of the men were farmers or labourers, which was also to be expected as it wasn't really an industrial area where she was focusing. There were also some Evelyn O'Haras, but as none of the ages matched what she might have expected, and none of them had a Francis in their family, it was very, very annoying.

A thought suddenly struck her which made her frown. Perhaps Evelyn had died before the census records were taken? 'Oh Evelyn! Is that why I can't find you?' Cordy got up, found the kettle and made herself a cup of tea while she considered it. Death records. That was the next thing.

She sat back down and scoured the church records, the death records; she even tried to find divorce records which she acknowledged was probably outrageous for the time she was researching. People just stuck with one another, even if they didn't particularly like one another after a while. Unless they separated and lived different lives.

'Ooh!' Her butterfly mind bounded off on another track, and she scrolled through the pages to the emigration records. It wouldn't be unheard of for people to catch a boat and travel abroad—

Her heart began to pound again as she remembered that

dream. The one where she'd been bouncing around on the sea, making a new life for herself. Then she battered the thought down again because it made her uncomfortable, thinking about the image of the lady in the green dress and the voice in her ear.

Green dress. Again, another image that needed battering down, because hadn't Sybill fetched her that green frock for the play ...?

'God, focus, Cordy!' she muttered, concentrating furiously on the screen in front of her. 'Passenger records – from Dublin to Liverpool. Or would she have gone to America?'

But once again, the passenger records came up with nothing. To be fair, there was an enormous number of them. And if someone really wanted to disappear, they could probably do so in those days. Cordy had a feeling that the record-keeping maybe wasn't as stringent as it could have been. If it had been her, for example, she probably would have chosen Liverpool over the USA. It was a relatively quick crossing. It wouldn't even have had to be a passenger boat – it could have been a fishing boat or something else travelling that way. It would have been cheaper. Then, once she was in England, she could have gone to London, and on to the Continent. There were many more places to disappear to, much more quickly, by doing that route.

However, on the flip side, it would make it easier for someone to follow her. But the Continent was a big place, and there were a lot of places to go ...

She was even more confused, and she acknowledged she wasn't getting anywhere fast. No matter if she looked east or west.

'Fine. Evelyn, I'm giving up on you for a bit,' she told the empty room. 'Lily Valentine. I'm going to look for you. At least I know there'll be pretty pictures of you at any rate.'

She pulled up the Google search and typed her name: *Lily Valentine*.

The first item was her Wikipedia entry – Cordy scanned it, reading nothing there that she didn't already know. She had appeared on the London stage in her first role as a chorus girl and worked her way up the ranks, taking lead parts by the middle of 1891. She had proven herself to be quick at learning lines, a naturally talented dancer and a gifted singer. Cordy skimmed past the notes on how she'd worked as a Tiller Girl, been in the Folies Bergère and eventually ended up as a singer in the Paris Opera. She knew all that. *Everybody* knew that. It was the real Lily she was interested in, but there wasn't a great deal about her early life at all.

The writer of the entry suggested she had come from a village somewhere near Stoke-on-Trent, an orphan with no family to speak of who had travelled to London to make it big as soon as she could. Her life on the stage was obviously well-documented, but she had, as they said, simply faded into the background after a glittering career. She had packed up one evening after a performance of *The Black Rose*, left Paris and eloped with Edwin Griffiths, an ex-military man who had haunted the audience of her show for a very long time.

It was quite a romantic notion – it was, after all, Edwin who she visited Pencradoc with. It seemed as if this was her last hurrah, the last time she made the headlines. But even Pencradoc got a mention in the Wikipedia entry, and Cordy clicked on the link, just to make sure it took the reader to the right page. It did.

Satisfied, she back-paged a couple of times, went onto the 'Images' tab and clicked on that.

Lily's pictures flooded the screen: Lily dressed as a showgirl, a gypsy and numerous other things. Cordy was astonished again to see how breathtakingly beautiful the woman was. She was the epitome of that Gibson Girl. One outfit looked particularly fun – she was dressed as a female pirate, hanging upside down from a makeshift rigging, complete with a knife between her teeth, her bare feet cleverly wrapped in the ropes as she patted a dashing pirate captain on the head, his arms folded, his feet wide apart. Despite the fact he was partially hidden in the shadows, Cordy could just make out that he wore his eye-patch at a jaunty angle as he looked at the actress wryly. She must have been quite the acrobat in her day – all that dancing training must have helped.

There was one picture, slightly more risqué than the rest, where she was semi-clad and, although the photograph was tasteful in comparison with, for example, Cordy's wardrobe malfunction, Lily looked quite young on it. Cordy enlarged the photo and zoomed in on Lily's face.

She was definitely young – probably not much more than a teenager. Despite the clever lighting, her face still had a little roundness to it and her hair was long, threaded with flowers as she gazed into the distance, dressed in no more than what looked a rumpled bed-sheet. For reasons she couldn't describe, the photo unsettled Cordy. There was something in Lily's eyes that spoke volumes – a hardness perhaps, or a conscious removal of herself from the situation; whatever it was, Cordy guessed the reason was because Lily didn't really want to be there, in that particular pose, but she knew she had to do it.

'Good old casting couch, eh Lily?' Cordy shook her head. Thank God that had never happened to her.

Then, as Cordy's finger hovered over the mouse, the screen flickered once, twice, then died.

'Ahhhh bugger!' she cried, clicking around desperately, trying every key combination she could think of. Finally, she switched the computer off and scowled at it for a few seconds before trying it again.

The machine hummed back into life, but refused to let her back on the internet. Cordy swore again and sat back in her chair. That was her stuck then – she couldn't look at Lily or Evelyn. It was typical that—

Then not only did the computer flicker again, but all the lights in the room flashed on and off, and a breeze whipped up out of nowhere. The window at the back of the office flew open, rattling the blinds in a frenzy; what *was* it with this place and their dodgy window locks? Then, for unknown reasons, Cordy scraped the chair back, and decided that she wasn't going to hang around any longer.

No – that was a lie. She hung on long enough to rush over and shut the window, then turn around, grabbing her notebook on the way out, but her way was suddenly blocked by a green column of light that flew at her, something that looked like a full skirt billowing out behind it.

Cordy screamed, put her head down and pelted out of the office as if all the demons of hell were after her. She slammed the door shut behind her, thankful that it was self-locking, and ran straight out into the gardens. It wasn't quite seven, but she didn't give a damn. She had to get out of that building and prayed to whoever was listening that Matt might be in the tranquility of Rose's Garden waiting for her.

Matt was enjoying the peace and quiet of after-hours Pencradoc, having listened to the upbeat chatter of the WI ladies for most of the day. He was lounging on the big, flat rock, overlooking the waterfall, just on the edge of the rose garden. He'd rolled his sweatshirt up into a makeshift pillow and was leaning on that, sketching the figure of a woman on a stage.

He knew it was supposed to be Lily Valentine, and if anyone asked that was who he'd say it was. But he knew in his head that it was really Cordy. He'd sketched the tilt of her head just so; that little quirky, quizzical look she gave him when she wasn't sure what he was rambling on about was lightly drawn on her oval face, her hair piled up into some complicated style, her figure draped in that Arts and Crafts style dress he'd seen—

'—Matt! Matt; is that you? Thank *God*! It *is* you. This *place*!'

The subject of his sketch was speeding through the garden

towards him, her hair wild and flying out behind her, her arms sort of flailing as she tried to keep her balance whilst pelting around the winding paths.

He quickly closed the book and stood up, putting his arms out automatically to catch her. 'Hey, what's the hurry? It's only quarter-to. I wouldn't count the minutes until five-past at least.'

'The hurry is I had to get out that house.' She pointed behind her, so he had absolutely no doubt about the fact that she was talking about Pencradoc. 'I was in the office trying to find Evelyn and Francis – a complete waste of time as I couldn't find a *thing* about them after the wedding – and I started looking at Lily Valentine because, you know, at least there's some stuff about her online. I was looking at her photos, and then the computer just went off. Twice. And then *she* came back – that woman – that one that's been bothering me.'

'Which woman?' Matt was confused. He didn't think Betty and her cronies had been that much of a problem, and Steph probably hadn't seen her since this morning – and Merryn or Sybill wouldn't cause an issue—

'The ghost woman. The one in green. Who was in my *bedroom.*'

'The one in green.' He felt his insides tense up. 'The ghost?'

'Like I said. I really don't know who she is – is it Lily? Is it Evelyn? Is it someone completely random?'

'I have no idea.' Matt was at a loss. 'Are you absolutely sure you saw something?'

'As sure as I am you're standing there.' She pulled away from him. 'Can we go out somewhere? To the pub, or something? I mean, I'm not really dressed up but The White Lady looks like it wouldn't mind.'

'Ah – the pub with the picture Kit hates hanging up. That White Lady.'

'What? Why does he hate it?'

'He says the girl on the pub sign looks nothing like Duchess

Rose did – and the pub was named after her. I suggested that unless someone came and copied the portrait of her from Pencradoc, he just had to stop stressing over it. He's got a total downer on that poor pub sign.'

All the time he was talking to her, he was guiding her out of the garden, distracting her with silly bits of useless information, just so she would get away from the area and, hopefully, think about something else. This green lady thing was getting out of hand – whoever she was, she certainly had some time invested in leaping out at Cordy.

Maybe it was Lily. Maybe the original pageant had been such a great memory, that she was determined to keep an eye out on what Cordy was doing – to make sure she stayed true to the tale?

He ran the idea past Cordy, who paused and looked up at him curiously. 'Maybe, you know, you could actually be right.' She turned back to face the house – which was exactly not the reaction Matt had hoped for. 'Perhaps she's overly-protective of it and she's frightened I'll spoil it. Maybe I shouldn't do it after all.'

Cordy looked downcast and shoved her hands in her pocket. Again, so not the reaction Matt had wanted. He had hoped, he admitted to himself, that she would have held his hand, or allowed some sort of physical contact on their way to their destination …

She's not one to give her heart easily. Give her time.

It was Matt's turn to stop in his tracks and look around. Who had said that? It had been a man's voice – was it his own subconscious? Because who said he even *wanted* Cordy's heart? Was a summer fling, a bit of a friendship they could build on, not enough?

No. For now, it might be but, even after just knowing her for a few days, he wanted to get to know her better, spend more time with her; learn what made her tick, made her laugh, made her chatter excitedly …

And even as he acknowledged that to himself, he heard himself reassuring Cordy. 'I doubt Lily Valentine has anything to worry about. You'll do a brilliant adaptation; I just know it.' Heaven forfend that she thought he had any interest of that sort in her – especially not after the Toby fiasco today. God, who would want to bounce into a relationship – any sort of relationship, serious or otherwise – after they'd just broken up with Toby Fowler? There was a quick, meaningless rebound and then there was … him.

He didn't want to be her rebound – if something were to happen with them, he'd want her to really want that. Not just fall into it through circumstances.

No. Perhaps for now, friendship was all he could hope for.

And as if he could ever expect her to 'give her heart' to him? As if! Whoever had said that really needed a reality check, or they were a person of very old-fashioned romantic notions.

Chapter Twelve

1895

Lily obviously knew that she was to learn one of Titania's speeches from *A Midsummer Night's Dream*, and that the girls were determined to stand about her in a *tableau*. Indeed, she had already been working on the speech; she had learned those lines for a play eighteen months ago, before Rosalee and *The Black Rose* began to consume her. It had been a short run, and she had tried to use the play to gain her more credibility, but certain audience members had still whooped and shouted and asked her to sing and dance for them, even at the most beautiful parts of the play.

But one day as she left Pencradoc, having had tea with Alys, little Lucy had come up to her. She'd approached quite shyly for a Pencradoc girl, and presented her with an almost pristine volume of the play from the library, which was quite dented on one corner.

'It's a very old book,' Lucy had told her. 'I had to climb upon a ladder to find it, and it was quite heavy, but I only dropped it once.'

'I see. Thank you. I shall take it back to the Mill House and I can study it quite well in the sunroom, I think.' She didn't have the heart to tell Lucy she knew the speech around the table and back again and she certainly wasn't going to send the girl packing. It was such a lovely, helpful gesture and the pride in herself that the little girl was emitting was wonderful to see.

'Elsie asked me to do it a little while ago, but I forgot. I hope it's not too late.'

'Not too late at all, Lucy.'

So little Lucy bobbed a curtsey and skipped off, whilst Lily took the book and headed home.

Home.

When had she begun to think of the Mill House as home? It was an interesting concept, but she did feel quite settled there. Whether it was because she and Edwin were settling into a routine of sorts, and the Cornish air and mystical atmosphere of Pencradoc was beginning to heal them both, or whether it was simply the fact that Edwin was ... there. Perhaps 'home' would be anywhere he was?

She pondered the thought as she unlocked the door to the Mill House. A few things had gone missing, recently – just oddments like a few coins, a china cup from the kitchen, some food from the pantry. She hadn't said anything to Jago and Alys because she had a feeling it was a village child, or even one of the workers she saw about the estate. She knew what it was like to struggle, and hadn't begrudged the food or even the coins. But one day she had gone to her room and her perfume bottle was missing.

That had made her feel uncomfortable – the fact that someone had been in there and possibly been through her possessions, even if it was a case of a child stealing the perfume as a gift for their mother.

'We have to lock the door when we leave the place empty,' Edwin said when she told him. 'I know you don't want to, but what if they hurt themselves when they're in here? What if they come in when we are asleep?'

So she had taken to locking the door behind her, just in case.

She put the book on the table in the sunroom and opened the curtains wider. It was a beautiful day, and the water-wheel was thrumming comfortably beyond the window. She was looking forward to Edwin coming back. He'd taken himself off to the Wilderness Garden with his camera after she had left him at the door of Pencradoc, and they had agreed to meet for a picnic. It was something to look forward to.

Lily intended to head upstairs to her room to change into something a little less formal, when she heard it.

The noise was unmistakable.

A bang, like a gunshot, right at her front door.

She screamed as she heard the door fly open and clash back against the frame.

'I found you. You can never stay lost for long, can you—?'

The voice made her scream even louder which was entirely the wrong thing to do, because now he knew exactly where she was.

Present Day

The pub was nice – not too busy, but still had a bit of a buzz to it. The villagers were enjoying a pint or a glass of wine in the sun-warmed beer garden before heading back to work the next day, or treating themselves to a meal out. It was too nice a day to cook, or at least that was what Cordy told Matt as she scanned the menu.

'You wouldn't be cooking anyway. Where could we cook in the attics?' he asked.

'Microwave. There's a miniature Marks and Spencer down the road. And a tiny Tesco.' She shrugged. 'But chicken-ding isn't on my radar tonight. I need something substantial after that situation in the office.' She shuddered, still feeling a little shaken but certainly not as bad as she had done. There was, as they kept saying, nothing logical about Pencradoc, but once Matt had suggested the ghost, or whatever she was, was simply worried about the show Cordy was planning, she felt guilty more than anything.

She resolved to tell the ghost not to be worried – but she'd pluck up the courage to do that another time. She had been just about to go back into the office and face her fears when Matt mentioned it, but sense had prevailed. 'One did not court trouble,' as they said. And spending time with Matt was certainly more appealing. She wanted some real company – company she could actually have a conversation with, have a laugh with, enjoy spending time with. With Matt she could do all those things and more. He was also pretty easy on the eye, and despite being certain she didn't want to fall into another relationship so soon after Toby, Matt was certainly ticking all the boxes so far. He could, she admitted to herself, be the one to persuade her otherwise …

She shook her head in an attempt to dismiss the silly thoughts and continued to look at the menu. She was torn between a jacket potato and an omelette.

' "Chicken-ding"?' Matt asked suddenly. 'I don't even know if I want to know the answer to that.'

'What? It's just another name for a microwave meal!' Cordy laughed at the expression on his face. 'The meals often have chicken in them, and the microwave goes *ding* when it's done. Simple.'

'Of course.' He bent his head to the menu, but she saw the quick smile on his face, and it made her smile too. He looked particularly nice this evening – slightly sun-burned from being out in the gardens with the WI ladies most of the day, his light brown hair looking a bit lighter where the sun had caught that too, and his dark brown eyes amused at the idea of her microwave dinners.

'I don't have them all the time you know. Chicken-dings.' She thought, somehow, it was important to clarify the situation. 'I do eat properly and cook and things, but sometimes when it's been a late night at work or a busy day, they're a godsend.'

'Oh no, I agree.' Matt raised his eyes and nodded seriously. 'I'm the same. Sometimes it's a chore cooking for one.' He wrinkled his nose.

'So you live alone then?' Cordy was curious. She'd never thought to ask.

There was the flicker of a smile again. 'I do. I lived with a girl called Layla until a few months ago. It didn't work out. She preferred my friend. Sorry state of affairs when we all worked together.' He scowled fleetingly and studied the menu again – she could tell he wasn't really seeing it though.

'Bad luck. I'm guessing you all don't still work together?'

'God no.' This time he laughed. 'I stuck it out, mind – they were the ones that left. Worst school-term of my professional life, though. I'm glad it's over.' He shuddered, as if remembering. 'They both got jobs elsewhere around about Easter time, thank God. I can be a bit of a pain when I'm rankled and I didn't make it easy for them, but I was determined to stick it out. I'm glad I did. I love the school and didn't see why I should leave when I'd done nothing wrong. I don't run away from things.'

'Sounds like they *should* have left. Poor you.'

'These things happen.' He shrugged. 'Life goes on. Have you decided yet?'

'What? Oh! My dinner. Yes. Mushroom omelette and salad, I think.' She closed the menu decisively.

'I'm going for pork and apple casserole with cider. Wine?' He stood up to go to the bar and order.

'White, please. Large.'

He laughed. 'Don't blame you.'

'Me neither, actually.'

Matt smiled and went to organise the food, and Cordy picked up her notebook. She opened it up and read the notes she'd made.

Then she turned to a blank page and started jotting down some more ideas on how she could really make the Lily Pageant shine. Mentally, she had made a commitment to Lily, or whoever that spirit was, and here in the pub, away from Pencradoc, she wanted to carry that commitment through.

'*A Midsummer Night's Dream*,' she muttered, writing the title down. Wasn't there a really good line in there – one of the fairies left the stage uttering it. It might be a good way for her to end the piece, and exit the stage. 'I go, I go ... faster than – what? What am I faster than?' Okay, so this wasn't as easy as she'd thought. She pulled her phone out and Googled it. 'Ahhh. "I go, I go. Look how I go, Swifter than arrow from the Tartar's bow".' She scribbled it down. 'Puck,' she said decisively.

'Excuse me?'

Cordy looked up and grinned at Matt. He was pretending to look shocked and clutching their glasses. 'Puck. As in the fairy. From the play.' She indicated that he sit down again, and, when he placed her glass in front of her, she took a long, satisfying glug of it, and set it back down. Then she pushed the notebook towards him. 'I thought I'd use that speech to end the Lily show. I Googled it to check.' She raised her phone in a salute. 'I would have considered using the computer at Pencradoc … but ugh. That … experience … put me off a bit.'

'I can imagine. You know, you could always use my laptop if you like. Or my iPad. I brought them both with me. I quite like using the iPad for creative stuff, and I've got some sessions in where I'll need to use it. I brought the laptop because – well – I'm always needing to plan lessons.'

'But school doesn't start for weeks!'

Matt gave her an amused look. 'Teachers never really shut down you know? Even over the holidays. Or maybe that's just me.'

'No, I think it's a fair thing to say. I'll not bother you with this then, will I?' She made to pull her notebook back, but he laid his hand on hers, stopping her from moving it, and sending one of those mad little *zing*s up her arm again. She looked up at him in surprise.

'No, that's fine. I want to help. I'd love to be involved – like I say, I've directed that play at school and know a bit about the stage. At the very least I can help with the props and the backdrop. I'm pretty sure Kit will be able to tell me where he's hiding some paint pots. I was thinking about a backdrop to look like an old-fashioned stage for the play, then if you're going to start with "Daisy Bell", we could cover it with a quirky Paris street scene, or a nice garden. It's up to you.'

'Wow. Well – I think either of those would work. We should see if there are any clues in the photos they have of Lily's visit. Maybe that one of the girls in front of the stage might help?'

'Good idea. We'll have a look tomorrow maybe. If you've got time?' He smiled at her. Then, as if realising his hand was still on top of hers, he suddenly moved it. Her hand felt cold now, which was rather sad – and also odd as it was the height of summer, and they'd been lucky with the weather.

Surreptitiously, she moved her hand under the table and rubbed some warmth back into it. 'And thank you. Yes, I think your iPad or your laptop would be great. I just pray I don't need to tell Merryn I blew up her computer … or how.' She felt herself flush. It wouldn't be an easy thing to explain. She hoped – she really hoped – that the machine would come back on when Merryn tried to use it.

'So you didn't get very far with your research? That's a shame, really it is.'

That little moment of intimacy was gone for now, it seemed. Matt had moved the subject onto more general things. He took a drink of his real ale, but his eyes were hypnotic and didn't leave her face. Cordy blinked. So the intimacy was still there then; just well-hidden for now. The thought made her blush again.

She cleared her throat and replied. 'Yes. Like I say, there's not much about Evelyn and Francis. The wedding was the only record I could find of them together.'

'No death records or anything?'

'No. They were last together in 1887.'

'1891 census?' Matt pulled a face. 'But you've probably tried that.'

'I found a few Francis O'Haras, but no Evelyns that looked likely.'

'I guess a lot of the population may have been itinerant

workers – especially if they worked on the land. They'd have gone where the work was.'

'Yes. So boarding houses or something might be likely?'

'Maybe.' Matt shrugged. 'Somewhere even like Pencradoc. It's a big house, on a big estate. I'm sure there were people who would have passed through here working.'

'Oh! Yes – Merryn said a labourer was killed here in about 1895—' She stopped and stared at Matt. '1895. That would fit, wouldn't it? With Francis? Hey – maybe he was the labourer? Wow.' She turned to the back page of her book and jotted it down. 'Thank you. You may have just sent me in a different direction. I wonder if they've got any records at the house for workers in those days? Surely they will have needed papers?'

'Cash in hand? Would they?' Mat shrugged. 'I'm not sure. But it might explain why the marriage certificate was here.' He raised his eyebrows. 'If that was him, though, Evelyn might have come with him.'

'But where did she go after that? Her husband dead, maybe a child or two … oh, it's a bit horrid to think about.' It was Cordy's turn to pull a face. 'So I'm not going to. It's for another day. I want my dinner and more wine.' She grinned. 'Let me know when you want another – my round.'

Matt laughed and raised his glass. 'Definitely. But I'm not getting in the state I was in last time you led me astray. I've got a workshop tomorrow afternoon. I have planning to do.'

'I don't particularly want to get in a state either.' She smiled, but inside she was thinking this: *if I get drunk tonight, my defences will definitely come down and I shall kiss you, and I don't think that's a good idea, because I don't think I'd want to stop with a kiss …*

And when she smiled again at Matt, and he smiled back, the look in his eye told her that he was probably thinking the same thing. Which really wasn't a great plan, right now.

She hadn't come to Pencradoc to fall for anyone.

But my goodness, it was proving hard not to sink …

Chapter Thirteen

Present Day

Cordy fell into a nice routine of helping out in the tea-room, working on her play, catching up with Merryn, doing bits and bobs for her and relaxing when she had the chance. She also fell into a nice routine of somehow being around the areas where Matt was, at just about the same time he was running a course or an open-air session.

He'd also seemingly found a nice routine of popping up at the tea-room when she was there, and most nights they met after work for coffee, or went for a drink in the village and something to eat.

One afternoon, when Cordy was inwardly congratulating herself for making a perfect flat white, complete with posh milky pattern on the top, a pretty dark-haired woman appeared: Sorcha, the lady who ran the place.

'Cordy! Thanks so much for holding the fort.' She smiled at Cordy. 'I felt a lot better knowing you were coming down to help.'

'Ah, don't worry. It's given me something to do.' Cordy smiled back. 'I've had fun. Here – have a flat white. Good pattern eh?' she pushed it across to Sorcha. 'It's good to see you. You look really well!'

'Thanks, honey. That *is* quite splendid. And thanks again for helping me. It's probably nice to have some downtime from your acting, I'd imagine, although I know working in a tea-room isn't the fluffy sort of job people think it is.'

'It's not. But like I say, it's been fun.' Cordy didn't want to go into exactly how much downtime she'd already had from acting over the last few months. It seemed to be harder and harder to secure a job and when she did, they didn't last very long. A chorus line here, an ensemble part there.

Nothing else decent had been forthcoming from her agent, Marion, for quite some time when she thought about it. And here, it seemed a world away from that life – and she hadn't felt quite so relaxed for some time, even though Pencradoc had its moments; it certainly wasn't the quiet, calm stately home everyone seemed to think. She supposed, knowing the character traits of creative people like herself, and being a home to artists like Teague, and even little Elsie, emotions would have run extremely high and desperately low at times in this beautiful place – even before Teague and Elsie arrived at Pencradoc, given Merryn's tales of the previous Dukes and Duchesses.

'Yes, the Tower Tea-Room has made a nice change, when I think about it,' she fudged to Sorcha and pasted on a bright smile. 'But what are you doing here? Aren't you supposed to be recuperating?'

'I'm almost finished with that rubbish.' Sorcha pulled a face. 'I'm not one to sit around – so as it's my business and I employ me, I'm allowing myself a staggered return.'

'Okay – well make sure you're up to it first. No point you rushing into it.'

'It's fine. I'm too bored otherwise. I thought I'd do a couple of hours this afternoon and see how I go. Is that all right with you? It'll give you a break anyway, if there's anything else you want to do. It's a shame you've come all this way on holiday and you're forced to work.'

'Nothing forced about it. My flat flooded, so I needed to get away anyway. I'll come back tomorrow morning though – you don't put yourself out, all right? No point in setting yourself back.' Part of Cordy was worried, she knew, that once Sorcha was back full-time and the Pageant was over, she had no genuine reason to stay in Cornwall. Matt's face flitted into her mind, and she batted it away. No. He wasn't a reason to uproot herself and come here permanently.

Not yet, at any rate.

Her face flooded with heat as she acknowledged that thought, then deliberately let it go.

'Two hours. That's all. I promise. Look, it's two o'clock now. I'll stay until four when we close and text you if I need any help this afternoon. Deal?' Sorcha grinned and held her hand out.

Reluctantly, Cordy shook it. 'Okay. Here's my number. Use it.'

'I will. If I need to.'

And then, within seconds, they'd swapped places and Sorcha was tying her apron around herself and checking over the work area, and Cordy was standing like a spare part on the outside of the counter.

Damn.

Well, she knew it was never going to last, she thought as she wandered out of the Tower Tea-Room like a lost soul.

But at least she now had the excuse of spending some extra time working on her performance, and hopefully doing a little bit more research. Her excuse to herself was that she wanted to find out as much as she could about Lily, but the reality was she *needed* to know about her. She needed to know what it was that linked her and the O'Haras. Because Lily had just appeared out of nowhere, blazed like wildfire then practically disappeared …

Around about the time Evelyn and Francis had disappeared—

'—Oh my.' Cordy blinked. Perhaps there were closer links to the pair of them than she'd thought. What if, for instance, Lily had eloped with Francis – *after* she'd picked up with Edwin – and the certificate was something she had found which had caused a huge argument? Perhaps Francis was still with Evelyn, and they couldn't get married after all?

He was always a charmer. Don't be fooled.

The voice that whispered in her ear was bitter and angry. Cordy jumped and flushed again, looking around for someone who had spoken. There was nobody near her.

Matt. Matt would be a good person to talk to right now, but of course he had a class this afternoon, didn't he? Damn. If only he was here.

Dare she go back to that little office and look at the computer there? She sat down in the stumpery near Rose's Garden, unsure what to do.

'Well hello. Fancy meeting you like this.'

Cordy spun around and there was Matt, standing with an iPad in his hand. *Thank you God!* She grinned at Matt, quite stupidly probably, and he held the iPad out to her, shrugging his shoulders. 'Tea break in the workshop. I saw you leaving the Tower and you looked a bit lost. So I thought this might help. Sorry, I've had to use it or you could have had it before now.'

'Oh, that's fine! I appreciate you have to work. Thank you! I love how regular your tea breaks are, Matthew Harker. And I was just thinking how good it would be to see a friendly face. Anyway. Sorcha's back.'

'Yes, I saw her go in, and she looked familiar – then I realised when you popped out and looked confused. It wasn't hard to spot you in from workshop rooms – so hey, I saw you and you weren't difficult to locate after that either. You looked as if you might *appreciate* a friendly face.'

'I absolutely do. Did you run? You look hot and bothered.' She smiled up at him and he flushed. He did indeed look hot and bothered.

'Maybe just a little.' He ran his hand through his hair and laughed. 'I'd say it was good to get some fresh air, but it's actually cooler in the house at the minute. I'd best go back before I'm missed. Some of them chose to stay there and help themselves to the stuff in the flasks. By now, they might have rampaged and mixed up all my paint tubes.'

'Hmmm. Squeezed the watercolours out to make a big blobby colourful mess.'

'And called it modern art. Jackson Pollock, eat your heart

out. Look – I would have given you the laptop, but the iPad was closest to hand. Hope that's okay?'

'It's perfect.' She pressed the button and glanced at the screen. 'Oh! Who's that?' She peered closer at the digital image he was halfway through creating. It was a picture of a woman in an old-fashioned green dress, striking a pose in the very garden she was in. Her face was clear, but her dress faded into the gardens and foliage around her, so she was almost one with the scenery, but she stood out as her own person regardless.

'Oh! Shit. Sorry, you weren't meant to see that. It's not really you. It's Lily Valentine – or the way I imagine her, anyway, floating around the grounds. Unfortunately, I didn't have much a reference point for her face, so I kind of borrowed yours. I'll change it once I have time to study her photos. I was just messing around as it's an advanced portraiture and figure drawing class – showing them how to create movement and impact with a painting of a person. It was easier to carry this around to the easels to show people. And using the Lily connection was ideal, with the exhibition being on. Makes people's imagination take flight …' His excuses petered out and he pushed his hair back again, then shrugged before putting his hands in his pockets.

Cordy smiled. She wasn't the only one fudging responses today. 'I see. Well, thank you. Do you want to save this properly so I don't lose it? I'm rubbish with tech, as you know –well, I was rubbish with my experience of Merryn's computer and it's scared me off a bit.' She handed the device back to Matt, whose cheeks were now flaming and he dipped his head, concentrating on closing the app down and getting the internet browser up for her.

'You're not rubbish. There you go. It's got plenty of data on it, so you'll be able to browse out here. No need to be stuck indoors out of the sunshine. Like me.' He paused for a moment, then gestured to the machine. 'I'll see you later to get it back. Or not. You can keep it. But maybe you'll want to chat about whatever you find …' Again his voice tailed off. 'Or not. It's up to you.'

'Matt Harker.' Cordy's voice was soft. She stood up and reached up, kissing him gently. 'I *will* see you later. I don't need an excuse. I'm just going to come and find you.'

Matt suddenly smiled. There was a brief pause, then he too leaned down and kissed her. It took her by surprise a little, as he put his hands on her shoulders and brought her closer in the gentlest movement she could ever imagine.

'Bye Cordy. See you later.' Then he stepped away from her and began to run back towards the house and his workshop. Tea break was over. More's the pity.

She wished the tea break had gone on a bit longer. Because he might have kissed her again if it had.

Matt bid farewell to the last of his pupils as the workshop ended and he closed up for the day. They'd produced some good work, and he was happy to see that they'd all come up with different representations of movement and impact. After seeing his iPad art, there'd been a lot of Lily pictures, and eventually he'd had to link his laptop up to the big projector screen and Google pictures of her to talk through composition and costume. The class had gone slightly off track, as they sometimes did, but Matt was a firm believer in being led by people who were enjoying learning. Usually the classes ended up even better and more engaging if he allowed that to happen. He was pretty adept at reining them in too, if he needed to, so it didn't worry him unduly if he saw it happening.

And today he'd been more than happy to focus on Lily Valentine, because every time he enlarged an image of her, he saw more and more of Cordy in her – which was mad, he supposed, but he was *really* looking forward to seeing his own 'Lily' later that day.

So he was in a very good mood when he went to lock up the room, and that only improved when he looked along the corridor and saw Cordy there, peeking around the wall. She waved at him and he waved back, then he gestured for her to come into the room.

'Is this a good time?' she asked.

'Always a good time when I don't have students,' he responded. 'You did say you'd find me. Well done.'

'You didn't hide very far. And I couldn't wait anyway. I wanted you to see this.' She held the iPad up, and he could see her pen was hooked onto the notebook so whatever she'd found she'd been making notes on.

'It's an iPad. A familiar one. I've seen it now.'

'Cheeky.' She nudged him playfully. 'It's what I found out using the iPad that's interesting. Let's sit down so I can show you.' She pulled out a chair and put the items on the desk at the front of the room. 'Nothing further on Evelyn, and I've been searching for days on my phone. I thought about using that computer in the office again, but I never got the courage up to go back in. Now I've got the iPad, I've dug a bit more and found some passenger records, just like we said, for a Francis O'Hara. Not sure if it's the right one, but these show him leaving Ireland and landing in England. Then a little while later, we've got some records showing a Francis O'Hara, with the same details, leaving England to go to the Continent. Not sure if it's our Francis, but it's likely. Because he came *back*, the same year Lily did her show here. So he might well have been the Francis who left the details behind.'

'So what are you saying?' Matt pulled the iPad towards him and scrolled through the information. It was exactly as Cordy had pointed out. The man had travelled well.

'I'm saying that I caught Merryn before and asked if there were any records about the people who worked here. She said she'd check it out for me. Also, I thought that Lily might have eloped with him, but now I don't think she did. Or at least, if she did, it didn't last. Look at this.' She opened her notebook and pushed that towards Matt as well. 'I decided to go way off track and look for Edwin Griffiths; the gentleman that was mentioned in Elsie's programme, and the chap in the Wikipedia entry about Lily. I found him on the 1901 census with his wife and their three children. And it seems he was still with Lily, as his wife's name was Lily Griffiths! Exciting, yes? Oh – there's also a news report about Edwin being honoured for his services to his country. It seems like he was wounded quite badly in the Semantan War, which I think was in Malaysia and it ended a while before Lily's visit to Pencradoc. I found this photo of him – it's not great, but it's like a studio portrait of him in his uniform. Poor man.' She pulled a face. 'However, I can't find a marriage record for him and Lily, which is annoying. She dropped off the radar after this event at Pencradoc and didn't do anything else high profile. What if she just retired with Edwin and had babies?'

'It's a nice theory.' Matt's response was guarded. The man was in the army? The memory of that dream he had about the bullets and the fighting came back into his mind. Surely it was nothing more than coincidence? 'I had a weird dream about being in the army and it wasn't pleasant. I feel for him.'

'The report says he sustained terrible injuries and spent some time abroad convalescing before returning to England.' She sat back in the chair and studied Matt. He began to feel a little uncomfortable under her scrutiny.

'He's got a *bit* of a look about him of you,' she said eventually. 'I think it's his smile. I wonder if there's more of a link here than we think.'

'Well, you've got the same colour hair as Lily Valentine. Doesn't mean you *are* Lily Valentine.'

He could see where this was leading and sure enough Cordy looked away, apparently embarrassed. 'True.' She sighed. 'I'm clutching at straws, trying to make sense of all this ... *weirdness*. You have to agree it's odd. We've both seen things and heard things. There has to be a reason.'

Matt shivered. No. He refused to go there. 'Look, just

because Merryn's told you this place is haunted doesn't mean that the ghosts are attaching themselves to us for any real reason. It's a coincidence.'

'I'm not necessarily saying they're attaching themselves to us. Just they seem to be making themselves known.' Just then her phone pinged. 'Ooh. A text. From Merryn.' She looked up at Matt and then opened the message. 'She's found some records for us. The estate manager employed a group of itinerant labourers in summer 1895. But then there's a few pages missing in the ledger. Must be when the accident happened at the Mill House.' She looked back at him, a challenge in her eyes. 'So that's why nobody knows who he was, and the records have been destroyed, I guess deliberately. But his papers were left in the Mill House, well hidden, it seemed. Tell me that one isn't a coincidence? That one of those guys wasn't the one who came all that way to find Lily – oh! Oh Matt, look.' She pulled her phone out and scrolled through the pictures. She showed him a set of three, all of the Mill House. 'See that weird shape on this one? Like a man. What if he's the one who got killed? Ugh. This *place*!' She shuddered, and even Matt felt a little unsettled at that one.

'Don't think like that Cordy! You'll have us both running scared from the place. And like I said, I don't run away from things. One of those men *could* have been O'Hara. He probably was. That, hopefully, is just a shadow on your picture.' He hoped, he really hoped it *was* just a shadow.

'Yes. I'm just a wee bit frustrated now with this whole thing. I think I've taken it as far as I can. I'm no nearer to finding the real Lily, or even Evelyn or Francis. Whoever they were, they were all bloody good at hiding their tracks.'

Her phone pinged again and she tutted, picking it up again. She read the message, and an odd little expression flickered across her face. Then she switched the screen off. 'I'd best let you get on then,' she told him, standing up. 'Just need to ring the insurance company. It's to do with the flat.' She half-smiled.

'Sorry for barging in on you. I just wanted you to know what I'd found out.'

'No worries. It was nice to see you.' He stood up as well. 'Do you want to take the iPad with you?'

'No thanks.' She shook her head. 'I'm just getting irritated with it all. I might see you later.'

'Okay. I think I'll head off to the stage area if you need me. Kit and I are going to go through what we might use for the show. I told him what we'd discussed, and we'll see if there's anything else in the old sheds we can use. Worth a shot.'

'Absolutely. Oh – here. If you're looking at scenery you might want these.' She shrugged. 'Just to help.' She opened her notebook and pulled out the photos they'd discovered in the Mill House along with a copy of the photograph of Elsie and her cousins.'

'Thanks.' He reached out to take them and their fingertips connected, sending another one of those little *zing*s up his arm. Cordy's eyes widened slightly, then she quickly withdrew her hand.

'Sure.' She nodded and turned away, hurrying away from the desk, out of the room and leaving him standing there, staring after her, knowing he shouldn't feel obliged to go after her – but he wanted to.

But for what purpose, he couldn't really say.

1895

'And that, my friends, is the end of the show.' Curtseying deeply, Elsie demonstrated to her cousins how the Pageant should end. Her cousins, however, did not seem to be as impressed as Elsie would have expected them to be. Indeed, Nancy had looked rather bored and had wandered off. She was currently a little way away, lying on her stomach, using a stick to poke at a worm who had made the mistake of crawling out of the soil and onto the lawn.

Elsie looked at them all in despair. Mabel was daydreaming, staring off into the distance, and Clara and Lucy were apparently engaged in a staring competition with one another.

'Really. You all need to take notice,' groused Elsie. 'This might be the only time we have someone like Lily Valentine here at Pencradoc and the only chance we have to put on such a splendid show. Nancy, put that poor worm *down*! He doesn't want to be dangled off a stick!'

'He's wiggly.' Nancy refused to put the worm down and Elsie sighed. It was very difficult at times being the oldest.

'But it's not our show,' pointed out Lucy, moving her head away and apparently losing the staring competition to her sister's great delight. 'It's your show, Elsie, and we just have to do what you say.'

'Well that is why I am the producer and the director.' Elsie was astonished that they could think her role lacked any importance whatsoever.

'And it's also why you didn't allow us to make the programmes,' grumbled Clara. 'It's always what you want, Elsie. You never let us do anything!'

'Clara. I'm the best person to draw the pictures in them. None of you could have done that, could you? And I did let you *write* in the programmes and fold them. You had the chance to help out there, didn't you?'

'Yes.'

'And Mabel also helped with the Pageant. Didn't she ask your mother where we could get some costumes?'

'Yes.'

'And Lucy. Lucy managed to find Mr Shakespeare's book in the library so we could ask Miss Valentine to say something out of it.'

'Yes.'

'And Nancy. She—' Elsie couldn't think for a moment what Nancy had done. 'She is too small, really, to help much, but—'

'But I thought of the "Daisy Bell" song,' the little girl

shouted, as she rolled over onto her back, growing bored of the wiggly worm. 'Mama sings that song to us quite a lot, and I *do* like it.'

'There. You have all helped then.' Elsie curtseyed again, inclining her head gracefully and holding the hem of her red dress up. It was quite her favourite dress, knee-length, with gathered sleeves and a pretty gathered bodice. 'Now, if you would please excuse me, I do need to go and speak to Miss Valentine. We have a few things left to discuss.'

'Then we shall go and play,' announced Mabel. 'I want to dress up. Mama said she would help us make costumes, and I do like to dress up. I really don't think Aunt Zennor would mind too much if we cut some of the things up a little, as they are all old things from the dressing-up trunk in the attic from when Mama lived here a long time ago. Aunt Zennor said just to leave the clothes for the children of the house, and that is what we are at the moment.'

'Please.' Elsie waved a hand regally in the direction of Pencradoc. 'Just go. I must go to the Mill House.' She sighed a little for effect. Really, a producer and director's work was never done, was it?

Chapter Fourteen

Cordy hurried out of the room and ran all the way downstairs. It was only when she was outside and a breeze was blowing, lifting her hair from her sticky, clammy neck, that she leaned her forehead against the old stones of Pencradoc and closed her eyes. She didn't quite know what was happening. There was definitely a connection between her and Matt, no matter how they tried to skirt around it or how much she told herself that she didn't want a relationship with anyone right now. It was getting ridiculous. She honestly felt as if she was seeking him out and then when she saw him her heart was banging around in her chest like a teenager with their first crush.

She was an adult! This sort of thing didn't happen to adults, did it?

But apparently it did and she didn't care how much Matt tried to deny it; there was *definitely* some sort of connection between them to Lily and, now she was beginning to realise, Edwin too.

The woman she'd sensed on the stage, the voices whispering in her ears. The images they'd both seen at the Mill House, her odd dreams and now Matt's dreams as well. And the bullet – the bullet she'd found by the river and the photographs with the strange figure on them that she'd taken that day. They were linked as well. She just wasn't sure how.

If Lily Valentine was still here at Pencradoc, what on earth did she want with Cordelia Beaumont?

Her phone pinged again and she pulled it out of her pocket. It was the same message as before; her agent, asking her to call back urgently. It wasn't the insurance company at all. Her agent wanted her, and that meant only one thing.

An audition.

Cordy dialled the number and closed her eyes as Marion answered.

'Cordy! Darling. How is your little holiday going?'

'Fine, thanks. But it's more of an escape than a holiday – my flat flooded. I needed somewhere to stay—'

'—yes, yes. Of course. Now, I know things haven't been great for us, and I'll not lie, I'm a little disappointed for you.' *Disappointed in you*, Cordy thought to herself, as she pulled a face at the wall. 'But I've put you forward for this part,' barrelled on the woman. 'It's a new stage show starring your old friend Toby. I think he's already spoken to you about it? Said you were happy to come along and try out?'

'No! No. Absolutely *not*.' Cordy felt her hand curl into a fist, as if she wanted to punch her old friend Toby's face, very hard. 'I'm not interested. He did speak to me. He came down here to do so, and hang on – how did *you* know I was down here? Did he tell you that too?'

'Darling, I'm your *agent*. I should be told when you're away or unavailable. I'm disappointed you *didn't* tell me, sweetness. I mean, what if an opportunity had come up and I needed you here? *Right* here. Straight away? Like now, for instance. Because I need you in London. One moment, darling, I have the schedule here.' There was a series of clicks as Marion apparently consulted her computer. 'I have you booked in for 9 a.m. tomorrow. You should be able to make it.'

'Marion – it's past five o'clock. I'm in Cornwall!'

'Of course you are. You can get a train tonight, then you'll be back in good time for the audition. It's at Royal Queens, on Shaftesbury Avenue, for *The Black Rose*. But you know all about it, I'm sure. You'll be playing Rosalee, obviously and—'

'—Marion! No. No, I'm not playing Rosalee opposite Toby Fowler!'

'Well you can't play her opposite anyone else. It's Toby's show.'

'I don't care. I have commitments here.'

'Rubbish. Your friends down there only put the Lily Valentine Exhibition on to build on the fact *The Black Rose* was coming out. We all read the same papers, love.'

'Maybe they did, but what's the harm in them capitalising on the interest in her? They've got more of a link to her than Toby bloody Fowler.'

'Cordy!' Marion was horrified. 'Now look here. Stop talking nonsense and listen to me. I have the agenda here, and the piece you need to learn is this one …'

Cordy squeezed her eyes shut and leaned her forehead against the wall as Marion's voice went on and on and on …

This was a nightmare. An absolute nightmare.

Stuff Toby Fowler and all he stood for!

Matt was in the gardens later that evening, feeling at a bit of a loose end. He and Kit had found some furniture and some paints and he had a good idea of what he could create for the show. It was only a few days away now, and yes, it might be a rush job as they'd all been busy and it needed to come together quite quickly, but the stage would look good. He owed that to her.

To whom? To Cordy? Or to Lily?

He pulled a face. He'd taken the liberty of calling *The Sunday Stage* as well. He hoped Cordy wouldn't mind, but he'd rang Rick – or at least he'd rang Rick's office. Cordy had mentioned he'd been interested so Matt had looked up the number and contacted him. A very nice lady had said she would pass the message on, so all he was waiting for, really, was for Rick to turn up on the day.

He was up a ladder, adding some climbing roses to a floral landscape, curling the image up around the side of the backdrop, when he saw her wandering towards Rose's Garden. It took all he had not to wave the brush madly and encourage her over. She might not even be coming over to the stage, and if he beckoned her, then what reason could he realistically give for having done so? '*I haven't seen you for a couple of hours and I really missed you*' would sound a lot more stalker-ish verbalised than it sounded in his head,

But he needn't have worried. She seemed to be heading straight to him, and sure enough she rounded the corner and climbed up the stage so she was standing next to him.

'Hello.' There was no preamble. 'I thought I might find you here.'

'Hello. What's up?'

'That wasn't the insurance people. I lied. It was my agent. In London.'

His stomach somersaulted. That could only mean she was needed back in the City.

'Oh. And what did your agent want?'

'An audition.' She pulled a face. 'But I don't want to go. I certainly can't make it for tomorrow when she wants me to do it. I've talked her into Tuesday morning. That gives me the weekend to do the show and Monday to ...' Her voice trailed off and she folded her arms.

'To what?'

'To plan my travel.'

'I see.' He daubed at a pale pink rose-bud, not daring to look at her in case his face gave away his feelings. He really didn't know what he hoped to achieve here. Her life was in London; his was further south again in Newlyn. Who was to say she even wanted to see if they could take the relationship to the next level?

'It's been nice here, hasn't it?' She wasn't looking at him; she was looking at the scenery. 'I like what you've done there.'

'Thanks. Yes. It's all gone way too fast. It's been great meeting you though, and sharing ... this.' He gestured to the scenery. 'It's good to know your milk frothing skills have been honed as well.'

He chanced a glance at her and there was a glimmer of a

smile. 'Sorcha's more or less back. She's not fooling me. I don't think I'll be needed beyond the weekend, to be honest. I've got no excuse not to go back to London. Or to try out for this show.'

'Indeed.' He added some pale green to a sun-kissed leaf. 'Can I ask what show it is?' He hardly dared to hear the answer; he thought he could guess.

'Funnily enough it's *The Black Rose*. Toby's new show. The one Lily Valentine starred in. They've updated it.'

He knew it. 'The one Toby tried to get you to go back for. Obviously. Rosalee?'

'Rosalee. The thought of Toby is putting me off. I feel a bit railroaded – first he comes here, then Marion rings me and demands I go back. I really didn't want to go back and go straight into something like that ... with someone like him.'

'But you're going to.' It was a statement, not a question.

'I should. It's a great opportunity.'

'Okay.' He changed the paint brush to one with dark green and worked on some shading.

'Anyway. I'm boring myself now.' She sat down on the stage, cross-legged, and put her chin in her hands.

Matt climbed down and sat beside her. He chanced putting his arm around her and was grateful when she leaned into him and rested her head in the crook of his neck.

'You don't have to go back. Not for this,' he said.

'I know. But maybe I should. My career hasn't been brilliant recently. It's a great opportunity.'

Well. Only you know what's best for you. I know nothing about theatre. I was a star in the Nativity at school. I fell off the stage.'

She smiled. 'A falling star. I like it. A bit like me and my crap career.'

'You're a rising star. You just need to find your galaxy, and you'll rock it.'

'I almost believe you,' she said. Then she turned to look up at him, and before he knew it, their lips had met and they were kissing.

And it felt as if he had come home.

'This really shouldn't be happening,' murmured Cordy, eventually.

'It really shouldn't.'

'The play is in a couple of days' time.'

'And the scenery will be ready. Have no fear.'

'It's not the scenery I'm worried about.'

'Well, what are your worried about?'

'Us.'

'Us? What do you mean by us?'

'The fact that there seems to be becoming an ... us. And I didn't plan for that.'

'Neither did I. It doesn't mean we can't just enjoy it though?'

'No. It doesn't mean that at all.'

'I'm pleased we both think the same then ...'

1895

Even from the edge of the path, Edwin could see the door to the Mill House was standing wide open, the lock shattered.

As he got closer to the door, his heart lurched.

He had seen enough damage from bullets in the army to recognise what had happened, and then he heard the commotion. 'Lily? *Lily!*' He broke into a run, heedless of the pain that shot up the left side of his body, unused as he was now to such physical exertion. The anger over that fired him up even more and he burst into the house, grabbing his cane as he stumbled into the small hallway.

The sounds were definitely coming from upstairs, a combination of shouting and swearing, male and female voices intertwined.

'Lily!' He grasped the handrail and hauled himself up the stairs, cursing the old wounds that, to his mind, impeded his progress. He tracked the sounds to the largest bedroom, Lily's bedroom – the one that looked out over the river and the water-wheel.

Throwing his weight against the door, he careered into the room. It was the first time he'd been in here properly, and along with the scent of lilies and the strong trace of her fragrance, he was aware of a gown thrown over a chair, and a brightly coloured blanket on the bed. But beyond that, he was horrified to see a man in front of the window, and Lily half out of it, but whether the intruder was trying to push her out or whether she was trying to climb out of her own accord was a matter open to interpretation.

'No you don't!' the man was shouting, grabbing Lily's hair and trying to drag her in. Lily was screaming, one hand flying to the back of her neck, one still on the window frame.

'Lily!' Edwin limped across the room. 'Leave her alone! Get off her!' He grabbed the man's shoulder, but he was younger and stronger than Edwin and easily threw him off.

'No! She's my wife. I won't leave her alone, She's my *wife*. I've every right to her!' The man's accent was a thick Irish brogue and Edwin suddenly understood. This was the man she'd wanted to run from in Paris. The man who had attacked her; the man who had somehow tracked her down to Pencradoc. This was Francis O'Hara.

Chapter Fifteen

Over the next couple of days, Sorcha did indeed take over the tea-room fully, quietly and efficiently – and by the weekend, Cordy was relieved of duty. She knew it would happen

Before that, for the couple of days when Sorcha was popping in for the odd few hours, Cordy had spent the time she wasn't working in the tea-room finishing off and practising her play. When Matt was finished with his classes, they'd meet up and work together on the set. Cordy was realising again just how much she loved the pace of life here, and the fact that she had more or less produced and designed her own show had boosted her confidence enormously.

Neither one of them mentioned the fact that she might be going back to London, but both of them had quite liked the kiss, and that was, to be fair, something they had indulged in again. Although the discussions surrounding the mythical 'us' had not been repeated.

Regardless, they enjoyed painting the set and discussing how Elsie might have done it, and neither one of them had minded too much when, out of the corner of their eyes, they had seen the hazy shape of a little girl sitting cross-legged in the wings, her chin in her hands, studying them carefully. They felt, somehow, that she was giving them her approval.

Cordy also abandoned the idea of researching Evelyn and Francis any more. 'What will be, will be,' she told Matt over drinks at The White Lady the evening before the show. 'If we're meant to find out about them, we will. It's not the end of the world.'

'And maybe it's not our mystery to solve,' Matt added. 'Maybe we just need to concentrate on Lily's show?'

Cordy had taken the old programme and photos with them

and they looked at them now, laid out in front of them. The photos were like old friends, especially since they now knew who was in them. But instead of the original programme, they had a copy of it. Cordy had felt bad hanging onto it, and had eventually given over its care to Merryn, admitting that she 'may' have found it squished down a floorboard at the Mill House when she was adventuring. Merryn had seemed to accept the explanation, and all was good.

It did mean that Coren had, within a day, organised some reproductions of it, and these were now on sale in preparation for the show. Cordy was impressed, and had bought one of the reproductions. It was just as beautiful as the original – and she wasn't so scared of damaging it.

'You've done so well, pulling all this together,' said Matt. 'I can't believe the show is tomorrow.'

'I know.' She pulled a face. 'Too late now to worry about it. It'll be fine. My dress is hanging up in my room all ready to go, and I know my part as well as I ever will.'

'And I called *The Sunday Stage*,' admitted Matt. 'I felt that they owed us for the Toby debacle, and the girl I spoke to said she'd pass the message on. Just thought I'd better confess now.' He smiled, almost apologetically.

'That's fine. It's good exposure for Pencradoc, and they say there's no such thing as bad publicity, don't they? So even if I mess up, Pencradoc will still be in the news.' She pulled another face.

'You won't mess up.' Matt took her hand and squeezed it. 'But I think you need an early night. Just so you're well-rested for tomorrow.'

'Well-rested?' Cordy raised her eyebrows. 'Seriously?'

'No. Not at all.' There was a twinkle in his eye, and she knew exactly where that one was going.

'Good. Because I'm not really sleepy, to be honest.'

'Are you not?' Matt looked comically shocked.

'No.' Cordy leaned over and kissed him, and his hand

tightened on hers – and yes. She knew exactly where that one was leading ...

Which was why the next day, Cordy woke up far too early for a Sunday morning – even if that Sunday morning was the 10th of August, and the day of the show. But the fact it was early didn't seem to matter too much, when she rolled over and stretched out and connected with a warm body.

After the debate on the stage about the 'us' thing, Cordy hadn't really been sure how it would all pan out.

But Matt had definitely helped her work *some* of that out at least, which was why she was here now.

'Good morning.' Matt's voice was quiet, amused, and he leaned across and kissed her. 'So, I hate to mention it again, but as our time is running out here, and London beckons for Rosalee, do you know if there's an "us" yet? A proper "us"?'

'In some ways there's very much an "us". In other ways – I don't know.' She sat up and looked at him. 'What happens after this little holiday? When you go back to your teaching job, and I go back to Kentish Town?' She frowned, not wanting to think about it. 'Newlyn isn't exactly Hampstead Heath. It's not like we can pop in to see each other on an evening, or spend any time at all together, really.'

'No. I know what you mean.' Matt lay back down, his arms folded behind his head. 'And believe me, I've been thinking about it too. The answer is, I *don't* know. I mean, long-term, if things go the way I would like them to, then I guess there are lots of schools in London that might need a teacher.' Cordy flashed a surprised glance at him, but didn't fail to see the fleeting expression on his face. He didn't want to teach in London. Of course he didn't.

But did she want to leave all that behind and come down here? She needed to be in London for rehearsals and opportunities and West End shows. There was absolutely no way she could travel up and down to the capital from

Cornwall all the time. Look at the problems she was having with Marion. Her stomach churned as she thought about Tuesday. It had to be at least five hours driving, a little shorter on the train. Merryn's situation was different. Although she had officially 'left' the art dealers in London she had worked for, she was still used as a consultant at times, but much of her work for them could be done from a base anywhere, and to be fair she had been used to travelling if she had to. That was how she had ended up in Cornwall. Being an actress was quite different.

Correction: being a *good* actress was quite different.

Cordy frowned. *Was* she any good? Really? Or was it all an illusion? Yes, she had done some decent work in the past, but could she really build a career on a non-speaking part in *Downton Abbey* and a few shows? What she needed was some stability and some long-term contracts. And that was why she temped.

She could temp down here. She supposed she could still travel for auditions if it looked as if it was worth her while.

But it was a five-hour journey.

Good grief. She really didn't want to think of any of that right now. Even if she got the train, as she had done to get to Pencradoc many a time, it was still about four and a half hours.

'I can't think of any of that right now,' she reiterated to Matt. 'My job is in London, and yours is here. But *here* is definitely prettier than London.' She looked wistfully out of the window at the summer morning. There were a few white, wispy clouds in a pale blue sky, but she knew that, given a few more hours, the rosy glow of the sunshine would reflect off Pencradoc's old, grey walls, and the sky would be a beautiful hyacinth colour.

Just like it had been the first time …

'Right! I'm getting up.' She slid out of the bed, trying not to acknowledge Lily or whoever it was giving her advice. Not today when she was already a bit jittery about letting everyone down.

'Don't go too far.' Matt's voice was teasing, lazy. 'You've got a busy day today, Miss Almost Valentine.'

'I have. I have loads to do first, not least getting the dress ready. It's in my room, so unless there's an undiscovered secret passageway between our two rooms, I need to make myself decent and sprint through the building and hang it up properly so the creases drop out.'

As Cordy quickly showered and dressed, the jitters subsided into a little thrill of anticipation which shivered throughout her body. The dress was the making of the show. She had already decided what her hair and make-up would be like – understated; the 'Lily' that wanted to keep her private life private, and relax with her family and friends. By the time she came out of the little en-suite, Matt had already made a coffee and she picked up the mug gratefully.

'I'll see you soon.' He raised his own mug to her in a sort of toast. 'Here's to Lily, Cordy and of course Elsie – who has made this all possible with her beautiful programme.'

'Definitely Elsie.' She smiled and, draining her coffee, reached up and kissed him. 'I know you've got loads to do as well, what with sorting all the scenery and everything, so I'm sorry, but I think I'll love you and leave you to it. Not that I really want to go, you understand.'

'I don't want you to go either – but "love me"?' He reached out and grabbed her around the waist, pulling her closer to him. 'Is that a promise?'

'Later. Maybe.' She laughed and kissed him again. 'I have to go. I'll take the photos too – make sure I know what I'm dressing up as.'

He released her, and she smiled. 'See you soon.'

She was still smiling when she got to her room and took the dress out of the wardrobe. She shook it out and hung it on the back of the bathroom door, then spent a little time running through the script and making sure she was clear on what she was doing for the extra little audience participation bits one final time over another coffee.

Eventually, in a bid to clear her head, she decided to wander over to the Mill House and check the staging out on her way back. The Mill House was a place she felt that she could think, quite quietly, about Lily – and hopefully present some of the calm, confident personality that lady seemed to have possessed to her own audience here today.

Cordy smiled to herself as she stepped onto the landing. Would anyone have ever known the real Lily Valentine? Anyone at all? Maybe Edwin would have known her—

'—Cordy! Good morning. Looking forward to it?'

'Oh!' Cordy jumped backwards, half into the bedroom as he thoughts were interrupted. 'Hello – Rick? Isn't it?'

'That's right.' Rick, the reporter from *The Sunday Stage* was standing in front of her, smiling. 'I told you we'd come to cover the show, didn't I?'

'Ah! Yes – you did! Matt said so as well.' Recovering from the surprise, she stepped back into the corridor and closed the bedroom door to. 'You're a bit early!'

'No – it's deliberate.' He looked around the corridor again and smiled. 'I wanted to get some shots of the Arts Centre before it got too crowded. Let people know what the studios and retreat rooms are like; make a whole … thing … about it.' He laughed, shrugging his shoulders. 'And I'm guessing these are the rooms I'm reporting on. I've stumbled on the right corridor.'

'Of course! Were you told they were up here?'

'Yes – yes that's right. In fact—'

'—Oh – Cordy! Do you need this … shit. Sorry, mate.' Matt's voice travelled down the corridor as he hurried along it, just as she had done, all the way from his room to hers. He was holding the copy of the programme.

'Matt! Thank you.' She felt her cheeks heat up. 'It must have fallen out of my bag when we were going through the schedule.'

'It must have done.' There was a twitch at the edges of his lips – they both knew they hadn't gone through anything of the sort last night. But it was quick-thinking on Matt's behalf. Whatever they did or didn't do together wasn't really any of the reporter's business.

But still.

She had told Rick that Matt wasn't her boyfriend and felt her face flush as she remembered.

'No worries. I guess that drink of ours really is off the cards now.' Rick shrugged. 'Not surprising. Like I say, actresses and me don't mix. Shame.' Cordy cringed a little. In another life, maybe she *would* have enjoyed going out with him, seeing where it led, having a bit of fun. He was tall and broad-shouldered and outdoorsy looking, which was at odds with his career when you thought about it.

'Oh, it's really nothing personal ...' Cordy began, but whichever way she chose to continue that sentence would sound pretty bad. He seemed like a decent man – just not the man she wanted to be with right now.

'That's okay. Honestly. If you change your mind – like I said – you've got my number.'

Then, as if a switch clicked on in his mind, something flickered behind his eyes which, truth be told, made her feel a little uncomfortable. But he blinked and it was gone. Then he turned away from her and looked around, seemingly interested in the surroundings.

'Ummm. Okay – the show starts at one. Be ... good ... to see you there,' Cordy said.

'It will.' Rick seemed to dismiss her presence and raised his camera to take a long shot down the corridor – and Cordy decided to take her chance and hurry away downstairs. She didn't want to get caught up in a photo shoot and, oddly, she didn't want to be that close to Rick right now. 'Bye for now. And Matt ... I'll see you later.'

'Bye, Cordy.' Matt's voice was still tinged with amusement. He winked and turned away, heading back to his room, and she ducked her head, hiding a smile.

But it was only when she was halfway to the Mill House that she wondered if she maybe *should* had stayed for the pictures? It was all good publicity, and she probably could have sat in the window or something, maybe done a little interview about it all ...

She frowned. A lost opportunity. But never mind – there would be more. She was sure of it.

Although, having said that, talking to a reporter with the man she'd just spent the night with in attendance was maybe not the best idea. If he was a good reporter, she was pretty sure any subterfuge would be teased out of the situation anyway. Plus, it was clear that Rick fancied her, so who knew how poor Matt might come out of the interview? Not that she felt they were in any way, shape or form ... subterfuging. But you never knew how things would be misinterpreted, and Matt was a teacher, after all.

A night spent with an actress was not the greatest publicity for a teacher, she reckoned – although she did find the idea quite amusing. The readers of *The Sunday Stage* and Matt's pupils' families, however, may not find it so funny ...

He turned and watched her walk away. She hurried down the stairs, her head dipped, red in the face, embarrassed. He knew what had happened between her and that man – it was obvious. He could have had her, right there, right then. Taken what was his by right. But then he *appeared. And dammit, hadn't he wanted to kill that man right there and then? But this was not the time. He wanted her first. And he would get her. He knew there would be another opportunity. He just had to wait ...*

Until then, this was her room, was it not?

He smiled. Taking the knife out of his pocket, he slipped it down the gap between the door and the frame and worked on the lock. It gave easily, and one step would take him inside.

Now he could visit her properly.

Matt hurried through Pencradoc, trying not to laugh. He and Cordy had done well to bluff their way out of that one.

Still, it was nice that *The Sunday Stage* had sent Rick over. The message must have got through to him, which was good. He just had time for a quick check of the stage, and to bring the props and extra pieces of scenery out of the shed.

Kit was there, moving the items out as Matt approached, and turned to greet his friend. 'Hey Matt. Just in time. We could have left them out – it didn't rain overnight like they forecast.'

'Daren't have risked it.' Matt helped Kit move a painted tree out of an awkward corner. 'Cordy is an actress after all, and although I haven't witnessed any diva-like behaviour, who knows what she might have done if all this had been ruined?' He grinned to show that his comment wasn't exactly serious.

'True! I wonder if Lily Valentine was a diva? She must have had a hard edge to her, to succeed in those days. But I guess fortune wasn't always guaranteed with that job though.' Kit eased a fake tree-stump out and dropped a garland of flowers onto it. 'Merryn told me that the original principal dancer in the ballet *Coppélia* died in poverty on her seventeenth birthday. Imagine.' He pulled a face. 'The Opera House just decided to stop showing the ballet due to the Franco-Prussian War. Closed itself down for the duration. And basically left her to rot.'

'Nice.' Matt felt a surge of annoyance run through him – the fact that they had treated a young girl like that – a girl no older than some of his students …

Lily did the right thing by leaving. She had to go when she did.

The voice startled him, and he looked up, ready to respond to Kit – but it was clear that Kit hadn't said that at all. He was busy chatting about ticket sales and the reporter who had come along to see the show on behalf of the *The Sunday Stage*.

'Oh! Yes. Rick Hoffman.' Matt shook off the thought about Lily.

'Rick Hoffman? No.' Kit turned to him, frowning. 'The guy I spoke to was Stanley something or other. Coleman. Stanley Coleman. That was him.' He dusted his hands down and shut the door. 'Unless they sent a posse of reporters and I just saw one. It's a possibility.'

'True. I'm not sure how they work it. Oh well. Thanks for this, by the way. It's great that we've got an echo of the past up here. The stage looks a lot like those photos, which is good for the people who'll be comparing it to them.'

'We'll just move them around a bit, make them look exactly like the photo, and we're good to go. Merryn says Cordy is really good. She should do well.'

'Hopefully we'll have sold a few tickets – I'm sure some people want to come and see the woman who binned Toby Fowler. She was right to do so, mind. The bloke's an arse.'

'So I've been told. Oh – speak of the devil.' Kit nodded towards a man walking towards them. 'That's Stanley Coleman. I'm off. This scenery is your glory, not mine!' And with that, he hurried away, vanishing into the gardens and leaving Matt alone. Matt knew his friend – he wasn't the sort to market himself particularly well, and whereas Coren would have smiled at the reporter and shaken his hand and invited him on a tour of the estate, Kit had clearly run off and left Matt to it. Ah yes, his friend may be part-owner of Pencradoc Arts Centre, but he left all the business stuff to Coren. Kit's heart was definitely in Marazion, with Merryn, in his own little shop with his own life.

Lucky man, to have found something so perfectly suitable for him.

'Mr Harker?' Stanley Coleman came up to Matt, smiling eagerly. 'I've heard so much about this event from my colleague – I'm absolutely delighted to be here to cover it. I understand you've been instrumental in bringing it together?'

'Errrr – no. Not really. I helped paint some of the sets, but I think you'll find the glory needs to go to Cordelia Beaumont. She's the one who's going to be up on the stage. And actually, she was responsible for designing the sets too.'

'Yes! Cordelia Beaumont. Now, what can you tell me about the play and the direction it's taken? I understand from the girl you spoke to in the office that it's not just a play, and we have some fun in store ...'

Matt thought he might as well sit down on the stage. Mr Coleman was going to be looking forward to a lengthy chat. He gestured for the reporter to join him and swung himself sideways so he was facing Stanley. He was just telling Stanley about the reasons behind the show, when he heard the unmistakeable swishing of a dress behind him.

He turned, ready to welcome Cordy to the stage – but was astonished to see that there was nobody there, although he felt the draught as someone walked past him, and the tickle of fabric grazing his knuckles as the train, or whatever it was, swept past him.

Good grief. He turned back to Stanley Coleman, ready to ask him if he had also heard or felt anything, but the man was sitting, eagerly anticipating Matt's answer to the next question.

'Umm ... sorry. Can you repeat that, please?' Matt asked. 'I didn't quite catch it.'

'Certainly.' Stanley smiled. 'I just asked if you could confirm if there really are five small girls playing the parts of the young Pencradoc ladies, as indicated in the photograph of the original stage?' He pointed to the display board, then grinned. 'I think they're quite excited, to be honest. I'm sure I heard them down by the river before. By the Mill House? I had a walk down there earlier, but I didn't see them.'

Matt squirmed slightly. 'No, as far as I'm aware, we don't have any child actors officially on the stage today. But that is one of the things Cordy is planning – so she can make it a bit of an audience participation event. I think what you heard was the sound of children playing across the river, in the wider estate.' He forced a smile, which felt hugely unnatural. 'It's not the first time we've heard them. Sound does carry at the Mill House.'

'Oh, it does indeed.' Stanley nodded his head. 'The sound of the water-wheel was particularly soothing today. It's a nice touch.'

'Yes.' Matt's heart was pounding, and it was difficult to keep his voice light and even. Of course there were no little girls around. Of course there was no water-wheel going.

Instead, the atmosphere was charged – completely charged – and whatever they were doing today had attracted the attention of every bloody spirit in the place, however they were related to the story—

A thought suddenly struck him, as clear as the water rushing downriver through the estate.

Shit.

'Stanley, sorry to ask you this one.' Matt tried to keep his voice even. 'Are you the only reporter here today from *The Sunday Stage*? Just so that we know we have to tell you everything, and we won't have to hold anything back to tell one of your mates.' It was poor reasoning and sounded ridiculous out loud as he stumbled over the words, but it was all he could come up with.

'One of my mates?' Stanley laughed. 'No. None of my mates are here today. I'm the only one. So please – feel free to hold *nothing* back. Our readers are eager to hear it!'

Oh hell. *Rick*. What on earth was Rick doing there then? In the corridor? Outside Cordy's room? With that weird, spaced-out expression on his face?

A vision suddenly came to Matt – a vision of a gun pointing at a man, but the gun wasn't held by him. Instead, he was holding a sword stick, and the man was big and brash and good-looking. Not a million miles away from bloody Rick Hoffman, if he was honest.

The gun was held by Lily Valentine. Not wavering. Steady as a rock.

'No!' He jumped off the stage, twisting his ankle badly as he fell, but staggering upright again, and cursing at the pain.

'Matt? I'm sorry – is everything all right?' Stanley was staring at him, horrified – as well he might be.

'No – no, it's not all right. I have to get to her. I have to stop him—' And he stumbled and limped across the grass, ignoring the waves of pain that shot up from his ankle, praying that his leg wouldn't give way beneath him.

Lily. He had to save Lily.

Francis was back.

Chapter Sixteen

Seventeen, she was. Seventeen and ready to be wed. Marriage to Francis O'Hara had been the last thing on her mind. He was a little wild and a lot dangerous, and he promised her the world. And it was all very well enjoying his company like that, but the time had come, they said, to be wed. She couldn't enjoy his company – like that – any longer without a wedding band on her finger.

It was unfortunate, really, that her pa had caught them and that there had been a terrible scene and a lot of shouting and a lot of talk about consequences and reputation and holding his head up in the pub again when he had a slut for a daughter.

But tying herself down like that had never been her intention, really. The man, however, had a silver tongue and could charm the birds from the trees with his pretty words and she'd found herself trapped by his promises and at the mercy of the menfolk in her life.

She'd just been carried along with it – red-haired Evelyn Sullivan, who had never wanted to stay here in this little village beyond the time when she had to. Evelyn Sullivan, whose ma was dead and whose pa was a drunk and who had no other family to speak of. She couldn't wait to leave, and damn the lot of them.

Tying herself down to Francis, to this awful little town, had never been her intention.

'We'll travel,' Frankie told her. 'I promise, Lynnie. I can do anything. I can train horses. I can work on the land from sunrise to sunset and you can be my pretty wife, my girl, the one I come back to every night, the one I make love to every night, after I've made all the money I can. You'll want for nothing, Lynnie, nothing at all.'

But she had wanted – she had wanted badly. She had wanted him home every night, not drunk in the arms of a whore or a farm girl. Not angry and abusive and yelling at her – God almighty, how he yelled at her! And he hit her, once or twice. Although he was always sorry afterwards, and she always spat on him and cursed him and swore at him and always, always refused to bow down and take it like a weakling.

She took it, to some extent, until the day she'd had enough – he'd spent the last of their money on a bet and lost badly. So Evelyn ran away before the landlord could come and throw them out of the rooms they were living in. She packed her one bag and she ran to Dublin, and she got herself passage on a boat – 'Don't ask me any questions sir, and I won't be telling you lies,' she'd said to the Captain. At least Frankie's silver tongue had rubbed off on her, and she'd learned from him that way, and besides that she knew what to do to convince a man to her way of thinking. It had even worked on Frankie at times.

But they'd adored her on the boat – she'd sang songs and entertained the passengers – and the crew – and they'd finally docked in Liverpool.

'What's your name?' the official-looking man on the docks had said. 'What's your name, girl?'

'She's with me,' one of the sailors had said, taking her by her arm and leading her roughly, but not unkindly, away from the officials. Money had changed hands, she thought, but she could never swear to it.

'Why did you do that?' she asked the man, the sailor, when they were in a tavern near the port.

'Because you look like a lass that needs to get away,' he said. He pushed some notes at her and pressed some coins into her hand and he kissed her briefly. 'Get away, lass. Live a new life.'

And she had kissed him back, and repaid him in the only way she knew how, and the next morning, before it was light, she'd left and she was on her way – somewhere.

'Your name?' the next official had barked at her when she went to a dancehall and asked for work; the chorus line, the ticket box, the sweeping up – whatever they wanted, she would do. She just knew she wanted to work there, in the warm, heady environment and earn money for herself by doing something she was good at.

'Your name?' he had repeated, his pen hovering over a piece of paper. She cast a glance to a vase of flowers nearby, thinking quickly. She saw the image in her mind's eye of Lillie Langtry, the woman she wished she could be like. She wanted to be strong and confident and successful in such a career ...

'Lily. My name is Lily.'

'Lily what?'

Her mouth began to form a word, then she clamped her lips together. Here, she could no longer be who she was. Nobody must find her. Nobody.

She looked down and saw that the man had dated the piece of paper. It was the fourteenth of February.

'Valentine,' she told him. 'My name is Lily Valentine ...'

Chapter Seventeen

Present Day

Cordy could see the stage in the distance. She saw that the flowers had been draped around it, and a couple of figures were beside it. Matt and Kit, possibly. Getting the set ready.

She loved the feeling of anticipation that was gently coursing through her veins today. She could well imagine what it had been like, that summer's day back in August 1895, when Lily had taken to the stage in a home-made pageant that Elsie had organised.

When Biscuit was in the wheelbarrow, and how he had tried to jump out, until Nancy had clambered into the wheelbarrow with him on the pretext of hugging him to make him feel safe but really so she too could get a ride onto the stage. How Nancy had waved at her father who was standing beside her mother as the Duchess played a gentle, musical tune on the old piano …

Cordy blinked. The whole place was buzzing today. Those imaginings were so *real*. It was almost as if she could remember being there and laughing at the spectacle; catching Edwin's eye and smiling, a look of understanding fleeting between them as they shared a memory – but a memory of what? There was something else there that bound them together …

She shook her head, afraid of falling any further into the Pencradoc rabbit hole. She had to focus on today. Merryn had told her strange things happened at Pencradoc – strange memories and events tripped people up when they were least expecting it, and Cordy had scoffed at her friend and disbelieved her. 'Nothing's ever happened to me, there', she'd said and Merryn had laughed, almost embarrassed, and agreed that maybe it was only her who could feel it – that Pencradoc atmosphere, all around her.

Today, Cordy regretted mocking Merryn quite so enthusiastically – there was definitely something here.

But the Mill House looked so pretty this morning it was hard to believe that it had seemed so … sinister … that first day. She wasn't even entirely sure that 'sinister' was the correct word. Perhaps 'odd' was a better description … ethereal? Maybe.

She stopped in her tracks, hearing the sound of children's laughter echoing around the place, a breeze as something ran past her, a wet nose snuffling at her ankle for a second, following hot on the heels of the little girls who were clearly still here in some shape or form.

She was standing in front of the Mill House now, looking up at the old windows and then she closed her eyes, not wanting to let the modern world intrude on what was surely an idyllic spot, despite what had happened there …

Her eyes still closed, Cordy felt the spray of water tossed up from the ever-turning water-wheel and, subconsciously, almost unwillingly, took a step forward as if she was drawn to the place. The logical part of her, the twenty-first century girl, didn't really want to go in for fear she'd fall down another hole in the floor, but …

'There's nothing logical about Pencradoc, is there?'

Cordy caught her breath and opened her eyes, staring straight into the face of Rick Hoffman – the reporter she'd left in the corridor of Pencradoc.

'Rick! What are you doing here – how did you get here before me?'

The man shrugged and looked over her shoulder, his eyes far away somewhere. 'Shortcut. I found it. After I'd been to Pencradoc.' His eyes suddenly slid back to her and fixed her with a direct, blue gaze. 'After I saw you there. There are plenty of ways around the estate if you know where to look. Plenty of places nobody else knows about.' He smiled, slowly, and Cordy caught her breath. This wasn't … right. Surely?

She'd only met him properly that day in the café and he'd seemed like a nice man. Now, here, outside the Mill House, she wasn't quite sure what she was seeing – or who. He looked … different. Her heart began to pound.

Something was wrong. Very, very wrong. This was not the man she remembered; the slightly gruff, ultimately cheerful man who had flirted with her and asked her to call him.

'Rick. Are you all right? Can I get you some water or something?' She actually didn't know where she could produce a bottle of water from. It was too far to the tea-room, but her gaze settled on the Mill House. There was a kitchen in there. She could maybe find a mug and do it that way. Hadn't they said the place was almost ready for rentals? Merryn told her just the other day that it was fully kitted out now. Cordy had meant to come over and see it, but she'd been wrapped up with the stage set and the tea-room and, let's face it, Matt.

'Come on.' She shook the thoughts away, blaming her imagination for being fanciful, and walked past the reporter. She tried the door to the property, and it opened easily.

She stepped inside.

It was as if the modern day suddenly dropped away, and she found herself in a different time. Even the silence within the house seemed to amplify; the sounds from the outside world had all but vanished. All the sounds, that was, except one. A regular *thump, thump, thump* gradually became apparent; a splashing sound that echoed around the place, just as if the water-wheel had sprung back into life.

Her skin began to prickle between her shoulder blades as she walked through the building, aware that Rick had also, seemingly, vanished with the outside world. But she couldn't seem to stop and turn around – it was as if she was replaying something that she had no control over; something that had imprinted itself on the very fabric of the building, etched into every brick and floorboard and window pane. Everything seemed to be hazy and unreal.

She knew this room. Part of her – a deeply hidden and long-buried part – was as familiar with the Mill House she stood in now as she was with her own flat in Kentish Town, with her own things around her and her own life carrying on as it did.

As she continued to walk through the rooms to the kitchen, the furniture looked like ghost furniture – right up until she passed it, then it seemed to take form and become real. As if in a waking dream, she gently touched a little side table that flickered nearby, yet was as solid as the ground she walked on. She stood, motionless for a second, trying to see through the haze into the world she understood.

She walked a few more steps and looked down, conscious of a swishing around her ankles; a sea-green dress, not unlike the one that was hanging up in her room waiting for her, skimmed the floor and she watched incredulously as the flash of a pointed toe from an elegant pair of white satin shoes peeped out with every step. The very same pair she'd seen that day as she sat on the stage and someone flitted past her. Now, she was even aware of the ribbon tied under her breast, the fabric of the dress draping softly over her body.

Cordy felt sick. She was hot and cold all over, forcing one foot in front of the other, tired and fragile and emotional … the prickling between her shoulder blades became an uncomfortable sweaty mess as she moved, silently, through the house, playing the scenario out.

All thoughts of getting water for Rick faded as she struggled to keep herself focused, telling herself it was silly and unreal and couldn't possibly be happening …

But it *was* happening, and there was nothing she could do to stop it.

As she drifted into the room at the back, the thrumming of the water-wheel seemed to become louder, and then there was an enormous *bang*.

Cordy screamed, jumping as what was apparently a gunshot echoed around the house. Then there was a crash as the door was forced open, and a shout as someone called out: 'I found you. You can never stay lost for long, can you? Evelyn O'Hara, you know you can't hide from me. I know you're in here – I saw you. I've been watching you. Lynnie? *Lynnie* – aren't you coming to greet your old husband? Your Frankie has come so far to find you.'

Another crash as something, maybe a chair, was picked up and hurled across the room, bouncing off the wall and shattering. That was followed by a sound like a vase breaking and a splash as water apparently spattered against the wall. 'All the way from Ireland, remember? All the way from home. Ah Lynnie—' Another crash, and the reverberation as a door was slammed open and heavy boots stomped onto the polished wooden floorboards of the front room. 'Lynnie. I know you're here. I *know* you are …'

Cordy pressed herself into the wall, looking for an exit. This was too real – far too real; she must have fallen asleep – or banged her head or something …

'I'm not Lynnie,' she muttered, still looking for a way out.

I'm not Lynnie. I haven't been Lynnie for a long time.

I'm Lily. I'm Lily Valentine …

And suddenly Cordy knew she *was* Lily. She definitely was. So she had to save herself and the baby. Good God – the baby. Because Lily was pregnant, wasn't she? That might explain the sickness and the exhaustion …

There was the door in the corner. If she ran, she'd be at the staircase. He was in the other side of the house, across the corridor, in the dining room. The windows down here were too small and if she ran to the front door, that was exactly where he would expect her to go. She knew, she just *knew* that he was coming back across that room, facing the hallway. She had to do it. She had to try …

Taking a deep breath, she pushed herself away from the wall and began to run – but she hadn't bargained on being hampered by the weight of the dress, or the slippery soles and cute little heels of the beautiful shoes. She caught the toe of the shoe in her skirt and screamed as she almost fell. Grabbing the arm of a chair was the only thing that stopped her face-planting the floor, but he had heard her and even as she burst out of the sunroom door, he was in the dining room doorway, filling the doorframe, pointing that damn gun at her ...

'Lynnie! You can't hide. You can't get away this time.' There was another shot, which, Cordy calculated, had glanced off the stonework in the doorframe from the dining room. He'd perhaps aimed for the door – hoping to scare her or, even worse, kill her.

God, what had she done to him that made him this angry?

I left him. I escaped from him. And I disappeared.

Then he found me again.

But it's too late, and I'm not going back!

'It's too late, Frankie!' Cordy could have cheerfully gagged herself – why the hell did Lily feel the need to answer the bloke? But my God! Lily's accent! It was pure, beautiful Irish brogue. But she had no time to think. She was hurtling up the stairs, and he was after her in an instant.

'Lynnie ... Lynnie. I have you now, you sly bitch. Think you can get away from me? Do you? *Do* you?'

Cordy threw open the door of the nearest room and ran straight across it, ignoring the dress slung over the chair—

She'd been trying it on earlier, it was her favourite dress, and she had been wondering if she could get altered in the months to come, because she loved that dress—

Cordy pressed her hands over her ears, trying to block out Lily's musings, and reached the window – the window was huge in this room, and it was right over the water-wheel. If she could climb out of it, she could shuffle down it and be outside. Then once she was out of this horrible house, the horrible house that had clearly retained this horrible memory, she would be safe ...

There was another crash from downstairs, and a voice,

dearer and more familiar to her than she had ever considered: 'Lily? *Lily*!'

Cordy started – *thank God, thank God!* – and froze momentarily. Would she risk climbing out of this room? Would she wait for *him* to come and help her?

Edwin.

'Lily!' She heard her name again, along with the sound of an uneven tread struggling up the stairs.

She couldn't wait. She just couldn't.

But stopping, even briefly, was a mistake. In a split second, it seemed, just as she threw the window open and got one leg outside, attempting to scramble as fast as she dared over the sill, Francis O'Hara grabbed a handful of her hair. 'No you don't!'

And that was the point that reality and Lily's strange, other-life blurred so badly, she couldn't make sense of one of the other.

1895

The familiar red mist descended over Edwin's vision and the anger burned through his veins; the anger and darkness he'd tried so hard to fight these last few years. For Lily, he had almost succeeded in doing that. And it was for Lily that the anger was going to win today: he knew without a doubt.

'No. No, you have no right to her at all.' He took hold of the man's shoulder and dug his fingers in to his flesh the way he'd learned in the army, his fingers finding the sinews and tendons at the joints and pulling hard. The man yelped as Edwin dragged him around to face him. Edwin's stomach lurched in the split second he saw the man point a gun at him, then he reacted as quickly as he had ever done in his life, finding strength to disarm the man, bend his arm behind him and knock the gun out of his grasp.

'You bastard – she's mine! The bitch needs to pay for what

she did!' yelled the man. 'I'll take a thousand. For now.' As he twisted free and surged towards Edwin, barging his shoulder into him, Edwin realised the man was the labourer he had seen around the estate, working in the woods. He'd clearly just been biding his time until he was sure it was Lily, sure that he could try and take her again.

'She's not yours.' Edwin hardly recognised his own voice. It was cold, stilted. He was back on the battlefield, staring death in the face, making a decision. 'She's not a possession or something to be owned. And she owes you nothing.' *Would it be him or his enemy who would die that day …?*

'Edwin! *Edwin*!' Lily's voice was pleading, but it seemed to come from a very long way away.

'She ran away from me. I found her and she ran away again. And I found her again. And I will keep *on* finding her! That child is mine. I'll come for *that*, if I don't get the money.' The man glared at them for a moment, then turned and vaulted out of the window.

'Francis!' Lily dashed over to the window and peered out. She turned back to Edwin. 'He's gone – he's gone!'

'Lily …'

'Hello?' A little girl's voice echoed up the stair. 'The door was open, so I came in. Miss Valentine, are you available? I do need to speak to you quite urgently.'

'Elsie!' Lily looked at Edwin, horrified. 'She shouldn't be here. She—'

'—Lily. I need to know if he hurt you.' His voice was urgent and he took hold of her shoulders, looking intently into her eyes. 'Did he?'

'No! No, he didn't. But I'm afraid he might have done if you hadn't come in.' She started to shake a little and wrapped her arms around her body. 'Edwin, I don't have a thousand pounds! He's blackmailing me. He thinks I made a lot of money on the stage. And I didn't, I didn't make that much. I could give him five hundred, but what if that's not enough?

Edwin, I'm frightened he comes back for the baby. What if he does …?'

'Don't, don't think of that. Right now, I need to know if you're all right?' He stepped away from her and looked her up and down. 'The child?'

'Miss Valentine!' The little girl's voice was getting louder. She seemed to be pacing the downstairs, her smart little boots *tap tap tapping* around the floorboards.

'I'm all right. I promise. We both are.' She looked up at him, her eyes worried. 'He might come back, though. He always had a bad temper. His dark moods …'

'Lily, I need to find him. I'll stop him.'

'Edwin – please. I know. I just … don't know what to do about it.' She took a deep, shuddering breath. 'But …'

'Miss Valentine!' the door flung open and Lily clutched Edwin. He turned around and Elsie stood there, her boots now sturdily planted in the doorway. 'I *absolutely* wondered where you were. I'm so terribly sorry, but there is something I need to ask you. Nancy is very small, as you know, and I'm a little concerned that she does not quite understand the role we've decided upon for her.'

'Excuse me, Lady Elsie.' Edwin steadied his breathing and took the opportunity and bowed to her. 'I have business to attend to. Please, may I ask of you a favour? My wife is feeling a little under the weather, and I'm sure she would appreciate a little company. In fact, could I prevail upon you to take her to see your Aunt Alys? I'm sure she will be able to make her feel better.' He really didn't want her left alone with an eight-year-old. That wasn't fair on either of them.

He, on the other hand, needed to leave the Mill House and track Francis O'Hara down. He was torn – but if it was the only way to stop him, and he knew for certain Lily was going to be safe, he would do it.

Francis had dropped down from the windowsill and landed

on the frame of the water-wheel. Cursing, he balanced on the wooden structure for a moment, then dived off. He could hear their voices above him through the window, and they disgusted him.

She was his wife, carrying his child, and she was living in sin with half a man. He didn't care that he was a soldier; he cared that he was using her as she was using him, making free of her body in that way *he* should be using it.

Once he got that money, he would leave. He wanted nothing to do with the brat and nothing to do with *her*. She'd never loved him, not really. She'd loved the stage and that lifestyle more – and she'd left him for that. She ran away and changed her name and tried to hide.

Well, he'd found the bitch again. That was a start.

But he had looked at that God-awful thing the Pencradoc brat had drawn and hated it. The photographs were worse. He'd stolen those as well, and he'd hidden them where they would never be found. Who the hell did that bitch Evelyn O'Hara think she was?

His lips twisted into a smile as he struck through the water and towards the shore by the waterfall. If he could get out there, he'd be hidden well enough. He could maybe hide out in one of the rough-hewn caves behind it for a day or so, then go back to the cellars of that Mill House. It was warm and dry there, and they'd never suspected he'd been there all the time, creeping through the house, looking through their possessions. Taking money. Taking things that belonged to her. Taking what he could.

He swam through the river and soon scrambled out on the shore, just beside the waterfall, slipping a little on the mud bank and swearing again.

But as he climbed up and hauled himself out onto the banks, he saw the man she'd been with, standing above him, glaring down at him.

Chapter Eighteen

Present Day

Matt was struggling, trying to get to that Mill House, gritting his teeth against the pain of his gammy ankle. He stopped, leaning against a tree, almost at the damn place as the pain seared up his leg. But he had to keep going – he just had to. It wasn't far now, and *she* was there. And she needed him, she needed him badly.

Him. Edwin Griffiths. And pray to God he found his cane soon – why the hell had he thought he could leave it behind? He hadn't gone far, but he still needed it and he cursed the weakness that defined him now ...

Matt snapped his head up, hanging onto the tree as his vision started to blur around the edges on the left side.

'Stupid. Don't be stupid.' He blinked, rubbed his eyes and looked around again. It was fine, all fine. But a cane – a cane would be a damn good idea.

Then he heard it. He heard the gun shot over at the Mill House, and all thoughts of his painful injury fled from his mind as he launched himself away from the tree and covered the ground he needed to, lurching that way, swearing each time his foot connected with the earth.

The door was damaged and flung wide open. All was darkness beyond, a strange miasma flitting around the building, like a grey mist creeping up from the ground and swirling around the open doorway—

'—Miss Valentine? Are you in there? I thought I saw a man ...'

From within the mist emerged a little girl, dark-haired, bright-eyed and dressed in a beautiful little red knee-length dress with gathered sleeves and a softly gathered bodice, a black ribbon tying her hair back, and black boots and black stockings.

She ran into the house in front of him, disappearing into the gloom.

He had no time to think about the little girl. Cordy was in there. She was in there and he had to reach her. He had to.

But his cane – thank God – there it was, just inside the door. He snatched it up.

As he stood for a brief second, getting his bearings, the little girl vanished into the dining room; then he heard the commotion upstairs. An anger erupted within him that he had no control over. But where she was concerned, he would do anything, absolutely anything that was needed.

Cursing himself, but unable to help the red-hot fury that was consuming him, he grabbed the handrail and hauled himself up the stairs, dreading what he might find up there but knowing he had to face it.

Lily needed him.

'Cordy! Cordy! Are you up there?' Matt reached the top of the staircase and saw the door open to one of the rooms. 'Cordy!' He barged into the room and what he saw made his skin crawl.

Cordy was in some sort of tussle with Rick Hoffman. She looked as if she was trying to get out of the window and screaming as the reporter reached out and tried to drag her back in. But it wasn't just Cordy and Rick he saw. He struggled to focus on them and, overlaid on the people he knew, were two blurred figures: a tall, well-built man, dressed in serviceable, labourer's clothes from a different era, and a red-haired woman in a long green dress – the red-haired woman he'd seen around the estate. This was unreal – what the hell was happening? The atmosphere was hideous, hatred and lust seeming to fill the room, emanating from the figures who were fighting one another

'Get off me! Get off!' Cordy was yelling at the man, trying her best to fight him off, but he wasn't going to capitulate.

'Hoffman! Leave her alone!' His ankle forgotten, Matt

launched himself at the man, but Rick was bigger than Matt, more well-built and a couple of inches taller to boot. He was an imposing figure, and Matt didn't want to think what he was capable of – but it wasn't him, was it? This wasn't Rick from *The Sunday Stage* – this was someone who was acting out of character, out of control.

Francis! Please!

Matt heard the voice as if it was a real person shouting in his ear – and he knew what he had to do.

This wasn't Rick Hoffman at all; it wasn't even Cordy. It was Lily Valentine and a man who was attacking her. A man called—

'*Francis O'Hara*! Get away from them!' Matt heard himself shouting the name, and he didn't even feel stupid doing it.

Then there was a shout from downstairs; a little girl's voice.

'*Hello? The door was open, so I came in ...*'

It was enough for Rick or Francis or whoever it was to pause and release Cordy long enough for her to wriggle free. Then, almost as if he had no control over it, and hoping Rick Hoffman would forgive him, Matt brought the cane down across his shoulders hard.

It was enough for Rick to gasp and shrink back a little. So Matt did it again, whacking the bigger man with the cane once more across his back, as he cowered away, swinging it for all he was worth, the thing landing hard on Rick's body.

Then Rick seemed to crumple and fall over, his face losing the horrible sneer and evil look behind the eyes and, suddenly, he was just a man again; a reasonably bruised and battered man by now, but definitely not the sinister person he had appeared to be moments ago.

'Matt! Thank God you found us.' Cordy threw herself at Matt, surprising him with the force of it. 'I've never been so scared in my entire life. I think he would have had me through that window if he could.'

'It wasn't him.' Matt held her close, his own mind whirring;

from his conversations with Kit and Coren, he knew there were dark secrets this beautiful house hung onto, until the time was right to throw them at you, and then it relied on you to bury them forever ... 'That wasn't Rick Hoffman.'

'It wasn't.' He was surprised at how readily she had agreed with him. 'I wasn't *me* either. I can't explain. But I think I was Lily. I was reliving something from her past that had happened, and it was obviously terrifying, and – well – the memory of it is still here.' She looked up at him, apprehension in her eyes. 'Does that sound weird? Am *I* weird?'

'No. Not at all.' He shook his head slowly, remembering the images and the feelings he had experienced in the Mill House and just outside it. 'Elsie!' He stared at Cordy, suddenly realising who the little girl had been. He clutched Cordy's arms. 'I saw Elsie. I—' Then he looked over at the silver-topped cane he had grabbed in the hallway. It was indeed a cane – not a branch, or a piece of wood. A genuine silver-topped cane decorated with a hornbill. How on earth had he grabbed that? It was awfully like the one he'd found outside his room. He tossed it onto the bed quickly, not really wanting to hang onto it in case he felt the urge to hit Rick again for any reason.

Instead, he looked around the bedroom they were in, trying to take in the details. It looked different – modern and freshly painted, despite the fact it currently looked as if a bomb had hit it . He could have sworn there had been heavy, old-fashioned furniture in here, and a blanket on the bed. 'I saw Elsie,' he said again, his voice quieter. 'She more or less told me to come up here.'

'Was that the little girl who shouted, just before?' Cordy's face was confused. 'I thought I heard someone, before you waded in.'

'Yes. I think so.' He looked at her. 'But Elsie was a grown woman when she died – years after Lily Valentine was here. So why on earth would there be a ... *ghost* Elsie ... here?'

'I don't think she was a ghost. I think she was part of the

memories here. A memory of this horrible incident.' Cordy shuddered, and Matt pulled her closer. 'It's like they were all replaying that scene – like a hideous encore. Good God – the first day I was here, I thought I saw something up in that window.'

'Me too.' Matt's voice was a whisper. 'Perhaps we just happened to be here – all three of us – and we gave Francis the chance to try again properly.'

'Of course – Francis!' Cordy let go of Matt and dropped to her knees beside Rick. He moaned a little, coming around from whatever spell he'd been under, and opened his eyes. Even Matt could see that the manic look had definitely vanished from them, and he was just blinking in apparent confusion as he took stock of his surroundings. 'Cordy? Where am I? What am I doing here?'

'Yes, it's me. I was walking past and I heard a crash from outside. You're in the Mill House – upstairs. It looks like you fell over something – maybe you bumped your head, perhaps? Can you sit up? The room looks a bit … well … messed up.'

And the room did look messed up, with the chair upside down halfway across the floor and the other furniture and items that were neatly placed there scattered everywhere. If one didn't think about it too hard, it was relatively believable that a man had wandered up here, caught his foot on something and tripped over, knocking the furniture awry as he did so.

But beyond that, Matt was stunned at how Cordy managed to sound as if nothing was wrong; yet moments before, Rick Hoffman had been trying to push her out of a window. Well – she was an actress, he supposed.

'Wow. Okay. Yes. I can sit up – I'm a bit sore. Feel like I've gone ten rounds in a boxing match.' Rick grimaced and rolled his shoulders, wincing. 'I think there was a man in here who pushed me or hit me or something. I vaguely saw him, but couldn't really describe him, I don't think.'

Matt looked away, knowing he should really keep quiet.

Then something caught his eye – a black mass that evolved in the corner of the room, turned into the shape of a man, then melted away, floating outside the window and hovering just outside.

This wasn't great. This wasn't great at all.

1895

'You need to leave, Mr O'Hara.' Edwin's voice was quiet and steady. He stared at the man. 'Shall I escort you from Pencradoc?'

O'Hara glared at him for a moment, dripping wet, his roughly cut hair sleek against his skull. 'No.' He spoke through gritted teeth, his voice dripping venom. 'I'm here for what's mine.'

'Are you quite sure about that, Mr O'Hara?'

'Quite sure.' O'Hara balled his fists and Edwin knew that the man was already sizing him up, judging how best to tackle him.

'You don't have a gun now, sir. I wouldn't recommend attacking me.'

'And what can you do to stop me?' the man hissed.

Edwin closed his fingers around the carved hornbill on the top of his cane and pulled. The sword that was hidden inside glinted in the sunlight bouncing off the waterfall. A muscle in O'Hara's cheek twitched faintly, and Edwin allowed himself a small smile.

'A pretty little thing. Yet I'm not leaving, *sir*. Where I come from, they say that a man may live after losing his life, but not after losing his honour. She took that honour away from me when she went away, but even if you killed me here, aye, I'd live on in that babby. And as it grew, every time you looked at it, every time you noticed it, you'd think of me. You may kill me, sir,' here he bowed mockingly, 'but I'd still be here.'

'No, you wouldn't. I was with her before you came back.

That child is nothing to do with you. It's mine. You're just passing through her life, as you always have done. So now it's time for *you* to leave. Sir.'

A strange expression flickered across O'Hara's face as he apparently processed that information, then he spoke: 'You lie. She said she'd had nobody since me.'

'She's an actress. Accustomed to telling the sad little men in her orbit what they want to hear, to make them leave. I, Mr O'Hara, do not lie. I'm a soldier. And more honourable than you could ever hope to be.'

O'Hara spat at Edwin; clearly for want of a reasoned response. But Edwin kept his expression calm and composed. He wasn't letting this miserable creature in. He'd faced worse abroad. This was only one man. *One man*. Not an army.

Yet, in his mind, it was the most important battle he'd ever faced.

O'Hara seemed to tense up, and Edwin knew the signs; knew he'd make his attack on him – yet in fact, if he turned and ran, there was no way Edwin could catch him. The man would be a fool if he launched his attack that way. An utter fool.

'Used to be a soldier, perhaps. Now, you're just an old, washed-up half a man,' growled O'Hara. 'You might have been a threat once – but look at you now. Just look at you. She wouldn't have gone with you. She wanted a *man*. Not a cripple.'

'I wanted *him*. Not a *slíbhín*. Not you. Never again.'

Edwin turned quickly, towards the sound of her voice. He'd never heard that word before – *sleeveen*. He didn't know what it meant, but he doubted it was flattering. Although he didn't have much time to ponder the issue as Lily was holding a gun, the gun O'Hara had left in the Mill House. And she was pointing it straight at O'Hara.

'Leave. Just leave now and never come back.' Her voice was steel.

'Lynnie ...' O'Hara's voice was wheedling now.

'I'm not Lynnie. I haven't been Lynnie for a long time. Just go, Frankie.'

But O'Hara just held her gaze and shook his head slowly. 'No. No I won't. We both know *that's* mine.' He pointed his forefinger at her stomach. 'And *he's* going to die today. A quick death and an easy one. For me, anyway.'

It all seemed to happen in one split-second – the world slowed down and O'Hara leapt towards him. There was a bang as Lily pulled the trigger and shot the gun. Edwin didn't know if it had found its mark or not, but it was enough to throw O'Hara off balance—

The sound of the gunfire and the relentless thundering of the waterfall drowned out all rational thoughts, and suddenly he was back there, back on the Semantan front, facing the Malay rebellion again ...

He must have raised the swordstick. He must have struck his target because, impassively, he watched the man's expression slide into shock and horror as he grasped the blade which was now buried in his abdomen, his face inches from Edwin's.

Francis O'Hara swore and staggered backwards as Edwin roughly pulled the blade from his flesh and stepped to one side. O'Hara fell to the ground choking, blood pooling on his clothing, from the wound itself and from the cuts on his hands where he had grabbed the blade. And more than that; there was a gunshot wound that had clearly ripped through his body. He started coughing up more blood and collapsed onto his side.

As he rolled over to, perhaps, try and stand and barge at Edwin one final time, he slipped. The side of the riverbank crumbled and O'Hara howled, like an animal in pain, as he tumbled down to the river in a mess of rocks and mud.

There was another scream and Edwin was vaguely aware of Lily hurtling towards him.

But he was frozen to the spot, unable to move, still clutching the blade in his hand, staring at the spot where the man had fallen ... and as the red mist cleared, the sudden silence pressed down on the world around him, broken only by the relentless rushing of the river and the tumbling of the waterfall.

But then one sound invaded the stillness, more horrific than before – the sound of a gurgling scream, the sound of the water-wheel crushing something between its massive teeth, almost grinding to a halt – then lurching back into life.

And Edwin found himself staring almost blindly downriver towards the wheel, then staring at Lily, not quite sure what had happened.

'Edwin – Edwin!' Lily held onto his arms, almost shaking him, almost terrified by the man who seemed to be looking at her instead of the Edwin she knew; the gentle, caring man she had found herself more and more drawn to over the last few months. 'Edwin.' She shook his arm one more time.

'Lily? Lily! What are you doing here? You should be with Alys ...'

'I shouldn't be with Alys. I should be with you. With you. If I had been with Alys, then he would have ... he might have ...' She couldn't finish the sentence.

He seemed to be trying to focus on her, to come back from wherever he'd been. 'But Elsie. She was taking you to Alys.'

'She was going to, but I sent her on ahead. I said I'd follow once I'd spoken to you.' She laughed, bitterly. 'I told her I was going to talk to you about taking a larger part in the production, and I didn't want her to be with us when I asked, because you might feel obliged and you had been very tired recently ...' Again her voice trailed away. 'And it was a lie and I didn't like lying to her but I had to. I had to, you see, because I knew what he would do.' She felt the tears begin and then his arms came around her and she lay against him, closing her eyes and letting the tears flow. 'And the water-wheel, Edwin. The water-wheel—'

'—I know. I know, my love. Don't look. He's gone. He won't hurt you again.'

'But the water-wheel. The Mill House. How can we explain that away? How can we tell them what happened?'

'But what *did* happen, Lily? What exactly *happened*?'

Lily looked up at him in shock, wondering whether he genuinely didn't know, genuinely couldn't recall what he had done. What they had both done.

Then she saw that it wasn't that sort of question. More so, that he was asking what story they could invent to explain the crushed remains of her husband, which were, even now she assumed, trapped in the mechanism of the huge wooden wheel, turning and turning until there was nothing human to be seen of him any more.

She took a deep, shuddering breath. 'He fell. It's quite clear that the edge of the pathway here has disintegrated. He was swept away downstream. He couldn't fight the current. It's not a lie.'

'He couldn't fight the current. No. He couldn't. Did you see it happen?' He looked at her sharply. 'Or did I?'

'We both did. He fell, and I screamed, and you tried to save him – but obviously neither of us could do it. I'm with child and you're still recovering.' She met his eye brazenly. 'But we tried. And we think he was a casual labourer, a traveller with no family we could contact. We didn't see him clearly enough.'

'No. But we need to report the accident. And necessary steps will have to be taken.'

'Yes.' She was silent for a moment, then took a deep breath and was surprised at how steady her voice was. 'Was it my bullet or your sword that killed him, Edwin?'

'Neither.' His gaze burned into hers. 'He died by drowning. And he was crushed further beneath the machinery.'

Neither one of them mentioned that bloodcurdling scream, just before the wheel ground its prey into a pulp.

'Yes. Yes. I agree. We have to keep the girls away from here. We can't let them see anything.'

Edwin pulled her closer. 'They'll see nothing, my love. We'll go and tell Jago now.'

Lily nodded. 'Thank you, Edwin.' Her voice was a whisper. 'He would have come back, you know. We would never have been free of him.'

'I know. But we're free now.'

'We are.' And she looked up at him, and suddenly the gap was closed between them and her lips were on his, and they kissed one another as if their very lives and loves depended on it.

And who knew, she thought as she fell, finally, into the abyss of emotion, gratitude and an all-consuming love for him – perhaps their lives had depended on it, and always would?

Chapter Nineteen

Present Day

Cordy patted Rick awkwardly on the arm, knowing that if she patted his back, she would probably hurt him even more where Matt had whacked him with that cane – it didn't really cross her mind to think about where the cane had come from. Just an item in the house, probably, to make it more authentic-looking. Maybe they'd used the one from the corridor, the one she'd seen when she'd helped Matt set up his workspace.

But what she did want to think about, and to concentrate a little on, was Francis O'Hara and the mysterious Lynnie. And Evelyn – hadn't he called her Evelyn at one point as well? Those names had come at her in a flash, even as she was reliving Lily's moments in the house, and now that she felt much safer with Matt here and Rick Hoffman being – well, just Rick Hoffman – her thoughts came back to them.

'Lynnie – it's not a million miles away from … *Lynnie*! Of course. *Evelyn*!' She looked up at Matt, light-headed suddenly, as the pieces fit together with a massive clunk. 'Evelyn and Lily. They're one and the same! God, why didn't I think of that before? Lily appeared in England, and Evelyn disappeared from Ireland! That's why there's no record of Edwin Griffiths and Lily Valentine marrying – she would have had to use her real name: Evelyn. I suppose the census with their children on didn't matter so much! It all makes sense now. Good grief!'

'And Francis. Where does he fit in?' Matt stared at her, and she saw the ideas and theories passing across his face as the pieces fitted together in his mind too.

'He was Evelyn's husband. And he came looking for her.'

'Hey – excuse me. Sorry, guys, but is it okay if I try to stand up? Wouldn't mind a Paracetamol to be honest.' Of course; poor Rick was still sitting on the floor.

'God! Sorry – yes. Come on – take my hand. Let's get you up onto the bed. You can sit there for a minute. Then when you feel up to it, we can take you back to the house. Are you dizzy at all?'

'Dizzy? No.' Rick shook his head in surprise. 'I feel fine – apart from the aches and pains in my shoulders. That fellow must have hit me with something then got out the window. That's what I want the tablet for.'

'Wow.' Cordy stared at him, her brain working quickly. 'Well, maybe you didn't really get a bump on the head. Maybe he just lashed out and ran away. A local kid, probably, meddling where he shouldn't be. But I can't comment as I wasn't in here.'

'Weird.' Rick shook his head again and stood up. 'Everything else fine. Not bleeding anywhere, am I?'

'Nope.' Cordy felt her cheeks heat up. 'Do you want to see a doctor at all? Get yourself checked out, just in case.'

Rick thought for a moment. 'Maybe it's best – but really. I feel fine. Look – I know you're a busy lady today. I don't want to take up any more of your time. It will have been a local kid, I'm willing to bet on it. I probably scared him off. I was like that when I was younger – always getting into places I shouldn't. Being places I had no need be, with people I had no reason to be with. One of the reasons I'm in this job.' He shrugged. 'And like I said, I'd go for a drink with you but, well, probably not great timing today.' He attempted a smile, and Cordy knew he was joking. He didn't, all things being equal and the shadows of the past notwithstanding, seem the type to be put out that a woman wouldn't go on a date with him.

'Honestly – it's fine. I'll call Merryn and see if someone can come and get you.' Cordy flashed a glance at Matt. 'Are you okay to wait here? I just need to call her.'

'Sure.' Matt nodded, but there was still a strange look on his face. He lowered his voice. 'Just ... stay inside the house when you ring, yes?' He nodded again, almost imperceptibly to the open window, then lowered his mouth to her ear as if he was going to kiss her gently on the neck as she went. 'Francis might still be here. I saw him go out there.'

Then he did drop a kiss on her neck and, despite the deliciously shivery sensation it set off in her body, her heart lurched. Her attacker was still here.

'Okay.' She walked out of the room, trying to look as if she was in control and not actually wanting to run screaming back to safety. Francis was still here – and the next time he tried to attack her, or Lily, or Evelyn or whomsoever she was meant to be, she might not be so lucky.

Heading downstairs, Cordy took refuge in the dining room. She closed the door, for what use that would be, and walked to the window as she dialled Merryn's number, praying that her friend would answer quickly. And she did, thank God. 'Merryn? We're at the Mill House. Rick from *The Sunday Stage* has had a bit of an accident.' She closed her eyes, silently praying that God would forgive her for lying in that instance. 'He swears he's okay, but I think he needs to see a doctor or go to hospital.'

'Oh no! Poor man. What happened?'

'We're not sure.' *Another lie.* 'We – Matt and I – were just at the Mill House and we heard a noise like a crash from upstairs. We went in and found him in the bedroom. Perhaps he was trying to get a photo for an article? He's a big chap – he might have bumped his head on a beam, or tripped over a carpet, or fell over a chair ...' *Stop. Just stop. You'll go too far! Just keep it simple!* she warned herself, and clamped her lips together.

'Right. Thanks. I know you've got your show to prepare for, but can you stay with him until we get there? Kit or Coren can take him to hospital.'

'Sure, yes. I honestly think he's okay, but you know ...' she trailed off.

'It's best to check. See you soon.' Merryn rang off, and Cordy tucked her phone back in her pocket. She turned back to the door and saw the little side table in the hall, just next to it. On it was something that looked very familiar indeed: the marriage certificate from Ireland.

'What the …?' She hurried over and picked it up. There was something scrawled across it, inked in copperplate.

Burn it.

'Burn what?' Cordy stared at the document, reading the words over and over, wondering what on earth it meant – and, more to the point, who had written it. And with what? There was no pen around. This was too much – too confusing – and the outlandish thoughts she was conjuring up were making her head hurt.

'*The marriage lines. Evelyn's story. My story.*' The voice was Irish, soft yet firm, coming from nowhere and everywhere, all at the same time. Cordy was frozen to the spot, clutching the certificate for dear life. There was absolutely nobody else in the room with her.

'Your story, Lily? But surely you did what you had to do,' whispered Cordy, still looking around the room, panicked. 'You needed to survive.'

'*I did. And I survived. But Evelyn O'Hara has been gone for a very long time. Please. Burn it.*' Then she appeared, right in front of Cordy; a shimmering, red-haired beauty wearing a green satin dress, identical to the one that had swept past her on the stage, the one she'd glimpsed in the gardens of Pencradoc. '*He needs to go. I need him gone. And you do too.*'

Cordy suddenly understood – she didn't know how she understood, but she did. The marriage certificate was the source of all this negativity. Francis, Lily's ex-husband, was clinging on to the past through that marriage certificate and he was never going to let it go – ever.

Destroying it was the only way to break his hold on Lily, on the Mill House and whatever he was lurking around Pencradoc for.

'Good God.' Cordy blinked, holding the spirit's direct gaze.

Strangely, she wasn't scared or freaked out. Lily was just ... there. And considering Cordy had walked in Lily's beautiful shoes not so long ago, she knew what she had to do and why. 'All right,' she whispered. 'I will.'

She looked around, wondering how she could burn the papers. Matches. There might be matches in the kitchen – so she opened the door quietly and headed back in. Rummaging through the drawers, one eye on the door and one ear on the men upstairs, just in case they shouted for her, she eventually found what she was looking for.

The kitchen door opened onto a small, terraced rock garden that led to the river – but she wasn't going outside. Not when Francis might still be lurking, when Matt had warned her as much. Her stomach turned over at the thought of that. Instead, she found a small earthenware bowl. That would do.

Much as it pained her to do this to something so old and delicate, she knew she had to. It wasn't a happy piece of paper. It was full of bad energy – she could almost feel it coming off the thing in waves; the hatred, the despair, the jealousy – ugh. Nobody, she realised suddenly, had even wanted to get married. They'd been forced down that route to save Evelyn's family's reputation. And he had used that certificate as leverage to – what? To blackmail Lily? To come after her, and scare her, and try to claim part of her fortune?

No. It had to be destroyed. Lily, she understood, did not want that secret exposed to anyone.

She struck a match and held it to the corner of the certificate.

Once the flames had begun to lick at it, she tossed it quickly into the bowl where it shrivelled and blackened.

There was a huge *whoosh* as the certificate seemed to ignite more than it would seem possible for a bit of paper, and Cordy swore, fumbling to unlock the back door before the smoke alarm started alerting everyone upstairs. She wanted it to burn and to burn well away from here – she wasn't even going to put it in the sink and turn the taps on.

When the door was open, she grabbed a pair of jaunty, pristine oven gloves that were hooked around the Aga and picked up the bowl, putting it quickly down on the little patio area where the flames seemed to get a new lease of life.

'Shit!' she stepped outside, meaning to use her toes to nudge the thing away from the house, when a big, black shape started forming out of the smoke. Her heart turned over as the thing seemed to evolve into the figure of a man, its arms reaching out for her. Its head seemed to develop features that glowed in the blackness – two bright red eyes and a mouth that opened in a silent scream.

But there was nothing silent about her scream as she yelled out in horror when it flew towards her—

'I've got you!' She'd never been so grateful to hear a man's voice before – and Matt's was the most welcome thing she could ever have imagined at that point. He grabbed her around the waist and pulled her forcibly into the house. Somehow, as she was being dragged backwards, she managed to slam the door shut – just in time, it seemed, as the thing flew at her, then engulfed the pane of glass in the door with blackness and red hell-fire, it's eyes burning into hers as she turned her face away and screamed again into Matt's shoulder.

1895

It seemed that nobody was going to mention the unfortunate incident with the water-wheel any more. Alys had clasped her hand over her mouth when they told her, and Jago had put his arm supportively around his wife.

The colour had drained from both the Duke and the Duchess's face as Lily faltered prettily over the storyline and Edwin supported her in the same way. She had been the obvious choice to tell the tale as Edwin leaned on his cane heavily, a man clearly in shock.

'I did see some terrible things in the war,' he told them.'

Things I never wish to speak of or think of again, and that – that just brought the memories back.'

'Oh Lily. What a dreadful, dreadful shock. Are you *truly* all right? I'm so worried about that little baby. I'm going to call the doctor, just to be sure.'

Alys was sweetly concerned, touching Lily's arm, but Lily simply shook her head. 'He's a fighter,' she said, 'just like his papa. We'll be all right.'

It was the most bizarre conversation Lily had ever had. She felt as if she was floating somewhere above it all, watching it as a member of the audience. She half-expected a round of applause at the end.

There was no applause, of course. Just a lot of people coming and going, taking information from them. The doctor confirmed the baby was, happily, quite safe. And, finally, people were brought in to deal with the wheel itself.

'I want it fixed in place,' Jago instructed. 'I can't take the risk of any of the girls falling in like that and being swept away.' The girls did enjoy paddling in a basin of water a little way from the top of the water-wheel, but it was shallow and safe and they were never unsupervised. The incident with the labourer just threw them all into discord.

'You must of course come and stay in Pencradoc itself for now,' Alys said. 'Wheal Mount will be ready very soon, and we have plenty of room there if you wish to come with us. You can't possibly stay at the Mill House after such a thing.'

'We won't be staying on much longer anyway,' Edwin told her with a smile. 'It's time we went home. Lily and I have discussed it. We have agreed that we need to build our own life and prepare for the child. If we do that now, we have four months or so before it arrives.'

They'd also agreed to share Lily's bed.

The day Francis had died, after they broke the news to Alys and Jago, they had taken a carriage to a deserted yet beautiful spot on Bodmin Moor. Edwin had driven and they had barely spoken; two lost souls, it seemed, knowing what would happen when they got there. And knowing, also, that it had to happen – it was the only way they knew they could deal with it; the only way they could seal the dark bond that they'd created that day.

And the inevitable *had* happened, with the scents of summer all around them and the warm breeze tickling their bare flesh as they carefully undressed each other. She had kissed his scars, and he had kissed the curve of her stomach and they had taken their time with one another.

It had been perfect. Everything, in fact, that she had ever dreamed of.

'It's not like last time, is it?' she had murmured into the crook of his neck as they lay close together, a blanket covering them, his arm around her protectively.

'No. Because this time I'm making love to my wife and she's carrying my child and we know it's going to be forever.'

'Your wife.' Lily laughed. 'Of course.'

Her mind drifted back to Paris – to a man sitting in the audience night after night, damaged beyond what he deemed repair, mentally and physically. To the bunches of lilies at the stage door. To the times she smiled at him, to the times he waited for her …

To that one time where they talked all night and those two lost souls had found themselves briefly again, and how one thing led to another. Then she had sneaked away in the morning, assuming he would never want to see her again.

And two days later, Francis had appeared.

She chose not to think of that – chose not to relive the horror and the shame of what he had done to her. Chose instead to think about the damaged man who had come back to the Opera House four weeks later, full of remorse for what he himself had done, saying he had barely been out of his lodgings, guilty as hell, battling his demons and unsure of what to do. He had made himself visit her, wanting to apologise to her and ask how could he ever make it up to her? It was around that time that she'd started to suspect she was with child – and she prayed, oh she genuinely did pray, it was Edwin's, although she felt her God had deserted her long ago.

It was soon after, once she knew she was pregnant, that she had confessed the full horror of her situation to him, and he had proposed to her. It wasn't the most romantic or magical proposal in the world at all. Rather, it was a practical solution and a way out. She had snatched the opportunity with both hands, not knowing what she was thinking really.

She flushed with sheer embarrassment and hated herself for using him as she had done. She had never considered him, never thought how he might feel if he knew what was in her mind. She was a terrible, terrible person. She was still, underneath it all, the wild, selfish, uncouth Evelyn O'Hara, the girl who went with men for her own gains, who cursed and shouted and hit back when she was provoked.

But was standing up for oneself a bad thing? Was it so wrong to be her own person? It didn't seem like such a bad thing now – not when she could appreciate who she was and how she had got here. Not now she had Edwin in her life. Not now they shared the most twisted secret of all. Not now they had both been party to a murder—

'—Lily, how long were you living with Francis?' The question broke into her darkest thoughts and took her by surprise.

'With Francis?' She blushed. 'Three years. It was three years before I left him. I married him when I was seventeen. We'd been together a year before that.'

'Hmm.' Then Edwin, surprisingly, turned to her, a wicked glint in his eye and a half-smile playing around his lips. 'I'm just thinking how highly likely it is that it *is* my child, then.' He flipped onto his back again and stared up to the sky. 'Not that it matters to me one bit. It's just a good way to look at the situation, isn't it?'

And Lily, despite herself laughed. 'Yes. Yes it is.'

And they went on to look at the situation in a good way several more times ...

Chapter Twenty

'I've got you. I've got you ...'

Cordy's face was buried against his T-shirt as the demon or whatever it was slammed against the window, then scattered into grey ash with one final contorted expression. Even as it broke apart and fell harmlessly past the window like snow, Matt's heart was thumping and he wondered if he'd ever be able to get the image of that thing out of his head.

'Matt. Did you see it? Did you *see* it?'

Cordy was shaking, and he held her close until she calmed down. 'I did,' he said. 'It's not something I want to see again.'

'What was it? Was it ... Francis?' Cordy pulled away and looked up at him.

The words sounded so strange and so surreal when Cordy asked that, but all he could do was nod. 'I think so. I don't think it was – *him* – exactly. More like, I don't know, a bundle of his emotions. His jealousy, his brutality – who knows? I don't think he was a particularly nice guy. I think those were the emotions attached to whatever you ignited there.'

'It was the marriage certificate. She asked me ... Lily asked me ...' Her voice trailed away and she flushed. 'I mean, I thought it best to destroy it. So nobody found out.'

'Odd how that certificate got to the Mill House, isn't it?' He didn't mention Lily's intervention.

'Very odd.' She compressed her lips and pulled away from him. 'Either a ghost brought it here, or, more likely, our friend the reporter did.' She paled. 'God. What if he knows what it was? We have to stop him printing that story—'

Matt lowered his voice, just in case. 'I don't think we're in any danger of that. I don't think he knows what the hell he's doing here, never mind what he did when he got here. He's

224

still in the bedroom. I came down to see if you'd managed to contact Merryn – and well. I saw … that.' He nodded towards the kitchen door and he felt Cordy shudder in his arms.

'I don't want to see anything like that ever again,' she said. 'I just wanted the stuff out the house. The flames …'

'Yep. They were pretty impressive. But you got it outside and Francis, or whatever that thing was, didn't get into the house.'

'Thank God. I—'

But whatever she was going to say was interrupted by the front door opening and agitated voices. It sounded like a whole crowd of people bursting into the Mill House. Cordy wriggled out of Matt's arms, and he understood why – no way did they want to be discovered in a clinch that could well be misinterpreted.

Quickly, Cordy grabbed a glass from the bench and turned the tap on. She began to fill the glass and called 'In here!' Matt was sure he was the only one who would notice the slight trembling in her hand. Once again, he had to remind himself she was an actress and combating stage fright was probably second nature to her. 'Just getting Rick some water – he's upstairs.'

Merryn, Coren and, surprisingly, Sybill all burst into the kitchen.

'Cordy! Matt – thank goodness you were here,' said Merryn. 'Is he all right?'

'He says so. But it's best to check. I was just going to take this up. We'll come with you.' Cordy's expression showed just the right amount of concern and brisk efficiency, and Matt was impressed. 'He said he thought it was a kid exploring where he shouldn't be and he got a shock when Rick turned up. He's long gone, whoever he is.' *And how right that was!*

'Little horror. Oh well, no harm done, unless we count poor old Rick,' said Merryn. 'Coren said he'll take him to A&E, just to be safe.'

'I said I'd go too – keep them both company,' added Sybill. 'And back-up is always good.' She smiled and whispered to Matt. 'Coren's a chap – it's not that I don't trust him to be *nice* to Rick, but sometimes the softer people skills escape him.'

'I'll take you guys upstairs then,' said Cordy, nodding to Coren and Sybill. 'Come on.'

She cast a glance at Matt, and he half-smiled and nodded. 'I'll stay here. It's not a huge bedroom, after all.'

He waited until they'd gone, then made to walk out of the room with Merryn, but his ankle gave way again and he sucked in a gasp of pain.

'Matt! What on *earth* have you done?' Merryn looked at him, horrified. 'You're hurting somewhere. Do *you* need to go to A&E too?'

'I turned my ankle a bit. It's fine. Honestly. And anyway.' He felt his cheeks heat up. 'I really want to be around to see the show. If it's still sore later, I'll think about it.'

'Matt!' Merryn tutted and shook her head. 'Can't you be persuaded otherwise? It might be worse than you think.'

'I just twisted it – it's a sprain. If I had an ice-pack, I'd use it. I know the drill.'

'But you don't have an ice-pack.'

'True.'

Merryn tutted again and studied him, then seemed to give up on the argument. 'Sit down. Just as well I've brought the first aid kit, isn't it? We'll strap it up for now, and see how you go. Wanting to see the show? My arse. It's Cordy you want to see, isn't it?'

Merryn pressed down on Matt's shoulder, forcing him to sit down. He wasn't going to deny it. It was true. So he just grinned apologetically at Merryn who rolled her eyes and shook her head and made him put his foot up on a stool while she felt the ankle and bandaged it tightly.

But no way was he missing this show – no way on this

earth. And if he had to submit to Merryn's ministrations to get there, he damn well would.

Even though she wasn't exactly the gentlest of nurses.

'So here he is. This is Rick. Not sure if you guys have met?' Cordy nodded across at Coren and Sybill. 'This is Coren, our manager and joint owner of Pencradoc, and Sybill, our friend from Wheal Mount.' She was surprised at how much better she felt, just by knowing there were more people here. And the atmosphere seemed to suggest that Francis had well and truly gone.

She prayed he was gone for good.

He has.

The words were for her alone, judging by the fact nobody else in the room seemed to acknowledge the voice. But Lily Valentine had one more thing to say:

May the road rise up to meet you. And may the sun shine warm upon your face …

Cordy felt her eyes widen as she searched the room in vain for the woman. There was, perhaps, the briefest shaft of sunlight flickering through the open window, and the curtains lifted ever so gently. She thought that might be Lily, trapped in a memory here from when she was a young woman, part of her forced to replay it again and again until someone … removed her ex-husband from the equation. Well, she was free now. She could forget it all.

But Sybill was talking to Rick, and Coren was looking around the room, straightening things out that Rick had – allegedly – disturbed as he fell, and then he looked at the dress which was still draped over the chair.

'That's yours, yes?' Coren asked.

'What? Oh – the dress?'

'Well not the chair.' Coren broke into a rare smile. 'Unless you carried your own seating down from the house?'

'Oh. Ha! No – definitely not the chair.' Cordy looked at

227

the dress. It was definitely the same fabric as the one she had loaned from Sybill. The same colour. The same ribbons that she could see trimming it ...

She moved across to double-check, but somehow she was reluctant to pick it up and shake it out – not with Coren and Sybill there. 'I – I brought it with me to try on. You know –a bit of method-acting to try and get into character before the show. With Lily being a guest here, I thought I might pick up some vibes, you know. Really get into her head ...' Her voice trailed away when she saw the odd look on Coren's face.

'Right. Okay. You're the expert on acting. I don't really understand all that. What I do know is that we'll get Rick here away and let you get back into character, or whatever you need to do.'

'I'm fine,' protested Rick. 'Just a bit spaced out. I mean I can remember coming in here, but not how I ended up on the floor ...' He looked around the room.

'All the more reason to go and get checked out,' said Sybill efficiently. 'Come on. We brought the car along the back lane so we can head to A&E straight away.'

And with that, Rick was ushered out of the bedroom, escorted downstairs and, presumably, bundled into the waiting car as there was a slamming of doors and raised voices – including Matt's, surprisingly – and then the roar of an engine, followed by the sound of the engine fading as the car drove away.

Which only left Cordy with the dress, all green and shimmery, and still draped across the chair.

'Is everything all right in here?' Merryn's voice behind her made her jump. 'I've just patched Matt up. He's determined to hang around and see your show, for some reason.' There was amusement in her words and Cordy turned around.

'Determined. I thought he would be. Even though I've probably made his day more dramatic than ever before the bloody show has even started.'

'It's nice that he's so enthusiastic. But I've banned him from coming back upstairs for now. He needs to keep the weight off his ankle as much as possible. They took him back to the house on their way to hospital. You probably heard him complaining – I think he thought they'd spirit him away to A&E with poor Rick. God, it's never straightforward, is it? Such drama, as you say. It must be you being an actress that attracts it.'

Merryn grinned but Cordy couldn't even bring herself to respond to the teasing. 'Whatever.'

'Ouch.' Merryn didn't sound that stung, really, but instead came up to Cordy and hugged her. 'You want to tell me what's really going on? Ooh – look, a nice cane. I think we can give that to Sir Matthew Hop Along.' She walked over to the bed and picked it up, weighing it in her hands. 'He could prove rather dashing, hobbling to your show. Bless him. Just like Lily's husband. We could give him an eye-patch too.'

'An eye-patch? And a cane?' Cordy stared at her friend in disbelief. 'I don't think Lily's husband had any of those?' She shuddered slightly, remembering the scenario that had unfolded not so long ago in this room. A man incapacitated like that couldn't really fight the way Francis had.

'Oh we think that he did. We know Edwin Griffiths was an ex-soldier.' *Of course.* Merryn meant Edwin, didn't she? 'Poor Edwin had been injured, so it's very possible. After Lily came here, you know that she sort of retired from the stage – she had a baby not so long after her visit, which was probably why – and Sybill's been rummaging through the archives at Wheal Mount to find things we can enhance the exhibition with. Anyway, she's found a letter from Elsie to her Aunt Alys, saying how delighted she had been to hear from Lily for her birthday, and that she'd never forget the magical summer pageant where they first met and how very happy they all were. She goes on to say something like how Mr Griffiths is walking so much better now, but it's a shame his poor eye will never get well again, but they can still tell Mabel he's a dashing pirate, so all is good.'

'Oh, to be as innocent as those children,' murmured Cordy. 'I really can't tell you right now what's going on, because the honest answer is, I don't know. I do know that we need to get ready for this damn play though.' She scowled and picked up the dress.

Shaking it out, she watched the fabric shimmer and unfurl ... and then cried out in horror as she saw how the skirt was all slashed and cut to ribbons, and hung there as limp as a dish-rag, instead of the beautiful swishy garment it had been.

'Oh my *God*! What's happened to it?' Cordy despaired as she stared at the shredded material. The bodice was fine – the damage was to the skirt. Someone had clearly lost their temper and taken it out on the frock.

Francis.

Or – and she felt a little sick as she realised what might have happened – Rick had done Francis' bidding. He must have taken it from her room and brought it here. The mess he'd made of it was a warning to her – a warning to let her, or Lily, more likely, know that he was here. He was around and he had access to her belongings, and *this* was what he thought of her new life.

'Bloody hell, Cordy! Something tells me it wasn't like that when Sybill gave it to you?' Merryn was just as shocked. 'Who would have done that? God! When did you last see it in one piece?'

'At Pencradoc. Last night. I just picked it up to bring with me this morning ... I ... I ...' But it was no good. She couldn't continue lying to her friend. Not about that, at least. Cordy shook her head. 'No. That's not true. I did see it last night, and it was in my room – but I didn't bring it here. It was on the chair when we ... I ... found Rick.' She lowered her gaze. 'I've no idea how it got here. I have no idea how it got damaged.' She raised her eyes and met Merryn's. 'I think I'm ready to believe your ghost stories, Merryn. I can't talk about it now, but I think I've sensed Lily around. I know you said it's happened before here. But there's too much I can't explain and can't rationalise. I—'

'—Don't say any more.' Cordy was spared from voicing the rest of her concerns and, therefore, potentially letting Merryn know about Lily's past life and Francis' behaviour, by her friend touching her arm and squeezing it. 'I don't want to know. I don't *need* to know. If I did – I would.'

'But—'

'No. Whatever Lily has or hasn't done, I'm damn sure she wouldn't have done this.' Merryn paused and fingered the fabric. 'It's the work of someone who is jealous. I'm not sure how we can pass this off to Sybill, but I think I know a way we can use it in the play.' Merryn frowned. 'Thank God Sybill and Coren are away with that poor man, they …' She paused, then shook her head almost imperceptibly. Cordy knew that one of the pennies, at least, may have dropped. She remained silent, and Merryn picked up her train of thought, perhaps a little too brightly, but Cordy wasn't going to stop her. '… they won't be able to see the mess of it. But I think we have a way to salvage it. I'm going to turn it into a fairy costume for the play – we'll rip it up a bit more and pin some lace and stuff on, and make it more old-fashioned yet floaty. Perhaps chop a bit of the length so it's uneven and looks more like petals. I've got some stuff back at the house. Come on. Let's go.'

'At least she said we could customise it,' said Cordy wryly. 'I hope she doesn't get upset.'

'She won't.' Merryn shook her head as if that was an end to the matter and began to lead the way out of the room. 'She'll just have to understand it needed to happen. You needed to be in character for Lily Valentine.'

Cordy shuddered again as she followed Merryn. How deeply she had actually been in Lily Valentine's character was not something anyone else needed to know – except, perhaps, Matt.

He, of all people, would understand.

Chapter Twenty-One

Matt had made his way to the stage, leaning heavily on the cane. The sense of urgency that impelled him forwards to save Cordy had dissipated, and now he was simply quite grumpy and quite in pain. But there was no way, no way on this earth, that he was missing the play. He knew how much it meant to Cordy, and by association, how much it meant to him.

The state of the dress had been a shocker, mind. He had opened his mouth to start asking questions, then quickly closed it again when Cordy made her eyes huge and round and glared at him from behind Merryn's back.

This, too, he understood, was Francis.

He was presently in the wings, hindering more than helping Kit sort the last few things out before the show started – to the extent that Kit had snapped at him to 'take a bloody seat, man. You'll trip me up with that damn cane and then there'll be two of us out of action!'

'Okay, okay!' He held up his arms in a gesture of surrender and limped off to find a seat. He had to smile, though, when he saw there were some reserved signs on the front row, and he was pretty sure, even from this distance, that one of them said 'Matt'.

'Matt! Before you go – what does the dress look like on?' Her voice was a whisper as she crept up on him. 'Is it okay?'

'Cordy!' he turned and saw her smoothing the frock down and looking concerned. 'It looks great. And so do you. Very … Titania … like.'

'Ha!' She smiled briefly. 'Better than looking like a bag lady, I guess. Poor dress. I feel so guilty – but Merryn is a miracle-worker. I'm just pleased Sybill won't be here to see it.'

'It wasn't your fault the dress got messed up.' He leaned

over and kissed her briefly. 'Is this the point I'm supposed to tell you to break a leg?'

'It is. They're all still at the hospital. Where maybe you should be, talking of broken legs.' She nodded towards his cane. 'Weirdly fetching, though. And kind of appropriate for the era.' She smiled briefly and he laughed.

'You're nervous. Look, I'll just be in the front row, there. See the names on the seats? If you need moral support look my way. I'll give you the thumbs up to let you know if you're doing okay. Oh – and see that guy there, the one with the glasses on?' Matt caught sight of Stanley Coleman, reading the names and working out where he was sitting. 'He's from *The Sunday Stage*. Genuinely from *The Sunday Stage* – so give him a nice smile if you can.'

'Okay.' Cordy grinned. 'But you'd tell me I was great even if I wasn't. Even if I messed it all up.'

'I would. But you're not going to. Where's the music coming from for your song? I never thought to ask.'

'Kit found an old recording of a music hall playing it. It's going to come through some speakers. But nobody will be looking at me – they'll be admiring the scenery.'

'They'll be admiring you.' He smiled at her.

'We'll see. I hope I do her proud.'

'You will.' He reached out, squeezed her hand, then thought that wasn't quite enough, so he kissed her as well. 'Go on. Your audience will be waiting.'

He popped his head around the corner of the stage, and sure enough, visitors were starting to fill up the seats, some curious, some excited – and a batch of ladies from the WI were chattering, led by Betty, who was striding along like the Queen Mary in full sail.

Matt turned back to speak to Cordy, but she'd gone. All he saw was a flash of oyster-pink satin disappearing onto the stage, and the hazy shade of five little fairies and a dog in a wheelbarrow, clustering behind the scenes, waiting for their cue—

'Lily?' He whispered her name, his stomach turning over as the logical part of him realised that Cordy was in green, and the girls and the dog were shadows from over a century ago.

It was suddenly a bit chilly on that August afternoon. He put his head down and hurried as fast as he could to his seat in the front row.

He didn't think he'd tell Cordy that Lily had come to share the stage. He had a feeling she'd know all about it anyway, once she stepped onto those boards.

The feeling of anticipation never left her. Every time she stood ready to go out on stage, she got that pounding in her heart and the horrid feeling that she was going to start sweating in some sticky places before she set foot on the stage.

Today was no different.

The sound of the music they had arranged for the grand entrance started to wrap itself around her, and she took a deep breath; then something caught her attention to the side of the stage: a flash of oyster-pink as a hazy shade stepped out from the wings onto the stage and walked to the front; more little shadows, flickering and glimmering, taking their places behind the curtain.

Five little girls suddenly all around her, their childish shapes forming out of shadows and sunbeams, and one of them hoisting a dog into a wheelbarrow. The smallest girl ran out onto stage and danced a little jig in excitement, before being dragged back behind the scenes. Then two others ran forward to open the curtains and one stood in front of Lily, ready to declaim something of great importance.

Cordy was stunned. She looked on as the drama unfolded and watched as the figures faded and disappeared within moments. She was filled with a curious sense of yearning for those people. She wished she could meet the little girls, talk to Elsie, stroke Biscuit – and share the stage properly with Lily.

Which she supposed, in some strange way, she was.

It was almost an echo of that other time she had stood here and the child had complained about being Mustardseed.

But Cordy wasn't scared this time. Whatever memories had been created there by Lily and her entourage were etched into Pencradoc as strongly as the emotions at the Mill House. A happy, happy time.

Cordy suddenly smiled and glanced into the wings again.

For a moment, she thought she saw Matt standing there; then she realised the man who stood there wore an eye-patch and a suit more appropriate for the nineteenth century than the twenty-first. She knew it was Edwin, yet he had a look of Matt about him – the same encouraging smile, the same stance, as if he was as excited as Lily was to be on the stage. He looked down as a small fairy tugged his coat, and then pointed to Lily again – and then he wavered and faded, leaving nothing but the bare wings of the makeshift stage.

But Cordy knew he had been there that day, watching Lily, loving her and waiting for her.

She smiled and held her head up high, pulled her shoulders back and took another deep breath.

'Lily. This one's for you,' she murmured, and she stepped forward as the curtains parted, and she faced her audience as the opening bars of 'Daisy Bell' rang out across the estate.

1895

The day the men came to deal with the water-wheel, hammering heavy nails and wooden beams onto it, was the day of Lily's Pageant. Edwin found her in the old rose garden, sitting on a rock and looking out at the waterfall.

She wasn't alone. Elsie was with her; Elsie and that dog of hers. Elsie was making the dog do tricks, but it was more interested in the treats it was getting, whether it was performing or not.

'Do you think,' he heard Elsie say, 'that Biscuit could also be on the stage today? I have seen, I am sure, pictures of dogs with ruffles around their necks. Performing dogs.'

'I don't know if Biscuit is a ruffle sort of dog,' Lily replied, quite seriously, 'but we can certainly try.'

'I'm wondering if we could roll him on in a wheelbarrow when you sing "Daisy Bell". It talks about a bicycle being made for two – I'm sure we could have Biscuit come on in the wheelbarrow and people would *imagine* it was a bicycle made for two.'

Edwin raised his camera and framed the shot. One press of the button, and the scene was captured forever.

'It's called a suspension of disbelief,' Lily said. 'We could try.'

'We shall, then. Miss Valentine – may I speak to you about a private matter, though, before we talk about our production?' The little girl was suddenly quite serious, and stood, arms behind her back, feet planted firmly on the ground. Biscuit, judging that playtime was over for now, threw himself gratefully under the shade of a tree, flopped down and immediately began to snore.

Edwin bit his lip to stop himself from laughing out loud. Elsie was quite serious, and Lily looked up at her, equally serious. He didn't know what a private matter might be to an eight-year old Lady, but he had enough integrity to turn away from them and continue his walk towards the wider estate. There was a particularly nice place where he had seen lilies blooming amongst the buddleias, and he headed there.

His cane had been left at the house. Today, he had decided to walk without it. It had been a different kind of crutch for too long and, in his heart of hearts, he knew that he had kept it more as an ingrained method of self-defence than a walking aid.

Besides that, Jago had mentioned he needed some help with moving something to the stage area – and he was more than willing to try to help, at least. He was a soldier after all, and soldiers did not give up. He looked ahead to the woods and deliberately thought about the good things in his life.

In fact, he made a conscious effort not to think about Francis O'Hara and all that had gone before. He wanted to, *needed* to, look forward; to concentrate on the future.

And with Lily's love, he thought he finally might be able to do that.

He hoped that the dark days were in his past, and his soul was no longer lost, because it had finally found Lily Valentine's – and her soul had found his.

Present Day

Matt had to admit that when Cordelia Beaumont walked onto that stage, she damn well owned the place. The dress had been patched up with lace panels so well that unless you knew the history of it, you'd think it was genuinely meant to be like that.

Cordy opened with 'Daisy Bell', which she sang confidently and faultlessly, and then, as she curtsied to the audience at the end of the melody, she smiled straight at him; then transferred that smile to Stanley Coleman – lucky sod. Stanley seemed to be entranced, as Matt knew he would be. The reporter smiled back at Cordy, pushed his glasses onto his nose, and scribbled something in his little book.

There followed a section where Cordy talked about Lily – she mentioned the Pageant and all the things Lily had been famous for and all the exciting places and cities she had worked in. In the background, a montage of photographs projected onto the back of the stage, and Cordy explained alongside it the parts Lily had played, and chatted about her time at the Paris Opera. As Elsie and her cousins appeared on the screen, clutching their hands together ardently, there was an audible *aaaahhhhh* from the audience. Cordy smiled out at them, and then talked about the children of Pencradoc, naming the girls as their beautiful little faces arrested everyone's attention. The final picture was the front page of Elsie's programme. The brushwork really was extraordinary when it was blown up like that – it almost came to life.

Matt was as entranced as anyone. Cordy said she'd been working on some extra parts, but he had no idea she had planned all of this. He sat forward, his hands gripping the top of the cane as he watched the spectacle unfold.

But she had more surprises in store. He laughed along as she gathered seven small children together on the stage; six girls and one boy. She asked the little boy if he would like a very special part that didn't involve dressing as a fairy or a sprite, to which he eagerly agreed. Kit came on and took the boy offstage into the wings, and Cordy placed the girls as she imagined the Pencradoc children had been placed around Lily Valentine – the girl she had designated 'Lily' had been equipped with a long dress she could put on over her own clothes, and Cordy recreated the *tableau* she imagined had happened in the real Pageant. Then she asked the children to try and recreate the photograph of the girls posing.

And, then, even better, Kit came on pushing a wheelbarrow – sitting in the wheelbarrow was the little boy, with long doggy ears attached to a head dress. Cordy wondered aloud if he could bark quite as well as Biscuit, the dog in the photos, could do.

The boy agreed enthusiastically, proved that he most definitely could, and earned himself a huge round of applause. The children were then ushered off the stage, and Cordy prepared for her Titania speech.

'But I need another volunteer for this one,' she said, smiling out at the audience. 'Titania, as you may know was a Fairy Queen. And every Fairy Queen needs her Fairy King. Sooooo ...' She pretended to scan the audience thoughtfully, and Matt's heartbeat quickened, even as he grinned and shook his head, knowing what would be coming.

'You – you'll do.' And indeed, there she was, holding out her hand to him.

Her eyes were dancing with mischief and he laughed. 'I don't think so,' he said, loud enough for the audience to hear. He folded his arms and shook his head as a ripple of laughter ran around the audience.

'Don't be shy!' That was Betty, accompanied by various whoops and laughs from the WI ladies. 'She needs her Oberon.'

'I do indeed.' Cordy held out her hand again and wiggled it. 'And there's a very special reason I want you up here.'

'Nope. Incapacitated,' he shouted back with a laugh.

'That's exactly *why*.' Cordy faced the audience. 'Lily Valentine married a gentleman who had been a soldier. Edwin Griffiths had been injured in the Semantan War, and as we understand it, he had quite terrible injuries – including the fact that he lost an eye and needed to rely on a walking stick for quite some time afterwards. My friend here has also been injured in a conflict – but the tree won, as I believe.' Another ripple of laughter ran through the audience. 'But regardless, I want you all to applaud him because he's the one who has kept me sane while I've been putting this together. And I do honestly, desperately, need an Oberon. Matt? Please?'

'How can I refuse after that?' He flung his hands in the air, helplessly, even as he was laughing up at her. The audience cheered as he heaved himself to his feet and limped over to the stage. Cordy rushed towards him and took his hand, helping him up the small set of steps.

Once he was at the top of the steps, she put her arms around his neck and drew him towards her. Then she kissed him, in full view of the Pencradoc visitors, and he could do nothing except hold her and kiss her back.

'Thank you,' she whispered as they drew away from one another – very reluctantly on his part. 'I mean it. You've saved my life. This morning was hideous.'

'You're doing brilliantly,' he whispered. Raising his voice, he asked the question he had half been dreading knowing the answer to: 'So what do you want me to do, my Fairy Queen?'

'I need my Oberon to read his part here. Kit?'

Kit appeared briefly to hand over a script. 'Your bits are highlighted. Obviously. Because you're kind of *not* Titania.'

'Smart man. Yet also a very sly man, if you knew about this already, mate!' Matt laughed and turned his attention back to Cordy. He squeezed her hand. 'Where do you want me?' His voice was low enough not to be heard by the audience.

She leaned in and whispered, "I'll tell you later – but for now, just stand next to me here.' And she led him to the centre-stage and positioned him carefully. 'It's as authentic as I can make it,' she said loudly, addressing the audience. 'We know from the original programme that Edwin Griffiths played the part of Oberon. We've got some copies of the programme for sale, so please – feel free to buy one to take home. You'll remember it from the montage, I hope, but I promise it is so much more special when you can study Elsie's artwork in your own time. But, this is the way I've decided to play *A Midsummer Night's Dream*. Welcome to the enchanted forest.' She curtsied again, and took her place. 'Oh – I almost forgot. We need a Bottom.' She looked comically stricken and placed her hand across her forehead in an attitude of despair. There was a roar of laughter from the audience. 'Any volunteers? Anyone at all? Anyone we can use as a Bottom?'

'I'll do it!' cried Betty, and there was an uproar as the lady stomped purposefully onto the stage. This time Merryn appeared with another copy of the script and Betty took it to a round of applause and cheering. Stanley Coleman, apparently completely swept away by it all, even gave Betty a standing ovation.

Matt shook his head and laughed. This was amazing. It was the sort of moment he wished would last forever.

But who knew? Perhaps the accompanying childish giggles he heard from the wings would ensure that it would.

It was, they seemed to suggest, a perfect pageant – and he was quite sure Lady Elsie Pencradoc would agree.

1895

'Come and talk to me then.' Lily patted the rock beside her. 'I'm listening.'

'Thank you. It's quite a difficult thing to say, so I think I shall just say it.' The little girl sat down, tucked her skirts under her legs, pulled her knees up to her chest and took a deep breath 'I know my step-papa is my real papa.' She frowned and stared into the distance, suddenly pensive. 'They think I don't know, and I'll never tell them I know, but I do. I'm hardly stupid.'

'You're hardly that,' replied Lily, trying to hide her surprise at the comment. 'But I'm shocked you should think such a thing.'

Elsie smiled slightly, looking for a moment like the woman she would become; not an eight-year-old child. 'It's not difficult to work out. I look exactly the same as my brothers and sisters. I draw quite as well as my papa does and nobody else in my family can draw. I don't … *like* the portrait of Ellory. The Duke who was married to my mama. It quite makes me shiver.' She pulled a face. 'It's hard to explain. But even if I didn't know, and I am *quite* sure that Mr Teague is my papa, it doesn't always have to be the gentleman your mama is married to who is your papa. So long as the gentleman you live with looks after you and treats you as his very own child and loves you like you are his, then I think a man who isn't really a papa can be a papa. Do you understand?' The little girl looked up at Lily, eight years old again and searching for validation. 'So Edwin can be your baby's Papa even though he perhaps didn't … make … the baby with you.' She blushed furiously. Some things, then, were still enough to cause Lady Elsie Pencradoc embarrassment.

'Perhaps you're right. But I'm not sure it's something we

should be talking about, and Edwin did … make … the baby, no matter what horrid things you overheard at the Mill House.' She fought down her own embarrassment and reached out, placing her hand on Elsie's. 'So we are not going to talk about it. We have, do we not, a play to put on? You have fairies to supervise. A stage to prepare …'

'Yes! Of course. But I am glad we talked. I've been wanting to say that about Mr Teague for quite some time, and I didn't know who I could tell. But I thought I could probably tell you, and I was right. It was quite easy to say to you, really. And I'm glad that I think, perhaps now, *you* can be happy too.' Elsie was suddenly shy. 'I think you *are* happier though. I think perhaps you feel safer now that man … died. I know it was him. And I'm glad, because he was a horrid man, he really was. I saw him, you know, looking at the Mill House. But I thought he was just looking at you like everybody does and I was pleased because you were my friend. I wish I had told a grown up.' She pulled a face. 'But now he can't hurt anybody any more.' She dropped her eyes and stared at the ground. 'I did hear him that day I came to see you. I heard him say the baby was his. But it's not, is it? It's Mr Griffiths' baby, isn't it?' She looked back up at Lily, hope in her eyes.

Lily shivered a little. Elsie was also astute. But Lily knew that whatever Elsie suspected would go no further.

'Yes, darling. Our baby belongs to me and Mr Griffiths.'

'Good.' Elsie nodded, apparently satisfied, and there was a pause, which might have been awkward, but, surprisingly it wasn't. Both of them were seemingly contemplating the mysteries of life and babies and papas. Lily certainly was.

As the thoughts tumbled around her head and she fought the worst of them away, she knew it would get easier with time. Francis was dead. She was free, and he wasn't going to come after her any more.

She looked across at the rose garden and the waterfall beyond, tracing the path of the river, refusing to think of what horrors the Mill House had witnessed. Those memories needed to be buried here – buried, perhaps with the old Lily Valentine. And definitely Evelyn O'Hara. Here, Lily Griffiths had been born and here she had finally found herself and stopped running away from the past. And if the memories and feelings of the past few months were burned into the earth around Pencradoc, then she could only pray they would stay that way. And if they didn't, then she had to trust that the people they revealed themselves to would understand why they had done what they had.

And the time now was not the time for regrets. The time now was to keep five little girls happy and to put on the very best performance she could muster.

'Lily – are you *certain* you are going to sing "Daisy Bell"? It's not going to spoil Titania is it?' Elsie's thoughts had clearly moved on.

Lily returned her attention to Elsie and smiled, relieved she was on slightly safer ground. 'Certain. I'm an actress, *acushla*. My darling, I can do anything my director and producer wish me to do.'

'Very good. Did you like the programme? I did three of them, but I gave you the very best. It was the neatest. I wrote it all myself. Clara and Mabel helped with the writing on the others and Lucy folded them. The audience will simply have to pass them around. I did not have time to do any more. I had to make sure my cousins knew what they had to do in the play.' She shook her head, now clearly a frustrated producer and director.

'The programme was beautiful. Thank you.' Lily hoped the girl wouldn't question its whereabouts. She'd gone to get it out of the drawer, but it wasn't there – she had a feeling who had taken it, and why, and that wasn't a pleasant thought … but she absolutely wanted another one. 'If you can perhaps rescue one of the other ones and let me have that too, I would be very grateful.' She thought quickly. 'I think I'd like to keep mine very safe. It's something I don't want to keep looking at and spoiling by touching.'

'Of *course* I can.' Elsie smiled. 'That's very sensible. Now, I think it's time to prepare the stage. I've already spoken to Mr Griffiths and thankfully he is quite clear on his role. I have also spelled it out on the programme. Mr Edwin Griffiths. Oberon. One of us can be Bottom. I haven't decided yet who. Which is why I haven't put the name down properly. I think, though, it will be me. It is a tragic name though, is it not?' She sighed and stood up and carefully brushed her dress down. 'Do you require some assistance in dressing, Miss Valentine?'

Lily stood up as well. 'No, thank you. You have much more important things to do.'

'Thank you. And thank you for listening. About Mr Teague being my papa, I mean.'

'You're very welcome.'

Lily was surprised to suddenly feel the girl throw herself at her and embrace her. 'Thank you for also making this the best summer of my entire life.' Elsie drew away slightly and gently rubbed Lily's rounded stomach. 'You're a very lucky baby,' she whispered and then looked up at Lily, professional again. 'I shall see you in the wings in one hour, Miss Valentine. *One* hour.' She held her finger up to drive her point home, then skipped away, towards the Hall.

Lily laughed, watching her as she disappeared, and was aware of a rustling in the undergrowth behind her, along with the scent of lilies.

'Miss Lily Valentine.' It was Edwin. He appeared out of a break in the foliage holding a huge bunch of freshly cut lilies, tied with a ribbon. He smiled and her heart skipped a beat. He was tall and handsome and so much more relaxed.

'Mr Griffiths.' She curtsied. 'How pleasant to see you.'

'I saw you were preoccupied with your producer, so I went for a walk. I couldn't let your comeback on stage go without marking the occasion somehow. As Elsie cornered me about her production to finalise the details a couple of hours ago, Mabel did take the opportunity to ask whether I would consider joining you on the stage as the Pirate King – until Clara scathingly told her we were not putting on *Pirates of Penzance*, no matter how many times she asked, and no matter that one of the characters was called Mabel.'

'Wise Clara. Or perhaps wise Mabel? I'm sure you would be a wonderfully dashing Pirate King.' She touched his eye patch gently and he caught her hand, bringing it to his lips and kissing it. Somehow, even that small gesture sent tingling up and down her arms and she smiled.

'Perhaps.' His voice was soft. 'But today is all about Lily Valentine. Now. I have been told that there will be a song, and then there will be a recitation. He dropped her hand, reluctantly it seemed, and pulled a piece of paper out of his pocket. 'I have been advised I am to play Oberon. And I have also been advised I can, and I quote, "hold onto the script as I'm quite sure you won't be able to remember it all as well as Miss Valentine".'

Lily laughed, delighted. 'I'm quite sure whoever told you that is correct.'

'Again – perhaps.' Edwin grinned and held out the flowers to her. 'But I wanted to give you these first, before I even contemplated looking at the script.'

'My favourite. Thank you.' She took them from him and buried her nose into the white blooms.

'The scent of lilies always reminds me of you anyway, but now I think the scent of them will bring this to mind as well. You, standing there, holding them at Pencradoc.'

'And whenever I smell them, I will also think of Pencradoc. And of you. Standing here, in the gardens. Where you rescued me from myself.' She felt her cheeks heat up.

'From yourself?' Edwin smiled, wryly. 'I'd say you were rescued from something much worse.'

'Let's not speak of it. Of *him*.' She still felt a little sick when she thought about what had happened. Although, she knew, there had been no other way they could stop him.

'I never meant him to die like that,' said Edwin suddenly. 'I want you to understand that. I couldn't help it.'

'I know, I know my darling.' She moved closer to him, and laid the flowers down on the grass, then put her arms around his neck. 'Neither could I.'

He looked down to where the curve of her stomach was gently touching his body and laid his hand on it, before reaching around her and returning the embrace.

She laid her head on his shoulder briefly 'He fell. He stumbled. That was nobody's fault.' She drew back and placed her fingers against his lips. 'And we are not to speak of it. I told you. Remember, he fell. Nobody incapacitated him – not a bullet nor a sword touched that man's body. I'm glad he's dead. I'm glad he has no claim on this.' It was her turn to brush her fingertips over her stomach. 'It's our baby, Edwin. *Our* baby. If you'll have us?'

She knew the answer, of course. She just wanted to hear him say it.

'Of course. It's all I've ever wanted. You. And a family of our own. But there is one thing, perhaps ...' He smiled down at her and the love shone in his gaze. 'I still have the marriage licence. Would you do me the honour of marrying me for real, Miss Lily Valentine?'

'Yes! Yes, of course. Some day, anyway!' Lily's laugh turned into a shriek as Edwin suddenly scooped her up in his arms and held her oh so close to him. 'Edwin! Your injuries. Put me down, I weigh more than a small elephant at the minute! But joking aside, should we do it soon? And quietly?'

It was Edwin's turn to laugh, then he kissed her. 'It is my opinion that we don't need a piece of paper to prove we are married – but propriety and all that may dictate otherwise. However, it'll be when *you* want to do it. And you're anything but an elephant. You're carrying our child and you've never been more beautiful and I've never loved you more. And my injuries can go to hell. I need to carry you over the threshold properly. I need to be fit enough to play silly games with our children and run around the lawn with them. And going back to our marriage or the lack thereof – who on earth would judge us here? It's not the logical thing to be judged at Pencradoc.'

'There's nothing logical about Pencradoc.' Lily giggled as Edwin put her gently back on her feet.

'Nothing. How many siblings has Lady Elsie Pencradoc got now? And how long have her parents been married …?'

'Shhhh again! Half-siblings, for a start. You're *not* to imply that Mr Teague is her papa!' Lily pretended to be horrified, but was surreptitiously delighted. 'That is Pencradoc's *greatest* secret and nobody is going to tell anyone that theory.'

'Of course not. My lips are sealed.'

'Good. But…' She lowered her voice and leaned very close to him, '…the answer to your question is she has three and a half siblings, and they have been married around six months, I believe.'

'Then we should try to catch up as best we can,' he murmured back, and she giggled again.

It was a delicious prospect.

Chapter Twenty-Two

Present Day

'Do you think you're still incapacitated enough to park close to the house?' Cordy glanced at Matt as they drove slowly along the driveway to Wheal Mount. Jago had built Wheal Mount for his Duchess, Alys, and there was a rather impressive run up to the building. Even from here, Cordy could see that the house was smaller than Pencradoc, but just as pretty. The first floor of the long, low, grey two-storey building overhung the ground floor, seemingly held up by an orderly line of pillars, and there were some signs for disabled parking going left and public parking going right.

Matt laughed and jabbed his thumb towards the back of the car where he had a pair of crutches, rather than the fancy cane he'd been using at Pencradoc. 'Just a bit.' He'd given in after the show and sought medical help, rather than relying on Merryn's rather slapdash nursing skills. He had a bad sprain and would be limping for a couple of weeks, but it was nothing insurmountable. He'd put Cordy on the car insurance for a month though, just in case.

And Cordy had put herself in his bed again that night, which had been delightful for all concerned.

'A month?' she'd teased, as he put the phone down on the insurance company. 'We'll be leaving Pencradoc in a few days.'

'Yes, but if you've got nothing planned, you might want to come down to Newlyn afterwards. It's up to you. You might still need an Oberon in your life. Unless you want a Toby in your life instead? Perhaps he's still desperate for a Rosalee?'

'Don't. Just don't.' Cordy shuddered. 'Ugh! The *thought*!'

In the end, she hadn't argued with the would-be Oberon, and much preferred him to Toby and his Gypsy King persona;

so here she was driving Matt's car to Wheal Mount to return the destroyed dress.

'It's really *not* destroyed', Merryn had said as she and Cordy surveyed the slashed material after the show, over a glass of wine or two. 'It's *customised*.' But even Merryn hadn't looked convinced that her handiwork would pass muster. So Matt had come with Cordy for a bit of moral support.

'Okay. I'll take a chance.' Cordy swung left and then pulled a face. 'Actually, we're here on official business, so I'm going a bit closer. Look, that bit says "Staff".' She drove a little further and tucked the car into a corner. 'I'll 'fess up to Sybill. Coren says he parks here, so I'm sure it'll be fine.'

'Coren. Hmm.' Matt undid his seat belt and opened the door, ready to hop out and balance until he got the crutches. 'Coren is subject to special privileges for virtue of simply being Coren.'

'Will those two ever get their act together?' Cordy came around and held the back door open while Matt got the crutches out.

'Act. Ha!' He looked up at her and grinned. 'There's no acting about how she feels about him. I just wonder how long she'll wait for him to make a move.'

'Well, why doesn't *she* make the move?' Cordy couldn't understand why Sybill hadn't already. Instead, she grabbed the dress and hugged it to her.

'Would *you* like to try and crack that exterior?' Matt raised his eyebrows. 'He's as thick as a plank. She should move on, really; give him something to fight for when he realises what he's lost.'

'You need to write the next Pencradoc play.' She nudged him playfully, her arms being full of fabric. 'Base it on those two.'

'I'd just lose my rag. No.' He laughed and turned. 'Come on. Let's go and find Sybill and accept our punishment.'

They made their way to the staff entrance and rang the bell.

Sybill herself pulled the door open and smiled at them in greeting. 'Well hello you two! Come on in.' She hugged them briefly and stepped aside so they could get through. 'Ouch.' She nodded to Matt's leg. 'You certainly did a number on that, from what I hear.'

'Gossip travels fast across Cornwall,' he said wryly. 'It's not bad. It'll be fine in a few days.'

'You should have gone to the hospital straight away,' she chided.

'No, I shouldn't. I would have missed Cordy's big debut.'

'Big debut!' Cordy laughed. 'It was a one-off show. Never to be repeated. Unless you write that one we were just on about?'

She raised her eyebrows and Matt shook his head, laughing. 'Nope. No way.'

Sybill looked at them oddly. 'Okay. Clearly something's going on I know nothing about.' She folded her arms, pretending to be cross.

'Sort of. We were just saying we've parked where Coren parks. I hope that's okay?'

There was a flicker of a smile on Sybill's lips as Coren's name was mentioned. 'That's fine. I hope the dress was okay?'

'It ... *was* ... okay.' Cordy frowned and hugged the dress closer. 'But I'm afraid it got customised a little more than we anticipated.'

'How so?'

'Hmm.' It was best, Cordy thought, to show her. She couldn't really explain it any other way. So she unfurled the dress and squeezed her eyes shut and waited for the tirade.

When silence greeted her, she opened one eye cautiously and looked at Sybill.

Sybill was still standing there with her arms folded staring at the dress. 'Oh' was all the curator of that precious dress said.

'I'm so sorry. When we got it out of the bedroom at the Mill House, it was damaged. We're not sure how – I think it was maybe vandals.' She felt herself flush as the lies tripped off her tongue again. 'That was why Rick had gone in to investigate, remember? He still can't recall much about it, except that he was pushed over by a young man. He described the man, and gave a report to the police, but said he wasn't interested in pressing charges, so I think they'll be dropping the case.'

'Oh.' Sybill nodded, slowly, still looking at the dress. 'Interesting ... customisation.'

'It was a fairy dress,' offered Matt. 'We made it more ... fluttery. For, like ... a fairy. A fairy – dress.' And Cordy couldn't help it. A giggle was threatening to erupt, and she bit her lip. Hearing Matt talk about making a dress more fluttery in a contrite voice that made him sound as if he was getting scolded by a disappointed adult was more amusing than it should probably have been at that particular moment in time.

'We're sorry,' she managed, before the giggle burst out of her in an inelegant snort she turned into a cough. 'No. Really. We are *so* sorry.' She bit her lip again. This was awful.

'Well so you should be.' Sybill was still staring at the dress, and then slowly transferred her attention to Matt. 'A fluttery fairy dress? *Really?*'

'Really.' He nodded, his eyes wide and far too innocent.

'Oh, stop it.' Sybill scowled briefly. 'That's a look you've borrowed from fifty million school children who are trying to wangle out of trouble.' She waved her hand at him. 'It's not going to work on me. I suppose we've got a fairy dress for the future though. I'm sure our designer could tidy it up a bit if she had to.' She sighed. 'Right. Thanks anyway for bringing it back. I suppose you want a cup of tea now, do you?'

'Yes please,' said Cordy composing herself. It really was dreadful when you thought about it. No laughing matter at all.

'If you can spare the time,' added Matt in a small voice.

Sybill flashed a look at them both then, surprisingly, laughed. 'These things happen. If it got messed up by a stranger in the first place, I can't really blame you guys for doing what you did. Although it's pretty tempting.'

'We really are very sorry. Look. Why don't you show me where the tea stuff is, and you sit down and I'll make it,' said Cordy. 'To try and make it up to you a little.'

'No thanks. I can't trust you with my tea bags after the mess you made of that dress. You sit down through there, in my office. I'll do it.' She stalked off and Cordy and Matt looked at one another.

'Close call,' he muttered.

'Nicely recovered,' she muttered back, and they high-fived before heading into the office.

But it was just as Cordy sat down by a small coffee table, nicely situated for informal meetings in Sybill's office, that she saw something which made her heart skip a beat.

The atmosphere shifted momentarily, and everything seemed to slow down. Matt took a moment to try to understand what had just happened. Feeling a little thrown, he eased himself into the seat opposite Cordy. She was leaning over the little coffee table, her hand hovering above something on it.

'Cordy? Everything okay?' He reached across and touched her on the shoulder. She seemed to be lost somewhere, staring at the items in front of her.

'Yes. I think so. Look – just look at this, though.'

He leaned in and saw what looked like a notecard and a photograph. The photo had two people on it at, he assumed, a fancy-dress event. The woman was dressed as a pirate with bare feet and a fetching spotted kerchief tied around her long, wavy hair, and the man was dressed quite similarly, complete with an eye-patch. He was standing behind her, and she was sitting on a barrel, daubed with the word 'RUM'. On her knee was a baby, dressed equally piratically, with a tiny tricorn hat on its head and little stripy trousers. Just nosing into shot, staring at the people, its tongue lolling out as if it was going to lick the baby, was a dog. It was the same dog, Matt could have sworn, that was in some of the old photos at Pencradoc.

'That's Biscuit, isn't it?' he asked. 'Surely?'

'It is.' Cordy nodded. 'And this is Lily and her husband and her baby. I found them you know – the marriage. *Evelyn* and Edwin got married a year after the Pageant. I checked last night after you'd dropped off. Sorry – I just couldn't let it lie. They must have proved Francis' death somehow, but I don't think the "how" of that is anything I really want to pursue.'

'I'm glad he made an honest woman of her,' said Matt wryly. 'I would have *liked* to have known they got married before now, I think… like this morning, perhaps?'

But Cordy seemed oblivious as she barrelled on, and he dipped his head to hide his smile. She'd never change – he knew that now, funnily enough. And he was happy to go along with her butterfly mind – very happy, actually.

'And I've seen a version of this photograph before. Look.' Cordy fumbled in her pocket and pressed the screen of her mobile phone. Scrolling down, she paused, enlarged the image and showed it to Matt. It was of Lily Valentine dangling by her feet from some rigging and the man standing grinning beside her.

'Where's that from?'

'It's on someone's Pinterest board – God knows whose. These things rarely have a reference.' Cordy shook her head. She clicked on the image and read the accompanying text. 'All it says is that it was sourced from a periodical – *The Tattle-Tale* – which was a student publication about the arts and entertainment, only in existence for a couple of years at a liberal arts college in the early twentieth century. I wonder where whoever posted this on the internet stands with the copyright? Who does the photo even *belong* to?'

'I've never even heard of the magazine.'

'You wouldn't have done – if it was just some kids putting it together when they were at college. But my question is why have they got one version of it, and Wheal Mount has this version of it—?'

'—Ah! You've found it. Fabulous.' Sybill came through the door, balancing a tray with three mugs and a plate of biscuits on it. 'I got it out of the family papers for you to see. We think Elsie took that photo of Lily and Edwin and their baby. They'd paid her a visit the summer after the Pageant and brought along the baby. Apparently, they put on a private little show as a belated birthday gift. It was a huge surprise for Elsie. Read the letter.' She nodded across to it.

'A letter? This must be the one Merryn told me about!' Cordy looked up at Matt and suddenly laughed. 'Brilliant! Lily and Edwin came to visit Elsie, and she sent Alys a letter about it. She must have sent the photo as well.' She took hold of the notelet and unfolded it. It had a small watercolour painting on the front of a dog – Biscuit, of course. 'Shall I read it out?'

'Please do.' Matt smiled. He was as interested as she was, but knew she would want to be the one who shared it with them.

'Very well. Here goes:

"Dearest Aunt Alys,

I hope this letter finds you well. I had a very good Easter, thank you, and I am very pleased the weather has kept so clement for us. The egg hunt you arranged at Wheal Mount was enormous fun and I do not believe I thanked you properly on the day, as my cousins and my brothers and sisters were most distracting and demanding of my attention.

Easter was a long time ago though, and I write to you today of some exceedingly good news! Lily Valentine, I am sorry, Mrs Lily Griffiths, and of course dear Mr Griffiths came to visit us last weekend! It was a huge surprise for me, and Lily (she said I could call her that) said she was sorry she had not been to see us earlier but Albert was still quite small and she did not feel it was good to come on such a journey with a small person. I said I quite understood as my smallest brother is still quite annoying when one tries to travel anywhere of a great distance.

However, Albert is now of an age to travel well, and they came to see us and it was a great surprise as I did not expect them! Imagine my surprise when I was blindfolded and led through the rose gardens, because I could smell it was the rose gardens, and then I was spun around five times at the very least, and I fell over Biscuit who licked my face, and then someone, I think it was my sister took the blindfold off me and I was facing a stage! A stage, just like the one we had last year, when you were so kind as to allow us the Pageant! And who should be on the stage, but Lily Valentine and Mr Griffiths! And Lily Valentine was hanging by her toes, and Mr Griffiths was standing there so tall and so proud and still looking like a Pirate King, (he is walking so much better now, but I fear his poor eye will never get any better, but you may tell Mabel that his is still a very good Pirate King), and then do you know what happened? Lily did a very flexible routine where she wound herself up in the rope and then dropped to the ground, the right way up, and then they both began to sing 'With Cat-Like Tread' from the Pirates of Penzance and I laughed so much! She said later it was a belated birthday surprise for me. I honestly could not think of a better birthday surprise. We also had a large cake.

Please find enclosed a copy of the photograph I took with my new camera. I took two, but this one shows dear little Albert who looks so much like Mr Griffiths, and do you see how Biscuit came to say hello as well?

I am sorry but the paper is ending so I must stop writing my letter. I hope to see you soon. Goodbye.

With great love
Lady Elsie Pencradoc."

'She got a bit of a birthday surprise then.' Matt was amused at the amount of 'surprises' the little girl had remarked upon in the letter.

'She did indeed. The other photo must be the one in that magazine ...' Cordy's voice trailed away. 'Oh! Elsie. Of *course*.' She looked at Matt and slowly she smiled. 'I bet Elsie went to whatever liberal arts college that was and gave them the photo for the publication. She would have kept the other one for herself. Of *course* she would!'

'Elsie definitely went to an art college,' added Sybill, settling down with them. 'With her talent, who could doubt that she would end up doing something like that. Why?'

'I think this is the other picture in the set.' Cordy held the phone out to Sybill whose eyes went round as saucers.

'Bloody marvellous,' said Sybill. 'That's fabulous. I didn't know anyone had a copy of that. It just shows what's lurking around the internet. Can you email me the link, please? I'm going to print it out for here.'

'Copyright?' asked Matt, raising his eyebrows in amusement. 'We've just had a discussion about that – or lack thereof.'

'Damn the copyright,' said Sybill. 'It was taken by *my* Elsie and sent to *my* Alys, so it's getting printed.' She looked so furious, Matt had to dip his head to hide his smile.

'Sure,' said Cordy. 'What's your email? I'll send it now.'

Sybill told her and the picture winged its way through cyberspace, back to where it should belong.

'It's home,' said Cordy, and smiled at Matt.

Matt smiled back. He hoped that Cordy might feel she was home too, in Cornwall – it would be nice to think so, at any rate.

1895

'It's a rather nasty thing, isn't it, to be crushed between the machinery of a water-wheel.' Clara's voice was musing. The girls were walking across the gardens, towards the stage, taking, of course, the long route which traced the length of the river.

They had also, of course, been warned not to go there, but someone had fortunately had the forethought to construct a makeshift barrier so small explorers might not take a similar tumble into the water.

'You know we're not to discuss it.' Elsie was prim, very much the older cousin. 'It was a Tragic Accident.'

'Do you think he was dead before he got to the water-wheel?' Clara was nothing if not persistent.

'Clara! Of course he was. He *drowned*.'

'That is good then as he won't have felt it squishing him—'

'—Enough!' Elsie stopped and stamped her foot, indignant. 'We are *not* to discuss it.'

'Very well. If you are going to be *boring* …' Clara stuck her tongue out at her cousin and skipped off, tossing her shiny, golden hair behind her.

Elsie shook her own dark head and glared after her cousin. Less than a year separated them, with the little ones following year on year behind – but sometimes she felt *so* much older.

And she especially didn't want to talk about the man who had died so horribly that day. And she had heard that gun shot echoing across the estate. She had mentioned it to her Aunt Alys, who had said it must have been a poacher or one of the estate workers shooting a pheasant or something and not to worry about it.

Elsie hadn't worried about it as such, she was just … uncomfortable … with it. But still. Her aunt must have been correct as it turned out that nobody had been shot, had they? A man, *that* man, had fallen into the river on the same day, but that was just an accident.

She looked at the side of the riverbank where the barrier was and pulled a face. Her cousins had all run off in front of her now, Nancy trailing behind them dragging a stick, but then she saw Lucy stop and bend down.

The girl stood up, something in her fingers glinting in the sunlight and Elsie frowned.

'Elsie!' Lucy came running back to her. 'Look! Look at this. What is it?' She held the item out to her, and Elsie took it.

She studied it for a moment, then pulled a face. 'It's a bullet, Lucy. One of the ones they use to shoot the rats.'

'Rats! Ugh!' Lucy backed away, and Elsie was pleased she had said 'rats' instead of 'rabbits' as then Lucy would have probably cried.

'It's nasty. Go on. I'll get rid of it.' She made a *shoo*-ing gesture with her hand and Lucy turned tail and ran off to join her sisters, the bullet forgotten.

Elsie, however, felt a little bit sick. The thing still had blood smeared on it. It must have really gone through an animal …

Or maybe a person.

'Oh!' Horrified, she remembered the gun shot again, looked at the sheer drop to the river, then recalled the gun she had seen on the floor in Miss Valentine's bedroom. She thought about the horrid man who had been shouting at Miss Valentine. How angry Mr Griffiths had been. The things that awful man had said … 'Oh no.' She stared at the bullet again, paralysed with uncertainty, then made a decision. Well, she made two decisions.

One decision was that she had to get to the estate ledgers just as soon as possible and make sure that nobody could ever think the dreadful accident had anything at all to do with Miss Valentine. She would tear that man's name out of Pencradoc's history.

And the second decision was easier and quicker to deal with, and she could do that right now.

Elsie walked as close as she dared to the edge of the riverbank and took a deep breath. Tossing the bullet away from her and over the edge, just as hard as she could, she truly hoped the nasty thing would go into the water and be lost forever.

She listened carefully for the *plop* that would tell her it had reached the water, but just then a crow cawed loudly above her head in the trees making her jump, and she ran as fast as she could after her cousins.

Chapter Twenty-Three

Present Day

After tea, they had been shown around the ground floor of Wheal Mount, which was still set out as if the family lived there. Cordy had loved seeing Elsie's paintings and drawings, and she exclaimed in delight when she came face to face with Alys and Jago and Zennor and Teague, whose portraits still hung on the walls. They'd been treated to a few extra Teagues as well, due to the exhibition, and then they had got back in the car and looked at one another.

'Back to Pencradoc?' she asked Matt, almost reluctantly. He smiled at her, and she felt her stomach flip.

'If you want. Or you could come to Newlyn. It's about the same distance, but you might be too tired to drive back afterwards.'

'To drive back to Pencradoc from Newlyn? It's quite a long way, isn't it?'

'It's over an hour. And this is an unfamiliar car.'

'Very true.' She sat with her hands on the wheel, thinking. Then she made her decision. 'It's a while since I was at the beach. I want to enjoy it properly. How about we go back to Pencradoc now, then we leave in a couple of days like we planned, and I come down to Newlyn then? For a bit of a holiday.'

'That would work.' She sensed the amusement in his voice. 'Unless you were desperate to get back home to London and your auditions? I'd understand it if you were.'

'London. Pah.' She pulled a face. 'It's still quite hot there, what with it being summer and all that.'

'It's hot down here as well.'

'I know.' She drummed her fingers on the wheel. 'I do prefer to be hot by the beach, though.'

'We have a beach.'

'I know.'

'You could even paddle. Or swim. And I'd take you for fish and chips afterwards.'

'Thank you.'

'We also have artists' cottages and little streets and museums and some nice gardens and things, just a little drive away. It gets a bit boring sometimes, going to these places on your own. It'd be nice to have the company.'

'I get a bit bored of doing stuff on my own in London. But we do have some amazing things to do there as well. I live near some good galleries and we have cool pubs too. Then there's the museums and the live poetry readings. There's a buzz.' She glanced at him. 'And it's close for me for work.'

'For the theatre?'

'Not just that. For the temping. The office jobs. The things I ... do ... when I'm not acting.'

'Okay.'

There was a silence, and she glanced at him again.

He glanced back. 'We've got offices in Cornwall as well,' he said, conversationally. 'Cool places to work, like galleries. And temping agencies as well.'

'And we've got schools in London that need teachers.'

'Yes.'

'Matt. We're not talking about holidays any more, are we?' She turned in the seat and looked at him.

'I don't think we are. No.' He looked back at her.

'A holiday is different to living here.'

'We're not talking about living here, though, are we?' He fixed her eyes with his. 'We're talking about an extended stay. Just to see how it goes. I know that it isn't ideal – like you say, your acting work is in London.'

'Oh *God*!' Cordy smacked her forehead off the steering wheel. She mumbled into the wheel, not looking at him. 'I can't lie any more. Matt. I thought about it, and you know what I did yesterday? After the show? I binned Marion off. I told her I didn't want to go to the stupid audition, and I didn't want to work with Toby. I told her I'm under no illusions and I know my acting life is rubbish. I haven't had a decent break for ages. I'm living on the fact I wore a fancy frock in one bloody episode of *Downton* bloody *Abbey*. I've been in precisely one stage show in the last year and it closed down after four weeks. I met Toby Fowler because he was a client at the PR firm I worked in. I don't have the sort of lifestyle that everyone thinks I have. I'm an actress, for God's sake, so I just make it *look* as if I'm good at what I do—'

'Hey! Stop it.' Matt's voice was unusually sharp. 'You're damn good at what you do. Your show at Pencradoc was brilliant – look at the write-ups it got. And what do you mean you binned Marion off?'

'The write-ups were in the local paper. And I told Marion she was fired. Ha! Listen to me. I've finally lost the plot. She even told me to calm down and ring her back when I'd come to my senses, then asked if I had sunstroke or if I was drunk.'

'The write-ups were also in *The Sunday Stage*. People will read that, influential people who'll want you on board. Maybe it's not too late to go back to Marion – the fact that *The Stage* is involved should give you more leverage, shouldn't it? For better parts? That don't rely on Toby Fowler. Anyway – *you're* the one that would make him look good. I'd put money on it.'

'Thanks Matt. I'm flattered, but maybe that's not *quite* the truth. Toby is actually pretty good at what he does. Well, at least he is when he puts his mind to it and has a good co-star to lean on. He'll have to work for this one, though. From what I've heard from Ash and Paul, he's already approached three other girls to play Rosalee – all ex-girlfriends, and they've all turned him down. Two of them he bloody well asked before me! Imagine! I was third choice, cheeky so and so.' She was indignant for a moment, thinking of it all. 'He must have been desperate to come all the way down here and drag Rick into it though. His reputation is looking a bit tarnished, methinks. Oh! And apparently the PR firm I worked at fired him for bringing them into disrepute, because he turned up down here and made a scene. That man needs a handler, not a PR firm. Good grief. I'm still wondering how the story got out about him being here though. Rick didn't run it.'

'Hmmm,' said Matt, quite uncommittedly. Cordy flashed a quick glance at him, but he was looking out of the window, scratching at a piece of dirt on the inside glass. 'Anyway.' She lifted her head fully and stared at him as he brought his gaze around to meet hers and their eyes locked. 'But you know what? I had more fun doing that little show, and having all that control over it, with my friends cheering me on and helping out, than I've had with anything else for ages. Before all this happened, I was thinking about starting a drama group or a theatre group back in London. And then after yesterday, I started thinking about doing the same thing but in Cornwall. Trying to find a niche down here where I can have my own little troupe, and travel to places like Pencradoc and put on my own shows, and maybe eventually take them a bit more further afield, and direct and produce and script write and all of that – but it's a pipe-dream at the minute. I really think I need to take stock of what I'm doing and what else I want to do. And you know what?' She took a deep breath and stared at him. 'I think I want to think about that here. With you. On that extended holiday.'

'I'm good at helping people think,' he said softly. 'Comes with being a teacher. I help people to grow and develop and reach their potential. Not that I'm saying you need me to treat you like a school child, of course – but what I *am* saying is that we could use a proper drama teacher at my school. Or at least start with a drama group and see where we go from there. I know they were talking about appointing someone a while ago – when my good ex-friends felt they had to leave. Nobody ever applied that was suitable. If you give it a go, maybe – go in and volunteer with the school and the pupils – who knows? And if it doesn't work out, what have you lost? You can go back to the city and back to your other life.'

'At this precise moment in time, I don't want that other life, though,' she whispered. 'I may be wrong basing my future on Lily Valentine, but look what happened to her. Look at that photograph. How happy did she seem with her lovely husband and her lovely baby, and still doing what she loved, but doing it at *Pencradoc* to surprise a little girl, for goodness sake? She was happy, I think. She was happy to be with her family and her friends and she'd done all of that. She'd escaped from Francis and whatever went on there, and found Edwin. And she still used her talent to do what she loved and made people happy – but her heart was elsewhere, I think, after that summer at Pencradoc. It wasn't with the acting or the fame any more.'

'And is your heart somewhere else now as well?' Matt's voice was soft and Cordy nodded her head.

'Yes. Yes, I think it is. I just have to see if it'll stay there. Or if it needs to fly away and be free again.'

'I can help you decide.'

'I want you to help me decide. Matt – in fact, just kiss me, okay? Kiss me right now. That might help me make the first decision.'

'Kiss you? Why, of *course* I can kiss you, Cordelia Beaumont. What decision is it you need help with?'

She just had time to smile, and suddenly she was smiling against his lips as he pressed his to hers. She pulled away briefly. 'To decide if we go to Pencradoc. Or to Newlyn. Or just stay in this car all afternoon, because I *really* want to be with you right now and I'm wondering where else we can go.'

'We're equidistant. But as I say, my house is at Newlyn. If we go there, we won't have our friends trying to get our attention. Also, we'll be a helluva lot more comfortable in my bedroom than we would be staying in the car, for example – and there's no chance of being disturbed by visitors or bumping into Coren in the corridor.'

'Newlyn actually *does* sound quite good,' she said. 'Thank you. Decision one: made.'

'Excellent.' Matt sat back and, smiling, clipped in his seat belt. 'I can't wait to see what decision I have to help you with next.'

'I might take a lot of persuading.'

'I'm very good at persuading.'

'I'll be the judge of that.'

And, later that day, as they sat on Newlyn beach in the evening sunlight, the warmth of the sun still on her skin, Matt's arm around her in a very safe and very wonderful embrace – an embrace she thought she could very well get used to – Cordelia Beaumont reflected that she was very well persuaded indeed …

Epilogue

10th August 1895

The thrill of the stage shivered up Lily's spine and she smoothed down her skirts. The oyster satin fabric shimmered in the light from beyond the curtain and she gave her lace sleeves a quick tweak, just to make sure they showed her creamy shoulders to their best advantage.

The publicity photograph of her supporting cast had been taken; the five little stars doing their best to pose beautifully on such an important day. Most of the shots would, Edwin had said, come out blurry due to the incessant fidgeting as the stars tugged at their costumes or looked vaguely around to see if anyone was watching. But one image, he had said, looked as if it might just be perfect.

Lily smiled to herself. She couldn't wait to see that one.

And as she stood here, ready to perform, she recognised that excitement building up within her – the feeling, she confessed to herself now, that she had missed over the time she had lived at Pencradoc with Edwin Griffiths. The anticipation of the crowd, the prickles of stage fright, then the moment the curtain swished open and she stood, centre-stage, all eyes on her …

But this time the curtain was a large bed-sheet suspended from a rail, and it was dragged open with much ado across a makeshift stage by two small girls who argued over who was in whose way. The smallest one fell over and began to howl and her older cousin, dressed in a made-over evening frock of her mother's, raced on and picked her up, then deposited her at the side of the stage before running back on and standing right in front of Miss Lily Valentine, star of the Paris Opera.

'Please welcome Miss Lily Valentine to Pencradoc Theatre of the Arts. Here, she will present us with her rendition of

"Daisy Bell", a popular modern song heard all over the *world*! And also especially accompanied at a Relevant Point by Biscuit. My dog.' Here, the confident young *compère* flung her arms out wide and surveyed the audience. 'Then, we shall have the pleasure of hearing Miss Valentine present Queen Titania's speech from *A Midsummer Night's Dream*, act two, scene one, complemented by Mr Edwin Griffiths as Oberon and a *tableau* of fairies and sprites—'

'—I want to be a fairy!' came a wail from the wings.

'Hush! You *are* a fairy.'

'But you said I am *Mustardseed*! I do not want to be *Mustardseed*!'

'Hush, Mabel! Mustardseed is still a fairy—'

Lily dropped her head and hid a smile as Lady Elsie Pencradoc continued her grandiose introduction in a slightly louder voice.

'Yes. *Fairies*.' Elsie cleared her throat. 'Anyway. Ladies and Gentlemen, *please* welcome, Miss Lily *Valentine*!'

A rousing fanfare was played on the piano that Jago and Edwin had brought out, and Lily glanced across at Alys, who gave her a mischievous wink as she finished the piece with a flourish.

Lily looked over the audience, and she smiled as she recognised the familiar faces of the servants and the family. Finally, she turned her head slightly and saw Edwin standing in the wings, the script in his hand ready for his big moment on stage, and in that instant there was absolutely nowhere else on earth she would rather be than here, at Pencradoc, with Edwin. Her soon-to-be-husband – when they got around to it, of course. And the only father of her child she would ever want or ever acknowledge.

And, with the future so delightful to contemplate, Lily Valentine took a deep breath, and stepped forward, waiting for the opening notes of 'Daisy Bell'.

Then she opened her heart, and sang.

Thank You

Thank you so much for reading, and hopefully enjoying, *Lily's Secret*. It's the second book in the Pencradoc series and I loved writing about Cordy and Matt, and Lily and Edwin. The story just "grewed and grewed", as they say, and I do hope you liked it!

However, authors need to know they are doing the right thing, and keeping our readers happy is a huge part of the job. So it would be wonderful if you could find a moment just to write a quick review on the retail site where you bought the book to let me know that you enjoyed the book. Thank you once again, and do feel free to contact me at any time on Facebook, Twitter, through my website or through my lovely publishers Choc Lit.

Thanks again, and much love to you all,

Kirsty

xx

About the Author

Kirsty Ferry is from the North East of England and lives there with her husband and son. She won the English Heritage/Belsay Hall National Creative Writing competition in 2009 and has had articles and short stories published in various magazines. Her work also appears in several anthologies, incorporating such diverse themes as vampires, crime, angels and more.

Kirsty loves writing ghostly mysteries and interweaving fact and fiction. The research is almost as much fun as writing the book itself, and if she can add a wonderful setting and a dollop of history, that's even better. Her day job involves sharing a building with an eclectic collection of ghosts, which can often prove rather interesting.

For more information on Kirsty visit:
Twitter: @kirsty_ferry
Facebook: www.facebook.com/kirsty.ferry.author/

More Choc Lit

From Kirsty Ferry

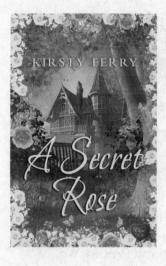

A Secret Rose

Book 1 in the Cornish Secrets series

"Wherever you go, I
will follow ..."

Merryn Burton is excited to
travel down to Cornwall to start
her first big job for the London
art dealers she works for. But as
soon as she arrives at Pencradoc,
a beautiful old mansion, she
realises this will be no ordinary
commission.

Not only is Pencradoc filled with fascinating, and possibly
valuable artwork, it is also owned by the Penhaligon brothers
– and Merryn's instant connection with Kit Penhaligon could
be another reason why her trip suddenly becomes a whole lot
more interesting.

But the longer Merryn stays at Pencradoc the more obvious it
is that the house has a secret, and a long-forgotten Rose might
just hold the key ...

Holly's Christmas Secret

Book 3 in the Cornish Secrets series

Once upon a Cornish Christmas …

It's almost Christmas at the Pencradoc estate in Cornwall which means that, as usual, tea room owner Sorcha Davies is baking up a festive storm. And this year Sorcha is hoping her mince pies will be going down a treat at 'The Spirit of Christmas Past' exhibition being organised at the house by new local antiques dealer, Locryn Dyer.

But as Locryn and Sorcha spend more time together, they begin to uncover a very special story of Christmas past that played out at Pencradoc more than a century before, involving a certain 'Lady' Holly Sawyer, a festive dinner party and a magical secret encounter with a handsome author …

Visit www.choc-lit.com for details.

Summer's Secret Marigold

Book 4 in the Cornish Secrets series

Can a summer secret from the past allow a new future to bloom?

For two people who run competing arts centres in Cornwall, Sybill Helyer and Coren Penhaligon get on rather well. So well in fact that Sybill often wishes the owner of Pencradoc Arts Centre would look up from his spreadsheets for a minute and notice her. Unfortunately, even that's too much to ask from workaholic Coren.

However, when the pair join forces to run an exhibition on the wild and wonderful life of Elsie Pencradoc, a talented artist who lived at Coren's estate in the early twentieth century, they're in for a surprise. How will a secret sketchbook and an exquisite gothic dress from a long-ago midsummer costume ball lead them to the scandalous truth about Elsie – and perhaps encourage them to reveal a few long-kept secrets of their own?

Christmas of New Beginnings

Not all festive wishes come true right away – sometimes it takes five Christmases …

Folk singer Cerys Davies left Wales for the South Downs village of Padcock at Christmas, desperate for a new beginning. And she ends up having plenty of those: opening a new craft shop-tea room, helping set up the village's first festive craft fair, and, of course, falling desperately in love with Lovely Sam, the owner of the local pub. It's just too bad he's firmly in the clutches of Awful Belinda …

Perhaps Cerys has to learn that some new beginnings take a while to … well, begin! But with a bit of patience, some mild espionage, a generous sprinkling of festive magic and a flock of pub-crashing sheep, could her fifth Christmas in Padcock lead to her best new beginning yet?

Visit www.choc-lit.com for details.

The Hartsford Mysteries

A series of atmospheric time-slip romances, all set in the same beautiful mansion house in Suffolk.

Watch for Me by Moonlight – Book 1

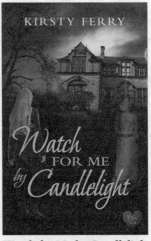

Watch for Me by Candlelight – Book 2

Watch for Me by Twilight – Book 3

Watch for Me at Christmas – Book 4

Visit www.choc-lit.com for more details.

The Rossetti Mysteries

A series of compelling time-slip romances set in the art world in Yorkshire and London.

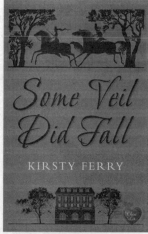

Some Veil Did Fall – Book 1

The Girl in the Painting – Book 2

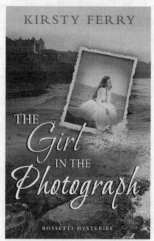

The Girl in the Photograph – Book 3

A Little Bit of Christmas Magic – Book 4

Visit www.choc-lit.com for more details.

The Tempest Sisters Series

*Cosy contemporary romances set in Scotland
and on the North East coast.*

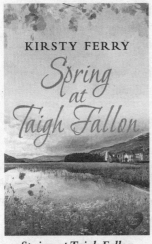

*Spring at Taigh Fallon
– Book 1*

*Jessie's Little Bookshop by
the Sea – Book 2*

**Summer at Carrick Park
– Book 3**

**Christmas on the Isle of Skye
– Book 4**

Visit www.choc-lit.com for more details.

Introducing Choc Lit

We're an independent publisher creating
a delicious selection of fiction.
Where heroes are like chocolate – irresistible!
Quality stories with a romance at the heart.

See our selection here:
www.choc-lit.com

We'd love to hear how you enjoyed *Lily's Secret*. Please
visit **www.choc-lit.com** and give your feedback or
leave a review where you purchased this novel.

Choc Lit novels are selected by genuine readers like yourself.
We only publish stories our Choc Lit Tasting Panel want to
see in print. Our reviews and awards speak for themselves.

Could you be a Star Selector and join our Tasting Panel?
Would you like to play a role in choosing which novels
we decide to publish? Do you enjoy reading women's
fiction? Then you could be perfect for our Tasting Panel.

Visit here for more details...
www.choc-lit.com/join-the-choc-lit-tasting-panel

Keep in touch:
Sign up for our monthly newsletter Spread for all the latest
news and offers: www.spread.choc-lit.com. Follow us
on Twitter: @ChocLituk and Facebook: Choc Lit.

Where heroes are like chocolate – irresistible!